ANGEL

Their dresses were gone. Bra and panty sets fitted tight on their trim bodies. All white lingerie with flesh stockings on tanned legs. High heels shed, they circled him. Something angry and all skewed off-course shone bright in their clever eyes. Smart girls with bad tempers.

Angel sat up and thought of defending himself. Those claws on their fingers could do damage to a country-club-gimp.

'Now, now, sweet boy,' the girl with the pussy tattoo said, ready for the big wide world and all the torture she could spread in it. 'Just be a good doggy.' They all laughed at that one too. 'With this belt –' she wrapped it through her fingers, the nails flashing like sport's car paint-work under the chandelier lights '– I want you to give us what for. You understand, doggy boy.'

You bet I do, bitch.

A NEXUS CLASSIC

ANGEL

Lindsay Gordon

This book is a work of fiction.
In real life, make sure you practise safe, sane
and consensual sex.

This Nexus Classic edition published in 2005

First published in 2001 by
Nexus
Thames Wharf Studios
Rainville Road
London W6 9HA

www.nexus-books.co.uk

ISBN 0 352 34009 6

Typeset by TW Typesetting, Plymouth, Devon

Printed and bound by
Clays Ltd, St Ives PLC

For James, Elizabeth and Zak

One

'Now remove your clothes,' she said, her tone sharp.

Angel hesitated. Grinned. Blushed medium-rare, then paled. His broad face was suddenly the colour of vanilla wax when interpreting her expression: not amused and impatient with him. Unmoving, and all set at pointy angles, it was a beautiful face; no creases on skin and definition exactingly prepared with cosmetics and frozen at an indeterminate youth by surgery in an enhancement clinic. Her mouth drew his stare more than any other feature; her lips were coloured dark red like a streak of blood on medicinal tiles.

'Your clothes, take them off,' she repeated, waiting with the rubber gloves on; squeaky-fingered, octopus-fleshed, red fingernails dim beneath the white rubber.

Now. Do it now. Rapidly changing snapshots of what he'd have to go back to if he failed the assessment flashed through his mind: his room with the two window frames, one swollen immobile into the walls, the other juddering loose; patched and peeled casements where the panes of glass were too grimy for sunlight, and the gaps at the bottom were wide enough for razor blade draughts to whistle gleefully through, intent on slicing his naked parts; the stained sink and spotted faucet that splashed thick ropes of cold water, the colour of unpasteurised milk, into his hands; the shower in the communal bathroom, shared with eleven others, that sprayed scalding piss at his face and gave his shoulders the feeling of sunburn once a day; carpet that cracked under his toes; bedclothes saturated with damp, and the bare light bulb he sometimes watched for hours upon end, his head as bare as the walls, his thoughts thick and sluggish as the air. Quickly, he began unbuttoning. Humiliation and wretchedness made his fingers fast though clumsy at their work.

She took a deep breath and by the time her long sigh of dissatisfaction had concluded, his T-shirt and watch were inside the stainless-steel tray she had placed on the bedside table. Now her eyes began to flick about, assessing the chest size and breadth of shoulder he'd developed swimming in the charity baths and freight canals. Day after day, week after week for three years he'd visited the baths, until the old glass roof – a beautiful green thing supported by a wrought-iron frame and made by the Victorians, they said – had been hit by lightning and fallen into the water below. Now that was closed too, like everything else in Binton, his township.

Down her eyes swept – so clear, so blue – to his stomach, concave and tight, from a diet of potato peelings, outer cabbage leaves, spindly carrots, beans in brine, rice, fish if he could catch it, and the black bread they made across the water with a crust like tarmac and the dry insides that smelled of old barns with their hooty owls and bales of sun-freshened hay. But her demeanour never changed when his top half was bare; she continued to look him over the way an analyst inspects a live specimen, seemingly on the verge of issuing the instant dismissal he so dreaded. The look of the powerful and successful he'd learned to dread. The look of his time.

But that was not enough; his best trousers, baggy and black and made from cloth like the sails on masted-ships, were expected to fall also. And they did, once his thick belt had been slapped out of its buckle, and the heavy-gauge zip yanked to the end of its runner. Owning just four pairs of shorts, he felt some relief at having the foresight to have cleansed these moleskin-grey smalls with a bar of soap against a pumice stone in his sink. His underwear still felt fresh against his pale skin and fell easily to his ankles. Off came his boots and he never dared look up to see her face; not wearing socks under his working boots was a symbol of his poverty that he did not wish to share with a woman who probably lived in Zone Two. There was no chafing, though; the soles and heels of his feet were thick but as supple as a pilgrim's sandal leather.

Now he was naked; all his clothes were folded into a metal tray beside the bed in the surgery: a room cleaner than the marble in the museums and brighter than the white tiles of the baths that he used to dive down to and sit cross-legged upon, for as long as his lungs would allow. But under his feet, this floor was warm, and against one wall, beside the eye-test chart, there was a mirror so clear he was stunned at the sight of himself. It had been years since he had seen his body with such clarity. Perhaps this was the first real opportunity as an adult to truly see himself. Straight away, he cringed inside at the look of wonder on his face and in his eyes, beaming from the reflection like he was a child in front of a toy shop's windows. Same as in the picture he'd seen in an antique shop; a child who could not afford anything behind the frosted glass, and whose presence was ignored by the man with cufflinks and a peppermint shirt who stacked and stocked things for the little

3

girls in fur hats to see. It had been called 'Urchin in the snow'.

'On the bed, please,' she said, breaking his reverie.

A lump formed in his throat as he sat on the bed. The single red blanket, with the crisp sheet folded over at the top, with edges straight as a ruler, was spun from fine wool, like the lady's jumper he'd once touched during a squash for the underground. He'd had an audition in Zone Three, where rich ladies shopped for old furniture, and he'd brushed up against this woman by accident who had cream skin, a perfect face from one of the labs, no doubt, a furry hat on her head, and a cloud of perfume around her like a protective force-field he'd stumbled into by accident and had to get out of real quick, before the dogs, torches and zappers made him feel a pain so great, it turned black hair white in under an hour. But she'd filled his head for weeks, that fine lady wrapped in the fine wool. Every night, he'd dreamed of her, and even now, after so many years, he still remembered her smell. No one had ever made him so stiff. He swallowed and then cleared his throat as he stretched his height along the memory of a strange woman's jumper.

Feeling thin and rubbery all over, and fighting the urge to close his hands over his thatch and cock, he watched the consultant wheel a gleaming trolley over to the bed. On the top shelf he could see cotton wool, shiny dishes, tubes of paste and measuring things. Along the middle shelf were boxes of stuff and white spray cans with blue writing around the circumference. He didn't look too hard at the bottom shelf; below the hem of her white coat, her legs could be seen and he'd made an effort not to look down there. It had been forever since he'd been with a woman and besides her neck and perfect face – which made him

4

think of drinking wine in street-side cafés, and of opera boxes, and strolls along cold rivers, hand-in-hand, and not sex – the consultant's legs were all he could see of the real flesh under all that doctor clothing. She was tall and her feet were long and compacted inside black court shoes. But it was the sight of those delicate veins along the top of her feet, and of the pale flesh visible through her stockings, the nylon shining like winter sunlight on a cobweb, that created the first tightenings of the dreaded stiffness. Something that hounded him on the streets and drove him blind and confused from Zone Five to Two – he'd never been allowed in Zone One and was relieved; the sight of those professional classes in overcoats and furs, all glossy and serious in clouds of scent would have made him faint by forcing all the blood from his body into the stiffness.

Fighting arousal – he'd not relieved himself for three days on account of his nervous excitement and abject terror at the thought of the examination – Angel tried to distract himself with thoughts of the charity library in Binton, which couldn't afford interactive communication, where he spent afternoons alone with books and their mottled pages. One place he was usually free of stiffness. The victory was only half won; his cock thickened like a sleepy snake against the inside of his thighs. Had she noticed?

Whether she had or not, it never seemed to concern her; she just commenced with the wetting of tissues and the uncoiling of wires and a tube – the rubber purple like a plum, and entwined like a jungle snake across her sticky, gloved knuckles. Electrodes with soft velvety suckers were padded against his temples, inside his elbows, on his neck, nipples, and the backs of his knees. This did nothing to allay the stiffness; he felt as if he were under water with lots of tiny feeders going at his most delicate parts with their tiny nutrient-seeking mouths. She then plugged him into a computer that had an orange screen. Green blocks built up into towers along the length of the screen. Curious about which block was highest and trying to guess which part of him the signal had come from (my knees, my neck), he turned his head.

'Stay still,' she said, curt.

Angel croaked the word, 'Sorry.'

But she did not respond. Indifferent, she tapped the buttons of the keypad, then took a speck of blood with a needle from the cleft of his elbow, and dropped it on to a glass slide which she slipped inside the computer, before leaning across him to run an X-ray lamp over his body from top to toe. During all this, the hard curve of her breasts became suddenly soft as they pressed his ribs and chest and, finally, his chin. This necessary contact was too much; blood started to pound against his temples; his throat went dry as if he'd inhaled sawdust, and his stiffness approached maturity. Her minty breath was on his face; he could smell the silvery perfume of her lipsticked mouth and the moisturiser on her girlie throat and see the tiny sparkles in her dark eye-shadow. They were close enough to kiss when she checked the canals in his ears. He tried to look through her when she shone a red pinpoint of light at his eyes, tried to focus on the ceiling when he heard her breath slip across her bright teeth, and went all taut inside when her body warmth melded with his own – his stomach vanishing when one of her buttocks squashed into his thigh. As there was no other sound in the surgery to distract his keen hearing, he was also forced to listen to all the tiny whispers coming from under her skirt as her smooth legs crossed, and as her breasts rustled in the black lacy cups he could see outlined beneath her blouse.

6

When his wayward mind imagined a thin bra strap crossing her pale shoulder, his stiffness clenched from the inside.

She'd sat back, pulling her warmth away, to tap more of his information into the computer when she noticed his discomfort – the distress in his face and the thickness between his thighs. Immediately, she turned her face towards his crotch to see what she'd done to him.

Thoughts of failure rang peals of alarm through Angel's skull and his entire body flushed hot. 'Better go,' he said, but hadn't the strength to sit up. Instead, he lifted his head off the pillow, found it too heavy with leaden embarrassment for his neck to support, and let it fall back down.

Something came alive in those clear eyes of hers. They seemed to grow wider. She said, 'Why?'

Words got stuck inside him. Sentences were washed away like frail bridges in floods. Out came the sweats. Cold went the sweats on his skin. 'Never ... You know ... Well ... Never happened before ... So ...'

Her laugh seemed to slap his face. Then she stopped the outburst, placed one sticky hand on his shoulder and said, 'I am sorry.'

'OK,' he said.

'There's a first time for everything,' she said. 'A shy one. It says on your chart you're an actor. Do actors get bashful? I'm afraid there isn't a category for humility on the assessment.' She looked pensive; devastating with her suddenly animate and clever face. 'Perhaps there should be. It might sell. Could be a winner. All the actors and dancers we get from the Zones are so full of themselves. To get one with humility ... Someone who blushes. From the townships too. You never see that.'

Anger smouldered red. The stiffness wilted. She thought him dumb. So fucking stupid, she'd

7

explained a word. She felt the need to give him a definition of *humility* because she thought him illiterate. Like the assessor and guardians at charity school, so many years before, who shook their heads at his mute incomprehension in front of the computer screens – the 'confusers', he'd called them at school, behind their ever-turning backs and ever-sighing mouths and ever-shrugging shoulders. 'I'm not stupid, you know,' he blurted out. 'I know what humility means.'

Silence in the surgery seemed to fall across him like winding sheets to bind him tight. What had he done? What was he thinking? He'd dared to raise his voice to a professional. This was the end. This should be the end after failing another interview for a High-Zone position – they were so scarce for those with unspecified skills. He felt ready for the final fall – the drop into the garden of sleep; no funeral, just the bin men to carry his useless weight inside polythene sheets towards the flames of that giant fire stoked by the environment agency, into which they put the meaningless and unsuccessful and unfulfilled. There was no smile on her face now. So he'd blown it. The assessment, the job, the chance of a better life out of the townships and all the broken glass in the swimming baths. He'd go back and stay in the charity library until he died of old age, reading his way to death, reading all about the world that the 'confusers' and the 'confuser' people had spoiled.

Her cheeks became pinky smudges. 'Sorry, I never meant offence. It's just –'

He finished for her. 'It's just that everyone from the townships is stupid. Too dumb to get out. Maybe my IQ is similar to that of a chimpanzee, but it's a measure of only one kind of intelligence. There are others, you know.'

She began to giggle, covering her nose and mouth with her rubbery hands, while she shook her head and tried to say sorry. Stop laughing at me, he wanted to say to the pretty woman in the white coat who had measured his inner workings with wires, and pricked him with a pin. Never had he felt so vulnerable or so alone. Inside him, the storm of thought and emotion, that made him go hot all over, found no expression. Like in acting class, it all spun about but found no 'balance', no 'articulation', no 'form', as the tutors had said. He failed in the defence of his soul as he failed at his acting as he failed at his life. The life he'd have to go back to. Black bread in a room with wet walls.

But then she surprised him. The smile that followed her laughter stunned him. The voice was softer than he'd expected. 'Relax, will you? And don't give up so easily. You passed the physical.'

He swallowed; the tantrum vanished as suddenly as it had reached meltdown. Now he felt foolish.

'My, my, my. Your heart rate –' she winked at him '– for a moment, I thought you were going to break the machine. Passion,' she said, narrowing her eyes – mocking him, perhaps. No, it was something else. He'd begun to interest this perfect, invulnerable woman. 'It'll come in useful in your new job. She'll . . . I mean, they'll like that, the clients.'

Elation surged through him; the weight was suddenly gone from his body. It was as if his spirit had expanded and filled the room with light; he could almost see it happening around him. She'd said, 'his new job,' like it was his for the taking now. 'I passed,' he said, his voice faint.

She nodded. 'Mmm. With flying colours. Great bone formation and healthy organs. Slight body fat. Could do with some nourishment, but I'd kill for muscle tone like yours. Do you lift weights?'

'Swim,' he said, confident now, a player.

'You swim? Which complex?'

'Not in a complex. In the baths at Binton, and the canals outside the limits. Sometimes up the river, too, against the current in the summer.'

She was stunned. 'A canal swimmer. I've read about that. Thought it was just a myth.'

He smiled. 'Swum all the major arteries.'

'Isn't it dangerous? What about the boats?'

'Stay deep, and claw the bricks when you hear the motors.'

She pondered his words; she liked them. Time for a compliment. 'Well, it shows. You have shoulders like a gymnast and lungs like a boxer. I've done those, you know, athletes. Before the Olympics in my last job. Do you compete?'

But she hadn't a clue. Athletes came from farms; from families who could afford the maintenance. 'Compete? Only in the inoculation queues,' he said, remembering those long lines and the silence that hid the panic as people lined up for a jab against a new strain of death created by another half a centigrade rise in the planet's temperature.

She blushed with embarrassment. 'Sorry, I forgot.'

He smiled. 'For a moment you forgot my residential code and IQ rating and thought I was good enough for a farm. And besides, since they purified the waterways, the safest place is under the water. Guess that's why I spend so much time down there.' Sometimes that happened. People were fooled by his vocabulary and took him for an educated man. If only they knew it all came from the books, stamped with the disease risk notice in the charity library. It was his joke at the world's expense.

She nodded, her head angled, her interest tweaked. 'And your blood is clear, besides a slight deficiency in

10

iron. Never seen anyone in such good shape from the townships.'

'Use your freedom wisely,' he said, quoting from the corporate billboards that preached to the township populace about charity education, about learning to use confusers, in order to spend all of your waking life in a cubicle, plugged into one.

She laughed, but checked her watch which disappointed him slightly. 'I'll do a detox and descale because I'm sure you'll pass the psyche. Your skin could use some work. A freebie for your humility.'

'And then the psyche?'

She winked. 'The finals.'

His balls shrivelled. 'Finals?'

'You need to be able to perform. Your responses must be tested. But you're an actor. I bet control comes easily.'

'What does it involve?' His question was genuine; the facial expression backing it up. Once again he was the 'Urchin in the snow'.

She looked at him dreamily – lost herself for a moment. 'Don't worry, it's the best bit. A consultant will try you out.' Then she looked right into his eyes. 'She'll assess your psyche and physical performance simultaneously, in an intimacy equation.'

'Stand before me,' she said, from where she was sitting, perched on the end of the bed.

This was a strange building. After a medical in the doctor's surgery, he'd been led through a maze of corridors that smelled of strawberry ice-cream to this place: a bedroom like those he imagined existed in a hotel for travelling professionals.

'Remove your gown. I'm on a tight schedule. This can't take long,' she said, and unfastened the bracelet of her watch. It was thin and made from gold.

11

Hesitation would be fatal. Fighting the rising fear and panic and excitement, Angel removed his robe and threw it on the bed beside her. A nice touch. The woman immediately shook her hair loose; it was dark and shone all the way down to her shoulders. 'Unzip,' she said, her voice still unfriendly, and stood with her back to him. Angel walked forwards and took the tiny zipper between the finger and thumb of his right hand, and pinched the material of the black dress between the woman's shoulder blades with his left hand. Slowly, so as not to catch her skin, or wrinkle the dress, he lowered the zip to her waist. Then she turned her face to one side in expectation of something else. Frantic, he tried to guess what he should do next; the zipper was down: what did she want now?

Against his crotch, she wiggled her backside. Take the dress off; of course. Slipping the thin black straps over her pale shoulders, that smelled so spicy and good, Angel worked the weightless fabric down her back to her hips. She pulled her ankles together to narrow her legs. Falling to his knees, he felt his body speed up; hands, heart, breathing. Over her buttocks he spread his palms and pushed downwards. Being so thin, the material expanded and then slithered down her legs to her ankles. For a moment, he went dizzy. Stockings, sheer and black, with the slim tops tucked under the bottom of her buttocks at the top of her thighs, coated her legs all the way down to her feet in the shoes made from two boot-lace straps – one around the ankle, the second across the bridge of the toes. Only the bra and thong were left.

It was almost too much to comprehend. He was being assessed for his suitability as a *companion* to the professional classes and, initially, he'd assumed that meant carrying luggage, or cleaning, or gardening, or shopping, or child-minding and so forth. But intuition had told him something extraordinary was about to happen when the pretty bio-consultant had measured his erection after the detox and said, 'No enhancement required.'

The woman in the studio walked away from him, back towards the bed. 'Pour me a drink,' she said, wafting a lazy hand towards a cabinet beside a full-length mirror. 'Dry with a sparkle.' Back on his feet, Angel made his way to the cabinet, confused. Refusing to drink the beer and spirits of Binton Town, on account of the damage it did – a social evil second only to the recreational 'fisties' and 'shoeings' alcohol usually accompanied – he guessed that 'Dry with a sparkle' would mean something fizzy with whisky or gin splashed in. With the concoction in hand, he then moved back across to the woman on the bed. With her lips parted and a look in her eye that shrivelled him up inside, but stiffened and thickened his cock, she pointed a foot towards him, spike-heel first. He gave her the drink and settled on his knees.

With fingers cold and trembly, the way they were after a long swim, he unfastened the ankle strap of her shoe and eased it off her foot. The shoe was so light he took a moment to weigh it on the palm of his hand and to marvel at it. Never had he held something so expensive. The other leg was extended. While he removed the second shoe, she pushed his cock against his belly with the underside of her toes on her free foot, and made a low hummy sound, like the stray cats he fed and nuzzled in the yard behind his housing block.

On his knees before the object of a lifetime's adoration, it was hard to think straight. After so many imagined scenarios with High-Zone women, and thousands of erections created by just the thought and not the sight of them, he found it hard to comprehend that he was actually touching one. And yet, it was real. In his lap, he was stroking the slippery foot of a professional woman.

'Fuck me now,' she said, her eyes so narrow he couldn't read anything beside a challenge in them. He shook away the instinctive shock of hearing her say that word, and rose to his full height. On his feet, something overcame him; it was quick, too sudden to stop, if he even wanted to, which he did not. It was like the power when he stood naked before flat water with the sun setting above him. Just before the dive and then the swim that could last for ever, everything fell into place in his head and the world was not so hard to understand any more. Tingling pinpricks passed through his stiffness; his belly went tight; every part of his body felt strong and good and complete. He fell on her. She was surprised.

Her breathing came fast. Her nasty, beautiful eyes flashed wide. Seized at the wrist, her thin arms, toned by the electric stretching and massage machines in the exercise complexes, became useless in his leather hands, and were pressed into the bed behind her head. As if cradling a glass full of rich brandy with a Christmas pudding taste, he slipped a hand under her bottom and moved her fragile body up the bed, where he would find the room and space required. Off came her thong, snapped off her feet like an elastic band.

'Slow,' she said. 'Be careful,' she muttered, a little scared.

He shushed her and then shook his head to refuse her request. Her eyes went wider and she tried to turn on to her front and crawl away. Angel slapped her buttocks hard. Couldn't help himself. After being taunted by all the money of the high zones and all the

14

beauty and comfort and peace it could buy, he'd lost control of himself and obeyed the zesty spirit that filled him up and seemed to engorge the room with hot body smells, and an invisible power that threatened to make the sound of thunder. Everything was a blur seen through a red lens.

'Ah,' she said, and screwed her face up when he sank inside her. So tight at first; she bit her fingers and then slapped her palms against his chest. Covering her entire mouth with his own, sharp with half a day's stubble, he sucked in her expensive air and glossy lipstick and plunged right to the back of her sex, straight and deep. He moved into the position he made for morning press-ups; her legs tightened around his waist. Like a tiny mammal hanging underneath a tree branch, her body rose with him, only to be slammed down to the bed over and over again when his hips made a thrust. Wordless, she closed her eyes and made soft grunty noises that he liked – even they sounded expensive. Then it struck him – her taste? What did a high-zone woman taste like?

After withdrawing from her, which was only achieved by a concentration of will, and which caused her to cry out and claw his shoulders to the point when they stung, as the thin sheen of sweat on his back ran through the diamond-stylus grooves her lacquered nails made on his skin, he then sat between her open legs and looked down. This wasn't tangled and crispy hair on her sex, this was a pelt. Shorn and level, it made him think of the teeny gardens with flowers you saw in Zone Two at the foot of the skyscrapers. Pink flesh was visible in the middle. A slit, wet and without a trace of odour until his mouth and nose were made shiny by it. She pulled a pillow over her face, like she couldn't bear to look at him.

Good; he would be able to take his time without the cold scrutiny of her eyes. Running his tongue, with the tip outstretched, between her lips and then inside her, Angel savoured the taste. Salty but perfumed with a meaty impression, he found a part of her not changed by money. Immediately, he glowed inside, thinking a vast chasm had been crossed in the simplest way.

Just inside the slippery reddish hood at the top of her sex, he used his tongue to find a part of her that was so delicate, her muscles rippled under her skin, all the way up her body when he pressed it. He could only just see this happen but, where he touched her with his mouth, he could feel her vibrations. Sucking lazily and then hard, he eventually pulled this part of her into his mouth, and rinsed it in and out between his lips. Warm and wet, she pooled on his chin and made his jaw slippery. While his mouth played, it was as if little bolts were being pulled through latches inside her, unlocking and freeing all the wild things she kept hidden. She began to produce a continuous series of rhythmic grunts, with a hard sound that didn't match the rest of her prettiness. Then she started to move her bottom up and down until she held her sex, with a slight pressure, against his mouth, pushing her lips against his teeth. After she began to jerk, and when she became silent, he took his mouth away.

Up the outside of her legs his hands slipped until they reached her thickish ankles. With one hand, he clamped them together and used his free arm to circle her thighs and to pull her sex and buttocks against his crotch. Shocked, she peeked from beneath the pillow, as if dreading the next move, but secretly wishing it too. Releasing her thighs, but still holding her up by her ankles so her tailbone was suspended an inch from the sheets, Angel pushed the fat bulb of his cock

16

back inside her. Moving his body over her, so her legs parted and passed over his shoulders, he pressed right to the back of her again, as far inside as he could get so even the base of his cock disappeared. From her pursed lips, she made a long 'oh' sound.

'Going to be really hard, miss,' he said. 'I can't help it,' he confessed. 'And I'm going to come,' he added, taking the greatest liberty, which made him want to come, just by saying it to a professional high-zone woman. In response to his audacity – something that only came out of him when he loved a woman – she squeezed her eyes shut and dug her fingernails into his forearms. And so to relieve the pressure of his entire adult life, of so many baffling journeys through the higher zones, of so many quick peeks at the pale breasts and long legs of the working girls, of too many dizzy spells on the underground and outside the windows of the salons where he watched them chat on teeny phones, drink frothy coffee in long glasses and pick at bits of leaf on their plates, Angel released himself. Allowing his longing to take hold, he enacted the hardest pounding he'd ever been capable of, right into this soft creature with a vicious face, until her hair was sticking out at all angles, and her enhanced features were red and screwed up into a sun-dried tomato thing, that was pretty all the same. Out came the deepest groan of relief as his seed scalded through him and vanished inside her.

He knew she would feel the presence of him when he was gone and would have to go to the strawberry-smelling bathroom to dab at her sweet pelt to catch drops of his love spilled for all of them, with the high shoes, arctic-sea eyes, bullet breasts, and shiny hair-styles pulled into tight buns under their little hats.

Nothing mattered now. He was inside her. Two more major pulses inside his cock than ever before,

17

three more small throbs than he expected, and it was over. Now he could breathe. Now he could lie on her and squeeze her soft body and smell her hair and kiss her cheeks and tell her a secret: 'At last.'

She never moved away, but squashed herself further into him with her eyes closed and her lips parted on his chest, so soft on the ticklish skin around his nipple.

But that was not the end. It was only the first of many trials for Angel. For soon the woman was cold again and in her high shoes and walking about the room, gathering herself, smoothing her hair back, spitting the drink he'd prepared back into the glass, breathing through her thin nose so it went even thinner, avoiding his eyes, while he lay on the bed, confused, with an ache inside him, wondering why she'd left the warm nest they had loved into the bed, where they could lie without talking and could communicate and bond through warmth and slowing breaths. How could anyone leave all that so abruptly?

'Be advised that someone is watching,' she said, and picked up a little remote that he imagined was for the giant tele-screen fixed into the wall opposite the drinks cabinet and mirror. 'And that, without your consent, you will be filmed and photographed. This may be used for the future training purposes of our staff.'

Angel blinked. His mouth hung open.

Pointing the remote at the giant silver screen, she pressed a button. From opaque, it went clear. Angel sat up, too shocked to do anything but stare. Four people sat on chairs; two women, two men, all dressed in the lab-coats of the bio-consultant. On their laps were tiny 'confusers' with flip tops. 'Companions are often required for group situations,' his intimacy assessor said, her voice flat again. 'Can you perform under scrutiny?'

18

Tricked. The lab-coats had watched their love-making. Feeling weak, Angel stood up, his gown clutched over his soft cock. Every face behind the screen watched him; their faces unmoving. His assessor placed her hand on his shoulder. 'Kiss me.'

This was the final; and they had selected him because of his social classification as an actor. He had only been given the interview card, on the street outside the community acting school two weeks previously, because the man who had followed him that morning, who he'd thought was a policeman, had connected his physique and good looks to his supposed ability as a performer. Before this test went any further, perhaps he should tell them that he was a fraud; that he couldn't act and got confused when people looked at him. And after passing the medical and then being permitted to sleep with a professional woman, he was now doomed. It should have been the greatest day of his life. But he should have known these people were tricksters; that everything was a calculation and an agenda; everything was measured and marketed and squeezed into a definite value, a quantity, even people whose births were manufactured, unless, like him, they were accidents. Perhaps the anarchists were right by claiming the flu that halved the world's population had been made by them – the professionals. And now they expected him to perform on a stage of their own making.

Pride made his body hard. His mind sought a refuge and he thought of the water and how it fell from the sky for him to swim in. No, they could not control or sell the weather. That had never worked. And he knew the secrets of the waterways. For some reason it gave him strength now, the knowledge of that. Enough courage for their challenge. He'd made a technocrat woman climax and hug him tight – a high-zone woman. He'd do it again.

'Ow,' she said, when he kissed her mouth hard. 'That hurt me.' Her face went sulky.

'Sorry. But you're so pretty. It's like I want to eat you all in one go.' And then his voice dropped to a whisper. 'Even with them watching us.'

She softened against him, ready to smile. Only her half-lidded eyes still betrayed petulance. 'There will be husbands who like to watch. Who will like to watch you inside their wives. There is such a demand. Very few companions can manage it.'

Then I will, he thought. Because I am lost when I see their wives, and I will perform. It will be different. Not like on the stage at school when I have to remember lines and suffer the faces turned towards me under the hot white lights. This is different. I will say the lines that come to me and be a swimmer. That's my secret; I'll fill up with the power of the currents, and the cold, and the depths, and swim to the heart of their city, because I want to see if it is heaven.

He carried the woman across the room to the mirror. She was surprised again. 'Maybe we should –' she tried to say, but he shushed her with a long kiss, and then stroked her ear with the tip of his nose.

Before the mirror he placed her, gently, on her heels and then bent her over, so she could see her face and his hard body behind her, and behind him the people watching them too, with his back turned to them – complying but snubbing too, and snubbing the technocrats was always good. And he went to the mirror because he suspected a watching husband would like to see the love-making more than once; for real in his marital bedroom and in a mirror at the same time. If you liked to watch such a thing for amusement, such as your wife with a stranger, then it would be good if the stranger had imagination. And

Angel always grew stronger when he relied on his imagination to get through difficulty.

Closing his eyes, he enjoyed the feel of her skin through the palms of his hands as he explored her; the delicate nature of her, the shape of her curves and dips and hollows. 'Yes,' he said. 'You are truly beautiful.'

'Mmm,' she murmured and pressed her bottom against his stiffness.

'This will take longer than the first time. It has been a while for me. That's why I was quick on the bed. I just needed to come in you. But the second time is always longer. Much longer.'

'Oh, yes. That's OK.'

Then a strange thing happened. What he had said made her giggle. Soon, they were both laughing. In the mirror, behind him, he caught a glimpse of the watching consultants. They were surprised and seemed to want to get closer and see more of what was going on in the studio. This gave Angel further confidence and he stayed hard and thick and solid. From behind, he then sank through the assessor. Making a long moaning sound, she dropped her perfect head between her shoulders.

'That's it. Slow at first. Then we'll go faster. Really fast.' He said the lines that popped into his head, that he felt were right for the situation, for the audition. He was acting before an audience, but he believed in what he was doing for the first time.

Making soft panting sounds, his lover rocked back and forth with his rhythm, that stayed constant and only paused at the conclusion of every slippery insertion he made deep inside her, so he could then grind against her bottom. In the mirror, he caught her peeking through all her hair, peering at the mirror so she could watch his body totally engaged in pleasuring itself on her beauty, on the final, peak-condition results of all her enhancements – dietary and surgical. Then, using his strength, he began to shake her about on his cock, planted to the root, as all the little shivery sensations passed through his arms and down the back of his calves. 'So soft. So soft on my hard cock,' he said.

'Yes,' she said, in a trembly voice.

'So soft it makes me want to do this,' he said and began to tug her, savagely, on and off his sex. Her head had dropped again and hung down by her knees. She held her thighs and rubbed her hands up and down her stockings until she lost control of her fingers and was content to be hauled backwards to his body and then thrust out so her teary face was closer to the mirror. 'Don't know where I want to come,' he said in a breathless voice. 'In you, or down the back of your legs.' She moaned even louder than before and began to bang her buttocks against him, accommodating his tugging, adding force to it.

'Or somewhere else . . .' he started to say, thinking of her breasts, swinging free: white with the dark nipples he hadn't even sucked because she said time was short.

'Oh, yes,' she cried. 'Yes, in my arse. Fuck it into my arse.'

Angel felt his body freeze. Did high-zone women do that? It was preposterous. Clearly preposterous. With so many degrees and credit cards and gene evaluations that made them capable of playing stocks and shares during the day, before playing grand pianos on high balconies at night, how could they do such a thing? He'd never done it, and the merest thought of it made him ashamed and hot and so aroused he experienced such a powerful dizzy spell, he suspected he might faint. But Angel kept his feet, slipped from her sex, listened to her frantic breathing, building with excitement, and then pushed his cock against the tight pink tissue of her anus. 'How will it fit?' he said, in a moment of clarity, but this only excited her further.

'Put it in,' she cried out, before whispering, 'you bastard,' as if he were tormenting her with the delay.

And he was a bastard too; orphaned, unwanted, but suddenly craved and loved by her. She hadn't been thinking of his birthright, so he forgave her the word, knowing it only came from excitement.

'This will hurt,' he said.

'Yes!' she shouted, her voice deep.

Wetting his length with both spit and the stickiness between her legs that he dipped his fingers into, he made a swift initial entry before the natural lubricant could dry, and slipped it, centimetre by centimetre, half inside her, because she was of a light physique and he knew, without a shred of immodesty, that his cock was thick. 'Fat,' his last Binton lover had said, so long ago, during their reckless loving in the townships.

Like she was walking across hot coals, his lover made quiet, 'Ah, ah, ah,' sounds, and in the mirror he could see her legs quivering.

'All of it?' he asked.

'Yes, yes, yes,' she said.

Amazed at the disappearance of his length inside her, and still wary of hurting her, or it being dangerous for such a slender woman, Angel pressed his remaining girth inside her slowly. He'd forgotten about the watching consultants, but as he raised his head to savour her tightness around him, he noticed how uncomfortable they had become trying to restrain their curiosity but failing to maintain their facial detachment and indifference. They were absorbed.

Pulling back, Angel waited until only his cock-head was still within her arse before pushing back in. It would make his cock feel even longer to her, and make her relive the initial penetration over and over again. What little weight the woman possessed now seemed to have vanished. She was limp, not beholden to gravity, while he felt solid and stronger than ever. Holding her hips tight, he pulled her back and forth, building speed and friction, no longer concerned about the moans she made, that sounded as if she were in pain as she kept saying, 'Yes. Fuck me. Yes. Fuck me.'

When his fullest realisation dawned – of what he was doing, where he was doing it and whom he was doing it to, while others watched – Angel knew he would come. That there was nothing he could do about it and that he was wrong about the second time lasting an age. 'Oh, I'm sorry, miss, but I'm going to come. Right now.'

'Yes,' she said, circling her fingers around her sex as if she was beating eggs in a bowl.

'All of it. Every drop,' he said, his voice gaspy.

She came, bending her head back, showing him her face in the mirror.

Little stars exploded inside his head while a long shudder passed through his body. Angel let go. She collapsed against him and he held her upright in order to keep his cock planted until every drop, as promised, had been released at depth. Still attached to her, he pulled her body up against his chest and then he kissed the side of her damp head.

'Stay inside me,' she whispered to him – just to him and not for the people behind the screen. 'Don't come out of me. Please.'

Another room; another woman. 'No income beside welfare? A charity stipend is paid to your municipal

24

account for the tuition of a community education programme, in acting. Is that all you receive by way of funding?'

'Yes.'

'No credit rating.' Her long fingers confirmed his destitution with one tap on a keyboard. 'Dependants?'

'Just the mouse in my room.' His attempt at humour failed. The woman's face was angled towards the computer screen and was lit up by a greeny glow. She just moved her eyes to the side to look at him. 'May I remind you that giving false information to a corporation will lead to criminal charges.'

'No dependants,' he said, colouring a hot red.

She looked pleased with herself. 'An IQ ranking of *disadvantaged*. And no employment record beyond public service for four years following a clipped education.'

Immediately, he smelled the turpentine, paint thinner, sewage and waste products of public service. 'That's right.'

She nodded. 'During the assessment, you failed on social intercourse. Your etiquette rating was zero.' Angel went cold. 'This incorporates the image rating. Also zero,' she said with apparent delight. Tired in body, mind and spirit and unable to listen to any more, Angel made ready to stand up and leave. 'But –' she raised her tone of voice '– those defects are superficial. Physically, you are more than adequate, and, surprisingly –' her eyebrows rose '– your psyche assessment and performance achieved top marks. A fluctuation in our forecast. Perhaps your IQ could be re-evaluated after a period of service. This would raise your social rating. Think seriously about the benefits.'

No, he thought, no more tests. If I get through this, I'll be an enigma and I'll surprise you.

Under the table her legs crossed with a hiss. She turned her whole body to face him, her entire face to wither him. 'Although you fall well below secondary selection criteria, we may overlook your failings if you agree to the following.' Then her eyes moved rapidly from left to right as they read from the screen she'd positioned between them. Speaking quickly, she said, 'When engaged in our employ you agree to a discretionary contract. This is rigorously enforced. If broken, you face criminal charges. By this I mean there is to be no discussion or revelation of your association with the corporation on any level, beyond your employ as an actor.'

He nodded.

'This interaction is being recorded. Your answer must be audible.'

'Yes,' he said.

She nodded. 'On an engagement you will be immaculate of appearance and maintain a premium level of personal hygiene, unless otherwise instructed. A client may prefer the natural odour of a companion. If this is so you will harvest it, as well as any image they require, to their specific brief.

'On an engagement you are technically and legally owned by a client. You will never make conversation or venture opinion unless explicitly asked. Never criticise a client. Never accept tips or accept social engagements outside of contracted service. Relationships of any physical nature are prohibited with any other persons while in our service. Masturbation, alcohol consumption, drug inducements are prohibited, as is any practice capable of undermining the constitution or professionalism of a companion.

'You agree to the inducement of pain within reason, scarification, bodily enhancement if required – although this is unlikely outside of an investment project – and you are insured for full bodily and psyche repair by the corporation should injury result within the specifics of our employ . . .'

There was more; list after list of what he should not do, of risks he would take. Unwilling to take on any further anxiety about dealing with a corporation, Angel stopped listening and became distracted by the woman's face and wondered if it too would soften under his touch. There was something about him they valued.

'May I remind you that a breach in this contract will result in the immediate termination of your employment for the corporation, and may lead to criminal prosecution. Under the terms and conditions recited to you, do you, Angel Smike, agree to serve as a companion for Leisure.corp?'

'Yes.'

Quickly, her fingers sped across a series of keys. 'A sign-on fee for four thousand units, International, has been credited to your account. Effective immediately, but repayable on the failure of probation.' As she continued to speak, finally, of the benefits, of the pieces of silver, thrown to him from the immeasurable coffers of the high zones, Angel wanted to weep. Something stuck in his throat and the room seemed to shimmer, ever so slightly, at the periphery of his vision. He wanted to breathe the cold air that settles over water to clear his head. This sign-up fee was more than the sum total of his life's earnings and handouts, and probably more than the cost of his free education. He'd often dreamed of what he would do with half of that amount.

'I suggest you move from the outer townships to a Zone address,' she added. 'It will aid our communications with you and assist your travelling. All of your work will be carried out within the perimeters of the higher zones. A wardrobe enhancement is provided by the corporation and deductible from future earnings. I suggest you take advantage of it; we have the best stylists in our employ. Medical insurance is granted during the period of your employ, as is the use of all Leisure.corp facilities at a discounted rate.'

Finally, she smiled. And only smiled because they, he and she, now worked for the same corporation. After that final key stroke on her 'confuser' to confirm his declaration of loyalty, he was something she could accept. 'Welcome to our family.'

Two

'She is waiting for you on the ninety-sixth floor. She will be alone. When the rendezvous is reached, perform. You have one hour. Assertiveness is required. Overpower resistance. Do not speak to the client. Touch nothing but the client, and then leave the equipment and uniform at reception on your departure ...' And there was little else, beside the address, transmitted to the communicator given to him by Leisure.corp and permanently attached to his wrist – in effect a mini-computer he'd neither the patience nor inclination to fiddle with or understand. Once his probationary period concluded, it was to be his only line of communication with them and he was to keep it with him at all times.

Pausing in his ascent to the rendezvous with his first client, Angel leaned against the wall of an upper stairwell in the giant Zone Two tower. This portion of the building had been developed to lull its occupants into the calm achieved by looking out at a great body of water. Even the scent vents pumped a cocktail of fresh ocean breezes throughout the three floors of the skyscraper, owned by Vision, a software corporation. Surprisingly, the pale marine colours and gentle smells did little to calm him. Beset by anxiety, he began to wonder whether his former life, the one he was about to escape on his first assignment, was a torment or a sanctuary. It was one of those moments when the mind played tricks, and the past, no matter how grim, was doused in warmth and golden light as the present created a new difficulty. His being here, thousands of feet above the ground in Zone Two, seemed unnatural. The terrain, what was done here, the sense of cleanliness, the scientific conditioning of an environment, was all too much to process; it was the present but seemed like the future to him. And to perform here, to meet expectations, when he could hardly feel his legs or breathe because of the tightness in his chest, and when so much could go wrong.

Clad in the black jump-suit of a security officer, with a gun, riot baton, torch and innumerable swipe cards on his utility belt, Angel proceeded upwards past the ninety-fifth floor. Knowing nothing of the client, he could only guess that she was important – she had to be, to work this high up – and enjoyed games; after-hours games with silent assailants in uniforms. Again, his comprehension was stretched. How could high-zone women do these things? It was not what he imagined watching them from afar for so many years.

At the top of the stairwell, he saw a plaque indicating that he had reached the ninety-sixth floor. He would have to overpower a woman – a stranger. The idea made him feel sick. There was nothing inside him that he could find and identify as excitement. It seemed to him that this was a game only to be played between lovers who were familiar with each other and who whispered their unusual yearnings in private; together in midnight confessionals between sheets made damp by love. This was not something to be played out between strangers; it was too random, too dangerous. And that notion in itself would impart a lesson to Angel about his new job.

A large, open-plan office opened out before him, free of clutter, decorated with sumptuous plants. Thin marble staircases ascended to platforms with thin steel railings around their edges, containing small dais-offices perched above the centre of the work space below. Promotion meant elevation, literally. Astonished by the space and design, made especially arresting when empty under subdued lights, Angel walked carefully in combat boots to the gigantic windows. They stretched fifty feet upwards to the ceiling. Pure glass, no handrail – just clear windows before the sight of a cityscape that stunned him. So far below in silence, each apartment light, every monorail snaking between the buildings, and each orange strip of street offered him a glimpse of the variety and expanse of life and lives – of so much occurring and changing below him. A new world.

His moment of wonder ended with the sound of capped heels behind him. They tapped on marble, then muted across carpet, before clacking against another strip of marble. The client. She was waiting for him: her excitement building; her game already begun; the anticipation suffocating her at moments throughout the long day, during the wait for nightfall, when everyone left for home and a stranger entered the building.

The sounds of occupancy were coming from the far end of the ground floor, where shadows crept under dim lights and threw dark rectangles up the walls to the creepers, spilling their arachnid legs over the sides of steel spheres. So it was there that she wished to be taken, in the dark. And it was a good place for prey to be overcome, in the cool of a strange forest floor, while the rest of the jungle slept.

Hugging the wall, he moved, silent, his eyes keen in the dark, one hand on his pistol grip, his jaw set, pausing when he picked up her scent. Opium. Heavy, spiced with mystery, settling at the top of his nose. Something pretty and delicate, wrapped in thin, expensive layers had given itself up with its aroma and careless steps on hard stones. Suddenly thrilled, Angel dropped to a crouch and then moved around a large desk to position himself behind a Grecian column that supported one of the platforms, making it look like a tree house in ancient Atlantis.

He saw her, from behind, as she stood before a small communicator screen fixed to a far wall, her slender outline lit up by the turquoise glow of the screen. Younger than he expected, she had coiled her blonde hair into a tight French pleat and dressed in black for her overtime hours: patent sling-back heels, a chic two-piece suit in a dark charcoal, lightly tanned skin just visible. Prepared for him.

For a moment, Angel was content to watch her, seeking clues and trying to understand why a young professional woman would feel the need to indulge in such a game. A game played so exactingly and convincingly by her with this pretence in being preoccupied with information on the screen, while beneath that was the desire to be taken from behind, to have force used against her, to have her intimacy stolen like plunder by a man who said nothing. Inside his jump-suit, Angel felt himself uncoil, and then stretch towards the prey. Maybe it wouldn't be so hard to perform this role.

Beside the occasional clack of her burgundy finger-nails on the keypad, there was only the sound of Angel's heart beating through the silence of his taut body as he approached. Now he was so close, he could see a freckle on the back of her neck, and the discreet velvet band that pinched her hair together. Her scent was stronger. Holding his breath, he brushed his hand across the front of his groin; his cock was hard and tingled after the gentle stroke. It was ready.

When he was no more than two feet away from her, she became aware of his presence and looked to the side, over her shoulder. A frown cut into her soft face; her lips parted; her blue eyes widened. She started. Both of her arms flailed when his hands seized her breasts; he parted her jacket, and clutched the heavy flesh of her bosom, held tight by a ribbed, lycra T-shirt. She twisted to the side and looked right into his face, the mixture of outrage and shock slapping him to his senses and making him pause, giving her time to twist around so she faced him but fell back against the computer screen at the same time. Now she looked surprised that someone with so handsome a face and with such gentle eyes would do such a thing. Why one so young and clean-shaven would risk chemical castration and life internment in Alaska for a grab of a professional girl. And she reacted as if she never expected him to do anything other than touch her breasts and this confusion kept her still as Angel fell to his knees and ran his hands up and down her long legs, making her stockings hiss between his hard hands and her shaven skin. They were glossy and sheer enough for him to see the tiny golden hairs on her thighs, and a birthmark, curiously shaped like a bat, on her right inner thigh.

'What are you doing?' she said, which made them both look askance at each other – her for saying it so softly, considering the situation, and him for hearing such a gentle voice and not being able to equate it with this kind of game. She wasn't acting; she was genuinely surprised. As instructed, he never spoke, but slipped his hand under her short skirt and rustly slip and pressed the palm of his hand against her

33

white panties. They were made from satin and slippery to the touch where they coated her tiny, clipped mound. Immediately she pushed her skirt downwards, and then seized his wrists when his hands refused to be knocked away. Speechless, she shook her head.

Angel stood up, and held her chin with finger and thumb. He kissed her. She kept her lips closed and her eyes wide open. Sinking his face into her neck, he filled his lungs with her perfume, and then held that breath to keep her inside him. She whimpered and pushed at his chest, to move him away from her tender neck. But Angel kept his face there and even bit the skin. She gasped and raised one leg, pushing her knee at his stomach. With one hand he cupped the back of her head and held it tight, so her throat stayed pressed against his teeth. His other hand ventured back inside her skirt and spread its fingers across her half-veiled sex. Against him, she shuddered, but continued to push at him, harder now.

Overcome resistance.

Angel growled and knocked her hands from his chest, before clamping her thin body against the rock-face of his torso. Inside her, his fingers then explored, two of them tickling the walls of this fresh sex. Wet between the fingers, his hand pushed up, gently but insistently, moving the woman up the screen she had fallen against. The knee dropped from his stomach and she stretched to her tiptoes, her thighs parted, her eyes closed. She made a sniffy sound, breathing through her nose in quick, random gusts that warmed his face.

Angel unbuttoned a portion of his jump-suit, and then worked his cock out. Cool air settled on his sex and around his hot groin; it felt good. He lifted her body from the floor by cupping his hands around the curves of her buttocks. From this elevation his eyes were briefly at the level of her mouth, now smudged from his kiss and open in helpless astonishment. At this height, he entered her, and then lowered her body down and against him so gravity would push his cock through her. No one had been this tight around his sex before and she expelled every jostling molecule of air from her body as her weight settled around his hips and her legs instinctively folded around the back of his knees.

Holding her aloft, so every muscle on his back hardened, he then eased her down to the marble floor, cradling her head to the tiles. For a moment, he nearly slipped out of her, and he thought she'd uttered a sigh of disappointment, but by moving his feet a fraction he stayed inside, and then moved his body across the top of her so she lay directly beneath him on the floor. Through the side of her panties, he then fucked her vigorously.

Not once did she open her eyes, or allow her fingers to leave his shoulders, digging into them at the top where he had strange pointy bones that people often used to stare at in the swimming baths. Content to be thrust into and moved across the floor, she kept her legs loosely wrapped around his waist, and just made sighing sounds that never rose or lowered no matter how hard he rammed himself into her, squashing her softness into the stone floor.

When his elbows ached from maintaining the position, and his knees rubbed uncomfortably on the marble tiles, he sat up and pulled her legs up his body so her heels spiked the air beside his temples. Having her long body stretched beneath him – the suit now dishevelled, the hairstyle now disturbed – and seeing the pretty face all lost and dreamy, with two fingers being sucked inside her mouth, Angel experienced a fresh, surging desire for this woman. For a woman who craved this experience and then requested it to be designed by his employers as an after-work treat, he wanted to be hard.

After knocking her shoes off, he licked the soles of her feet, bit into her ankles, and squeezed the back of her calves, wanting to consume all of her sweet parts instantly. Then he slapped her buttocks, hard, from the side. This she liked.

She said, 'Yes.'

One hand following the other, he spanked her white cheeks pink and then red, making her squeal and yelp and finally grin.

Twirling her over, desperate to be moving in and out of her again, he pulled her to all fours. A ladder ran white up the back of her leg and one stocking slipped down her left leg, wrinkling in dark, thin folds at the back of her knee. Still inside her, with his arms passing over her shoulders, and his lower body supported by the toes of his boots, Angel threw himself into her from behind. And she kept her body firm beneath him, taking his weight too, so every bit of his power would slap and then judder through the rest of her. When her head dipped between her shoulders and she began to make a neighing sound, that he thought unusual but exciting, Angel rocked back on to his knees and began to slap her buttocks again – from both sides, one hand following the other as before. As he smacked her bottom, half-concealed by a shiny slip and disordered panties, with the sound of his hand on her skin echoing wetly through the cavernous office, she began to bang her backside against him.

Gulping at the air, she started to shake. Her elbow eventually gave way and she fell against the floor, palms spread, cheek to the stone. Angel followed her down to the cold slabs and stretched along her back, so his mouth was close to her ear, allowing her to hear his rhythmic grunts; savage sounds so close to a perfect head. Building his rhythm into something fast, they moved across the floor to the wall, so she had to place her free hand against the blue plaster to protect her face. Angel came in her there, biting down on his desire to tell her to expect a gush inside her womb. But she was lost to him, as she spun through her own world, peaking, and swallowing the temperature-controlled air.

Wet beneath their clothes, they lay on the floor for a long time, cheek to cheek, he still on her back, covering her, squashing her, protecting her. When she finally opened her eyes, he moved off her and lay beside her to stroke the loose strands of blonde hair off her cheeks. Then he tucked himself away, kissed her, and stood up. Thinking it right to go – to leave her with her thoughts and calm – Angel walked away.

'Wait,' she said, folded away inside the darkness behind him. He turned and walked back to her. She was sitting up when he reached her, legs curled underneath her, side-saddle. 'Who are you?' she whispered. Through the dark between them, he sensed her trembling. Smiling, Angel ran his hand up her exposed thigh, offering to love her again as he suspected their hour had not yet concluded.

'No, not now,' she said. 'I shouldn't be here. It's too risky. But come and see me.' She handed him her card with a home address on it. Already, a client was asking him to break rules. Not wanting to upset her by refusing the card, he took it, but remained silent. 'Come and see me again. You don't have to knock. You can let yourself in. At night is best. Or on Sundays.' Then she stood up and skipped away, straightening her clothes and looping the straps of her sling-back shoes over her ankles as she left, vanishing through the door through which he had originally entered. Angel cocked his head to one side, thinking her escape odd. Part of the game, to be where she should not, perhaps. After savouring the last of her scent, he slipped her card inside the thigh pocket of his jump-suit, and ran his fingers through his hair. Time to go.

But Angel never made it to the door. Up above him, on one of the hovering platforms, another woman had appeared. She sat with her back to him, glancing at her watch before peering down over the side of the platform, expectant, but puzzled by the sound of the girl's heels. The blood slowed in his veins. His skin went cold. Unable to move, he stood and stared at the real client.

How long had she been there? And who had he just overcome against a wall and then taken savagely on the floor? Hot and then cold, Angel passed through every stage of terror until he arrived at panic. What had he done? Should he flee? Had the client heard him with the other girl? Did he even have the right building? His heart felt ready to seize.

Gradually he calmed himself; the girl had offered him her card. And it was not his fault; the building was supposed to be empty. No one else should have been working late. If it was at all possible to salvage his time in this strange new life, he would have to act immediately. Punctuality, the agency had said, was as important as performance. Checking his watch, he saw that he was twenty-five minutes late for the liaison, but maybe – and he had to think positively – the delay could work in his favour; it could suggest unpredictability and add to the client's pleasure. Straightening his jump-suit and utility belt, Angel made ready to correct his mistake.

Sweeping the ground floor from the sides, he made sure no one else had entered the complex. Upstairs on the dais, he could hear the client's heels tapping now, as she circled the platform, the altar on which she demanded to be sacrificed. Her shoes made an impatient, annoyed sound. Underneath the dais, Angel moved to the foot of the spiral staircase. Testing the first step, he felt relieved that it didn't creak. Unless she looked over the side of the platform at the moment he circled that point, he should be able to reach the top without detection. Holding his breath, he began the ascent.

He knew she'd sat back down by the time he reached the top quarter of the staircase, because her heels no longer made any noise. Climbing from the stairs, Angel hooked his hands over the edge of the dais. Choosing not to look down, he hung free, and moved his hands from side to side, around the platform, until he reached a point he guessed was directly behind both her desk and her back if she were seated. Holding his breath, so as not to give himself away with a grunt from the exertion of the climb, he pulled himself up so his eyes peeked over the surface of the floor. His estimation of her position was correct. He could see her clearly but only from the rear. Slightly overweight, but carrying it handsomely beneath a good tailored suit, with short blonde hair, she spun from side to side on her chair, sighing and blowing.

Effortlessly and silently, Angel pulled himself aloft until everything from his waist upwards was exposed. Still, she never turned, or even seemed aware of his presence. Looping his legs on to the platform would make some noise, though. While he thought of how to complete the final part of his manoeuvre, the client turned to her computer screen and began stabbing the buttons of the keypad. One of her feet kicked up and down too, making her chair squeak. Realising she was probably about to call his employers, Angel wasted no more time. Using the sounds of her annoyance to his advantage, he eased himself over the rails of the dais and then stood behind her.

At the very last moment, like the girl he'd just taken by accident, she became aware of him – must have seen him in the reflection on her screen. She spun her chair around until her foot hit his shin and brought her to a stop. With no expression on his face, Angel stared down at her. Like the other rare women with a large build he'd observed, the client's face retained the pretty features of her younger self. A healthy complexion had not aged taut and pointy like so many women in the city. Overweight women were scarce in the High Zones – genetic modification and effective bodily enhancements had all but removed the natural, maternal shape of women that was now so ardently sought after by a growing number of men. Angel was lucky – his client was an exotic. Small lips, painted dark, parted to release a gasp of shock. Eyebrows arched over lively green eyes, framed by mascara and shadow. Thick but shapely legs uncrossed.

But her moment of surprise quickly passed and it seemed his efforts were in vain. While he stood silent before her, fascinated in his study of her shape and the way she dressed to both conceal and reveal it, she began to tap the thin gold watch on her wrist. 'I requested an hour. On my timetable, one hour for leisure without sleep is worth the earning equivalent of six months for you, young man. In another thirty minutes, I have to leave for China. Punctuality is something I prize. If we can't keep our appointments, do we expect to be rewarded?' She gave a look to wither. 'And what will your superiors think?'

Being so accustomed to diffidence and confusion recently, when faced with the professionals, Angel managed to maintain an inner calm. Especially as it seemed his new job was to be terminated on the first night. That was her intention – this powerful woman whom he'd kept waiting for the time it took for washing water to heat in his home. So he was to be fired, for not delivering, for not performing on time. With her surprise spoiled, and her anticipation turning to frustration, she'd slipped back into her 'work mode' – the attitude he imagined her adopting with younger, prettier women, and swaggering, professional men, as she guarded her perch, her Olympian platform, like a giant bird of prey. He enjoyed the thought; this woman disciplining him for tardiness, staring him down with her pretty, clever, devious eyes, with her body so solid above her Cuban-heeled shoes. Manipulative, and in command of his future, she was about to snatch the keys from his hands; the keys to this city of light he'd dreamed about for all of his life.

His cock thickened.

Maybe all was not lost. Perhaps he now understood a little more about her. Bullying her minions and killing her way to power; perhaps it made her dream of a juxtaposition, of being taken forcefully by an underling. Inspired by the memory of his latent ability, the resourcefulness he'd discovered with the intimacy assessor, Angel removed the riot baton from his belt in one long movement. The client stopped talking. He walked behind her chair, followed by her eyes, casually eyeing her large bosom, so she could see his flagrant and wilful delight at them. Never had he touched so large a bust, and the way they appeared compact beneath her blouse of white, unpatterned silk made something clench inside

41

him. With a clunk, his utility belt dropped to the floor.

Her mouth opened and her eyes widened. 'How dare –' she began to say, but stopped as he nonchalantly – insanely – unbuttoned his jump-suit. Horrified, she watched it fall from his shoulders to his waist and then down to his combat boots. Stooping over, without taking his eyes from her round knees, so shiny in flesh nylons, below the trim of her slip and the shiny fabric of her underskirt, Angel peeled the jump-suit over his combat boots. Ignoring the sudden movement of her hand to her chest and the way she tilted her body back and away from him in her chair, he took his time to eye the layer after layer of softness up her skirt, rustling over a greater, heavier softness he wanted to seize in handfuls and then thrust into.

When he pulled himself back up to his full height, she remained speechless but was unable to prevent herself from looking at his cock – thick and extending from his body. Her eyes eventually moved up to his. What he saw in them was hard, frightening even. He guessed for some it must be a joy to serve her, to look up to her platform and to imagine doing just what he was about to perform. Slowly, with incredulity, she shook her head from side to side.

Now or never. Do something dramatic or the moment is lost.

Stepping up to her, over her, wearing nothing but his combat boots, laced tight up his strong legs, he placed a hand, gently, on his cock and focused his stare at her mouth so she could not fail to see his intention. She swallowed. Cupping the back of her head, gently at first, but then more firmly, by applying pressure through his fingertips against her scalp, he turned her open-mouthed face towards him. Bending over, he kissed her. Almost immediately, her mouth opened and he had a sense of her large body relaxing into the chair beneath him, as if it opened before him.

She broke from the kiss. 'The surveillance cameras come back on in less than twenty minutes. There is no time. It's too late now.'

Too immersed in their game to stop, Angel smiled and let her know that the time was of no concern to him. He kissed her again and she began to whisper, 'No' repeatedly, before saying, 'The time, there's no time.' But she made the sound of one eating something delicious as he pushed his cock between her lips. Her eyes, with their long and girlie curling lashes, closed as he sank into her mouth. Holding her head still, with both hands on the base of her skull, he held her in position, but had to do little else. His cock was taken almost gratefully, and was sucked so well by tight cheeks and an expert tongue that he feared he would climax before long.

Working fast, she kept him in her mouth while hiking her skirt and slip up to her thighs. Wide but firm, there was no gap between her legs at the top. Shiny and tinted a smoky colour, her stockings stopped where her French knickers began. With one hand she tugged her underwear down to her knees and held his buttocks in place with the other to continue suckling him noiselessly. Wetting his skin and making it darker with her plum lipstick, she seemed to take so much of him inside her mouth and enjoyed him in a vigorous, enthusiastic way, making humming sounds with the bones at the front of her face as if he tasted good.

'You're a bad boy,' she said, smiling broadly, after reluctantly releasing him from her lips. 'Do you think you can do what you like? Mmm? Think you can have me?'

Angel went cold. The balance was redressed. There was something cruel in both her voice and stare. Almost grateful they only had twenty minutes together, he feared whether he could cope with such a woman for longer, and the thought of her as an enemy turned his stomach. Now he knew why she disdained the use of diets and toners; she stayed big to complement the vastness of her ambition and temper and vision. Was this world too much for him? If she had not continued to beat his cock through her hand, while kicking her knickers free from her feet, he was sure that fright would have frozen him inactive.

'Want to get this cock inside me?' Her eyes widened; there was a recklessness in them now. 'Umm? Want to fuck me?' She said 'fuck' slowly, relishing its harsh sound in her plump mouth. 'Think you're man enough to just take me, boy?'

Holding her arms by the elbow, Angel pulled her out of the chair. She said, 'Oh,' and began to smile. Her heavy breasts knocked against him, making him take a step back. Unable to blink, with a loud rushing sound between his ears, he kissed her and worked both hands inside her blouse. Rolling her head back with her eyes closed, she moaned as his hands pressed her breasts and as her nipples were rubbed, softly and then firmly, by the palms of his hands. 'Yes,' she said, and her claws nearly drew blood on his back. Angel yelped.

Slitting her eyes, so he could barely see them, she looked at him and her smile widened. 'I can fuck you over, boy. Finish you. Do you understand?'

He could not let her overwhelm him; she was testing him. Although forbidden to speak, he said, 'Do I look like I care, lady?'

Throwing her head back, she shrieked a wild, loud laugh. 'You'll be good at a party with that attitude. You'll be eaten alive.'

Invigorated by fear becoming excitement, he let a savage desire guide him. 'Turn around,' he said in a stern voice, too old for his years.

She liked it and said, 'Oh,' again, and then, 'Oh, sir,' in a sarcastic voice, but complied instantly with his demand and moved her hips about, taunting him. As she shoved her skirt up to a ruffle around her waist, her broad backside was revealed. Hesitantly, he patted it, making a little slapping sound with his open palm – the spanking had served him well so far. He smiled at the thought. She moaned and pulled her head back between her shoulders. Rubbing her wide cheeks, he bent her over the desk and then pulled the cuffs from his utility belt. Just the chink of steel in the air, so far above the ground, seized her attention. 'Bastard,' she said at him, turning her flushed and angry face to him. 'You fucking –'

He cut her short with a mighty slap against the right cheek of her backside. Huffing and moving her feet around, she offered no resistance as he snatched her arms up and cuffed them behind her back. Not only was she surprised, but genuinely pleased with him too. 'Oh, yes,' she said. 'Do it. Fucking do it.' The voice was deeper now, impassioned. Cushioned by her breasts, her body sprawled across the desk. He took up position at her side and then spanked her buttocks until his hand smarted.

Shaking his hand in the air, he took a moment to look about himself, dumbfounded by what had befallen him in less than a month. High above the city, he suddenly saw himself from outside of his body, slapping the buttocks of a professional woman. This moment was defining; he would never forget it despite its excess, the grotesque nature of it seen through sober eyes, the meaning of it.

Annoyed with its knocking against his leg, he kicked the swivel chair away from her desk. After skittering across the dais, it slammed into the railing and then toppled on to its side. The violent sound delighted her. 'Do it. Please, do it,' she said, her voice suddenly softer and more feminine. Slipping his hands under her hips, he clenched his teeth and then yanked her into position. He spread her legs by putting his booted ankles against the inside of her calves. Now she just breathed heavily; there were no more words at this point. Using his fingers, he cupped her fleshy sex and then rubbed his hand against it and through its lips. Withdrawing the sticky hand, he raised it to his face, feeling the need to insert those digits inside his mouth. Salted and thick in his mouth, he relished her taste, mixed it with his saliva, and then swallowed it. He then smiled at the night he could see through the giant window panes. She had turned her head to watch him, puzzled by the pause after so frantic a spanking and so sudden an introduction of a hand against her sex. They caught each other's eyes and became truly close for the first time. She nodded. Glossy and moist, her lips moved. He thought she had said, 'Yes,' to herself.

Entering her became effortless. Fucking her hard, without a pause to reposition himself or to catch his breath, was easy. Finding a rhythm in his breathing and in the supple push and pull of his body, Angel focused on taking her – just taking her – concentrating like he did on the toughest part of a swim when his stamina and strong muscles were required to pull him through the cold water and stiff currents.

Friction from so hard and deep a thrusting, added to the force of his thoughts, of where this sacrilege was being performed, and gradually he ascended to the climax he knew would make him blind with pleasure. On the very altar of wealth and power that surveyed the expanse of the world as a series of quick plane journeys, where the whole planet could be circled in six hours, and on the lectern that paid in privileges, that carved the very earth beneath him into ever-changing territories, Angel loved the stranger so hard that her feet left the floor and the computer crashed over the side of her desk.

Moans became grunts; animal but unavoidable. Ancient noises – sounds that seemed to have come from the bottom of her stomach – drove him along her back to be closer to her until they were both sprawled on the wood. At the moment when his vision dissolved into a universe of tiny lights and his seed burned through his cock, in one long draught after another, she began to sob and say, 'Hurt me. Hurt me. Oh, Richard, hurt me. Please, Richard, hurt me.'

Not caring who Richard was, or what the man had done to this woman to implant such cravings inside her – underneath the part of her mind she used to make money, to generate and to destroy in turn – Angel ground himself into her, so the cheeks of her bottom were flattened against his hips. And there he waited, until every drop of passion from the poor boy who came from the townships, down there with the rest of them she never gave a thought about, had fallen inside her powerful body.

When he withdrew from her and uncuffed her hands, she grabbed him and kissed his face, hard, making his mouth and chin and nose wet with her fragrant plummy spit.

'Love you, baby,' she said over and over again, and then she placed the side of her head on his chest and sniffed a little, like she was happy but crying too. Wary now his heat had cooled, Angel held her tight, but never dared to kiss her.

And, soon enough, she returned to her prior self. In a few of the valuable seconds that kept time with her effect on the world, she had straightened her clothes, thrown her crumpled knickers inside a briefcase, smoothed her stockings up her legs and fixed her hair into its original shape. 'Don't stand there. Get dressed,' she said, quick and harsh, without looking at him.

Angel stepped back inside his jump-suit. She checked her watch, her eyes keen, like someone who watched the spin of a roulette wheel, or the inching forwards of a racehorse's nodding, straining head across a photo-finish line. Just as his night-stick slipped through the leather loop that hung from his belt, she said, 'On time,' and swept her briefcase from the desk. Running for the stairs, she said, 'Get my cases from the mezzanine, by the conference screen, and take them down to the lobby on your way out.' She disappeared from view and Angel listened to the sound of her clattering heels, descending the stairs, musing on the fact that she had not looked at him once since he came. If his instincts did not tell him otherwise, he would have been fooled into thinking he had disappointed her.

Three

And over the next month he was allowed to live his
dreams. It seemed every pair of breasts he'd ever
stared at on the underground was suddenly his to
unwrap, press, caress and covet. Up and down the
long legs of the high-zone strutters, his hands brushed
and squeezed. Inside the many mouths – pink, red,
purple, wide, thin, thick – he would put his tongue
and taste wine and caviar, or insert his cock and feel
his soul sucked from his body in a stream of white
vigour the new goddesses of this planet would
swallow and grow wilder upon. And their sexes, so
trimmed and tight, were plundered. Unprotected by
the thin walls of panties, secretly left unclad beneath
tight skirts, or accessed through the slits tailored into
underthings by craftsmen who had no brand or
signature, Angel dipped his untrained meat, made
hard as cartilage through worship, and prolonged its
slow work for hours when required, or hastily thrust
to the point of physical collapse when a client
required quick favours on her way to a conference in
a long car. There was plenty of work.

And sometimes he served drinks naked, or carried
a silver platter wearing a collar around his throat,
and no word left his lips for an entire evening, or no
pair of eyes met his whenever slender, white fingers
plucked a delicacy or the thin stem of a champagne

flute from his tray. Once he was beaten across the buttocks with a switch by a Japanese woman who wore red high heels and spoke broken English. And the beating was endured in a boardroom before twenty gaping men and women as a new motivational policy was demonstrated to a sales team. And, on their way out, one of the women seized his cock and gave it a quick, merciless tug, without even looking him in the eye. Another scratched his buttocks with cruel finger-nails, painted purple, and spat between his eyes when he looked at her with shock in his still innocent gaze. Left alone, buttock-sore, saliva-eyed and cock-hard in this boardroom, he fulfilled the final task of the assignment. Facing the window, through which he could see the skyscrapers of blue glass and cold metal, and imagine the hot winds wrapping and howling between them, he thought of the Japanese girl's high heels, fire-engine red, and ejaculated into a small pink carton, the size of a cigarette packet, made from rubber, with a nozzle in one corner that looked like the reed of a woodwind instrument. After dressing, he left the strange carton on the boardroom table. And minutes later, as he walked from the building, so smart in his black suit with his rangy body weakened from the ordeal, he saw the Japanese woman in a passing car with the pink container clutched in her small hand, and the nozzle tucked into the side of her mouth. She met his stare with a blank face, her eyes covered by sunglasses, and at the last moment before her car turned the corner, he saw her cheeks go flat.

Once his role was reversed. High up in the sky aboard a penthouse made from marble and filled with the bronzes and stones of museums, a husband, dressed like a butler, served him food and fine wines while he sat at one end of a long table, opposite the wife who talked at him relentlessly, and told him her opinions of everything as well as all the incidents in her long life: a life made long from the new genes they could afford. Although she looked a handsome forty-five, he was staggered to learn it was her seventy-seventh birthday when he was paid to call on her. And the husband's long face never twitched when Angel took the wife to her marital bed and stretched her across the black silk-sheeted mattress. Under the canopy of iron, she told him matter-of-factly to be assertive with her, 'because that's just what I like on my birthday,' and she never bothered to undress much beyond the black corset and stockings on her white body – her flesh as firm as those of the twenty-something girls he'd enjoyed. It was not difficult to perform; he liked the lady, her friendly manner, and the way she said, 'Ooh, you, ooh, you,' repeatedly, as he held her shoulders tight and ground into her bushy sex. With her he'd managed to come four times, and came just where he needed to, more than where he thought he should. Once in her mouth, his cock still wet from her sex, when she sucked it hard as if it was a toffee apple with the caramel coating going thin over the fruit skin; in her sex with her legs pushed so far back, her knees gripped her temples; on her heavy breasts where she dabbed her fingers into his come, and looked embarrassed when she then stuck them in her mouth, before saying, 'Sorry. Was that allowed?'; and finally up between her big white buttocks so she had to bite the pillow and her mascara ran in powdery splodges down her cheeks. That was her favourite place. She told him so when the butler helped him into his coat and then held the door open for him. He looked forward to her next birthday.

But he never managed to get over his shock behind the scenes in the High Zones amongst the wealthy.

Something would happen or something would be said that would leave him dumbfounded, or perplexed, trying to figure their motives for days afterwards as he waited for the next assignment, doing all kinds of things with his hands to stop them reaching for his erection. That was not allowed.

Like the time at the country club, when he collected tennis balls, poured drinks, and offered clean white towels, smelling of apricots in wooden baskets, to three blonde girls just out of university. They never really paid him much attention throughout the day, made hot and sunny by the ecosphere that covered the grounds, tennis courts and open air pool he longed to swim in. Occasionally, they would say, 'Be a darling' and do this or do that; run and fetch this; tell so and so we're ready to go in now; 'There's a good boy, place these orders with Chef'; 'Take these bags upstairs'; 'Oh, my God, you simply must fetch the stylist this instant.' And all he did was nod and say, 'Yes, ma'am,' in between his scurrying about in the sun, that felt as warm as the real sun on his skin. It seemed he was not to touch the girls or love them, and was not disappointed by the arrangement, because it was another beautiful day inside the sphere and the money he was to receive was more generous than he deserved.

But then they began to drink; before dinner, all through dinner, and then after dinner at the dance – where he saw the specialist companions of the resort, in white suits, whose faces had been enhanced to resemble the Spanish men who used to kill bulls, and he wondered what their old faces must have looked like before the laser knife got busy. The girls' drinking continued after the dance too, when he followed the trio up to their rooms, where they were still restless, and the drink had taken away their refinement he'd become so accustomed to throughout the day.

Upstairs, they began to look at him with hard eyes that became laughing eyes. And they said vile things to him, until one of them, his favourite with the pink irises and the pussy cat tattoo on her ankle, threw a drink in his eyes and then started to cry and say she was sorry, but he did remind her of a polo player who'd broken her heart clean in two. But Angel kept his face straight, as he'd been trained to do at etiquette periods with Leisure.corp, and carried on with the yes and no ma'am routine until midnight had come and gone.

Trouble was close, though. He could sense that. Especially when they crowded into the bathroom together, in a huddle, whispering and giggling and plotting. When they came out, tottering tipsy on their heels, the classic deportment gone from their smooth bodies in the blue and pink dancing gowns, they told him to take his clothes off. He obeyed and stood naked at the bottom of the bed they all sprawled upon, drinking from the bottles that looked so heavy against their thin wrists.

And when they told him the first story, his cock stuck out and his favourite with the great backhand on the tennis courts, who had the cat tattooed on her ankle, called his cock a 'diving board', which they all found incredibly funny. In hushed tones they then talked amongst themselves as if he were a statue with no face, and told each other what they had done with men, and other girls, in something called 'the overseas year'. The one with the rainbows painted on her toenails complained that she 'had never had it up the bum' and was teased by the other two for being a 'virgin'. While they laughed at her, she looked at his cock twice – damn it, he saw her do it – and then she put her hand under her bottom as if to test something.

The discussion changed then. Pussy Tattoo told the other two she had been spanked every week for three years by her hall mentor. She'd liked it, especially with a belt. They all oh'd and ah'd at that one. Angel felt his shoulders go broad and a shivery ripple had run up his back. But Freckly Cheeks, the third girl, who could speak twelve languages, and who didn't know whether she wanted to be a diplomat or a classical violinist now exams were over, refused to be outdone. She told them how she'd been flashing her naked pussy at someone she called 'canteen gimp', who Angel presumed was a township servitor in her university refectory. She also sent her old panties to the kitchens, taped inside little packets, addressed to gimp. At first it was a 'teaser', a joke, and gimp would blush whenever he served her table. He was terrified, she told the others, and would say nothing when she cornered him and sucked his cock in the dark area behind the kitchens, where gimp had to empty slops bins. She started going every day, after lunch, or dinner, to experiment with gimp. 'He had a huge cock,' she said. 'Used to choke me.' The other two girls on the bed fell silent and let their pretty mouths stay open, because they knew Freckly Cheeks was telling the truth. When Freckly told them about how she made gimp fuck her against a wall, with her wrists pinned against the bricks and her legs around his waist, they all began to look at Angel, their faces flushed and not altogether pleasant-looking.

It was then he knew, in a fraction of a second, that trouble was due. And it came fast.

Suddenly, Rainbow Toes put out the lights and said, 'Hall orgy.'

They all shrieked with delight, understanding the ritual. In the darkness, he could hear their shoeless feet bumping around the floor near him, and he could hear their hot breaths whipping like ghosts through the air. When someone said, 'Fuck him over' – he thought it was Pussy Tattoo that said it – three pairs of hands slapped his body. As if he was in the middle of a cloud of frightened birds, these girls came up against him with their hard, swiping hands. They turned him red all over in the space of a minute. One of them got her claws in his hair and pulled him down to the bed. He couldn't understand this anger. Why were they enraged? At who? Him? Why?

Tears in his eyes, he was pressed into the bed and one of them sucked his cock back out hard. Another, he didn't know who, rubbed her little milky pussy on his face. The third said dirty things into his left ear. All about him in the pitch blackness, the swarm of soft bodies, rustly dresses, slippery underthings, and nasty girlish whispers assaulted him, finally blowing itself out like a hurricane that had flattened every building in a coastal town. When they finished, he heard Pussy Tattoo say, 'Everybody had a taste?'

'What, of his noodle doodle?' Freckly Cheeks asked.

They all laughed at that. And then the two who had missed out took turns to expertly suckle his cock. Only their mouths worked on him down there; he never felt so much as a finger on his shaft.

'He's going to spunk in a bit,' Rainbow Toes said.

'I want to see it come out,' Freckly demanded. The lights blew on.

Their dresses were gone. Bra and panty sets, graduation finery, fitted tight on their trim bodies. All white lingerie with flesh stockings on tanned legs to co-ordinate. High heels shed, they circled him. Something angry and all skewed off-course shone bright in their clever eyes. Smart girls with bad tempers.

Over-achievers with fat bank accounts, they circled him like the off-shore predator gulls that now and then pulled fishermen into the air to shred them red. Angel sat up and thought of defending himself. Those claws on their fingers could do damage to a country-club-gimp-gopher.

'Now, now, sweet boy,' Pussy Tattoo said, ready for the big wide world and all the torture she could spread in it. 'Just be a good doggy.' They laughed at that one too. 'With this belt –' she wrapped it through her fingers, the nails flashing like sport's car paint-work under the chandelier lights '– I want you to give us what for. You understand, doggy boy.'

You bet I do, bitch.

'Will it hurt bad?' Rainbow Toes asked.

'No. It feels good,' Pussy Tattoo told her friend with a ludicrous expression on her face: an attempt to be sincere with eyes unable to focus.

Don't listen to your friend. It's going to sting real bad.

'When's he going to spunk?' Freckly asked.

'Soon, and in me first. They always do more first time.'

The girls bent over and Angel stood behind them with the belt. Three pairs of buttock-cheeks in silk white panties jostled. The girls giggled. Their mirth was short-lived. When Angel carefully peeled each pair of the panties down to the top of their thighs, a hush descended in the room.

When he flexed the leather belt with a crack, Freckly had second thoughts. 'He's going to hurt me.'

That's right.

'Don't be a chicken,' Pussy Tattoo told her. 'He's done this before. You can tell.'

'I can't wait,' Rainbow Toes whispered.

You won't have to. Walking slowly behind them, he trailed the loose leather across their bared bottoms. It tickled the skin. Walking back the other way, the end of his swollen phallus brushed their cheeks. A ripple of alarm spread through them. He saw their backs tense, but no word of objection was raised. Rainbow fiddled a painted fingernail between her legs. Her eyes were closed.

Shlack! Two backsides whipped red. Shallack! The third not forgotten. Ouches, whimpers, Ahh sounds.

Dog boy, aye?

Shlack! Shlack! Shlack! Shlack! Shlack! Shlack! Six times the belt whipped across them and they understood leather could produce fire. Only Pussy Tattoo, an old hand, remained bent over; the other two stood up and began mincing around the rug on their pretty stockinged feet, hands clutched to red buttocks. Angel threw the belt to the ground. His nose flared; his jaw clenched. He seized Freckly by her French pleat and pulled her against his body. She slapped his face. Up close, he could see the pale red rims of her teary eyes. He kissed her mouth hard. She tried to pull away. Rainbow Toes skipped over to offer help but Pussy Tattoo, now on her feet, her face flushed with pleasure, her eyes wild for something fundamental Angel understood, caught Rainbow by the elbow and held her back.

'No,' she said. 'Let him fuck her. I want to see it.'

Twisting around in his arms, the freckly captive looked at her friends with open-mouthed horror. The two girls smiled back at her. Before she had a chance to struggle or shout, Angel had his hands on her breasts and his mouth in the cleft of her neck, between jaw and collar bone. She relaxed back into his body. His cock passed between her white thighs and protruded the other side. The other two girls looked at it, their emotions hop-crossing between terror and delight. Had they gone too far? Was the companion dangerous? They had been awfully mean to him all day. He deciphered the unspoken thoughts. But Pussy Tattoo nodded at him to begin. The empress had asked the gladiator to finish his job.

Down to the rug, he swung her; white arms with a light brown down about his strong neck, shiny-hosed legs over his taut buttocks. Wide-eyed, her speckled breasts rising and falling, her expensive heart thudding so her temples moved like a bubble beneath the surface of heating milk, she waited for him. Between her thighs he began to eat at her sweet, odourless fig lips; his brawny hands moulding those tiny pink nipple-heads at the same time. Head back, using the top of her skull like a pivot, she made the lamb sounds of a girl driven to passion. Hiding her face from his wild, red-brown features and bared teeth, but with her slender musician fingers fisted in his hair, she opened her legs wide, feet flat on the furry rug. As he pushed in, cooing at her, slow moving, the other two dropped to the floor – observers on all fours.

'Oh, I can see it going in,' Pussy Tattoo said.

'All of it. I can't believe he got all of it inside,' Rainbow Toes added.

Slow, because she was tight and pulled at his hair if he dared speed up, Angel speared his freckled fish, adoring the sight of her screwed-up face, sun-burned with pain-ecstasy. And her little sweet toes were bent right back and her polished calves hugged his ribs. On her side, he swivelled her, and took her much harder with one of her legs held up, hand under hot knee. At this she squealed and slapped a hand at the rug. Perhaps she was thinking of another gimp with a thick cock, because she never once opened her eyes. Even when he shot a full six pulses right up and on the ceiling of her birth canal, her eyes stayed shut.

She kissed at his face for a long time afterwards, and had to be prised off Angel by the other two, eager for their turn. He patted her freckled bottom as she was pulled free.

On the bed, Pussy Tattoo and Rainbow Toes rubbed their slinkiness and silkiness all over his body. Two hands stroked his cock. Two voices whispered private school obscenities in his ears. They wanted him hard again. They liked their meat prepared and filling, spiced and juiced. It wasn't long before the dish of his body was ready to satisfy their strange appetites. Pussy wanted to be sucked and the rainbow girl was determined to lose her 'virginity'. Together, they managed to have their way.

Hands swishing up and down Pussy's lovely legs, planted on either side of her friend whom she stood over, Angel lapped and tickled and pushed at her sex with his tongue. Before him on all fours, breasts supported on pillows, her wrists seized by Freckly's hands so she could not pull away, her face buried in a goose-feather duvet, Rainbow Toes presented her unbroken anus and Angel slipped his cock, lubricated in champagne and lipstick, into it. Her quick, frighted breaths, words of caution, words of threat, and finally words of bestial encouragement, filled the room, above the rhythm of the deeper moans the pussy-tattooed girl issued from her pursed lips. At least her claws were easier on him too; they stroked his ears and cheeks lovingly while he supped at her long, brown, tangy lips.

'I love it. It's so fat. Oh, it's up inside my tummy. I can feel it,' the girl who painted rainbow colours on her toes cried out, her white buttock-cheeks spread, the tight mouth of brown-lipped anus strangling his sex.

'Come in her. Come in her. Do it in her arse. Make her scream,' her evil friends commanded.

Angel obeyed. Foaming out inside her backside, squeezing him like a fist in a rubber glove, his face showing every sign of abandonment, he buried his head in the gartered stomach of the tattooed girl. Skin-shivers, heart-thumps, a dizzy vertigo spin swamped him in body and mind. He collapsed across the collapsed back of the lover he'd penetrated, his cock softening as her anus squeezed itself back into a more regular shape. As the sweat dried on his body, the other two stroked him, kissed him, thanked him, and asked him for the same.

When he was allowed, finally, to leave the country club with its shimmery air, its blue canopy mimicking the dead skies of yesteryear and its thick green grasses, he walked off-balance with his back straight so the fine linen of his shirt would not worry the welts their nails had cut across his ribs. Around the bite-marks on his shoulders – purple berry clusters on brown skin – a pleasing ache issued whenever he moved his arms to operate a swipe card. Worn flat and rubbed sore, his cock snuggled in hibernation inside his white cotton shorts. Stuffing out his pockets were three napkins, with phone numbers scrawled upon them in black eyeliner, plus a pair of white briefs the freckly girl insisted he took with him, and an instamatic snap-shot of three thickly painted mouths, fighting like piranhas for what looked like hot wax spilled from a long candle.

He was left uncharacteristically idle for one week, but following the frustrating recess Angel met two women who would alter the course of his companionship for ever. The apprenticeship was over.

Four

After your entry to Dr Madelaine Sutton's office, lock the door and draw the blinds. Then proceed with your assignment. Use one hand for her wrists and silver cuffs for her ankles. The cuffs can be found in a brown paper envelope, marked FEDERAL POST: URGENT, on top of a toilet cistern, third cubicle, fifth floor, Gents' bathroom. Your attentions are to be vigorous. Stay no longer than one hour. Begin the assignment at two p.m.

This was his first instruction from the corporation in seven days. It had been transmitted to his communicator and included with it was an address in Zone Two. It signalled an end to a period of tortuous privation. Besides peeing and washing, he'd learned not to touch his temperamental genitals. Even the faintest pressure of his underwear against them caused giddiness. Twice, he'd been forced to dip his sex into icy water in a wash basin after becoming aroused with thoughts of his previous clients. It made him both ashamed but curiously pleased with himself too. This period of restraint from self-pleasure, imposed by his contractual obligation, reminded him of previous feats of self-discipline – during long swims, or periods of lengthy concentration while reading in the charity library. It was like taking a pleasure in the punishment of hard labour; a life of solitude and contemplation, like a monk or visionary living outside of the world, separated from the sight of the high-zone girls, to be removed from that which he could never have, because he was worthless and deserved punishment in celibate exile. A masochistic and self-pitying stance that somehow made him feel better.

But now, the situation was much improved. The delights were double-edged; while he took this curious flagellating pleasure in following their unnatural and punishing rules on masturbation, he was actually earning the far superior pleasure of entertaining their princesses.

Indeed, he'd come to realise his feelings for the continuance of his work were truly ambiguous. From this prohibition on masturbation he experienced an unease. The first major quiver of discord with this self-proclaimed ideal life he now led. He knew himself now to be owned. Before he became a companion, poverty had been his master and had largely governed his existence. Now he suspected he might be serving something that threatened his freedom with an equal power.

As he prepared himself for the assignment, he became so distracted by his thoughts, he never really felt the hot water when he showered. He couldn't even recall dressing in his customary black suit, complemented by a white shirt and black tie. Watched by the grimacing faces of his neighbours, he left Binton still deep in contemplation.

Before him on Thatcher Boulevard, where the onyx marble matched the gleam of the dark windows in the passing cars, two women, dressed identically in black suits, walked in step. Their eyes were concealed by sunglasses, contoured and streamlined like their slicked-back hair. Slim attaché cases were clutched by their leather fists against tight-skirted thighs. Around each of their left wrists, they wore a silver handcuff bracelet with the corresponding cuff locked into the case handle. Between glove and sleeve he saw thin seams of pale flesh. He fancied he could smell the perfume dabbed across the fine green veins and the white skin. His eyes dropped down, arbitrarily drawn to their patent leather shoes, sleek in the sunlight. He tried to look away and keep his sex soft, but became mesmerised by the chiselled ankles and lathed calves of their legs, shining like glass in dark hose. Looking straight ahead, chins up, shoulders thrown back, indifferent to admirers, the girls marched to their appointments. And they were hardly noticed, because the men that passed them were equally focused and purposeful in the way they strode down the sidewalk of power.

Only Angel was preoccupied with them. Were their fingernails, mummified in those fine leather gloves, painted? he wondered. Or their perfectly formed toes tinted blood-red in those confining, shining heels? They must be; the girls were dressed in the fashion of business, and red nails, as if just dipped in the rents of recently broken hearts, were everywhere in the Higher Zones. As were the transparent black blouses they wore, peeking through the V of their parted suit jackets; a sheer tint over the round swell of milk-white bosom, divided by a dark cleft where a soapy scent would continue to waft all day following their morning cleansing in the steam clouds of shower units.

His gaze lingered too long. There came a swarm of bees to his head, dark blood surfaced in his eyes and a pressure emerged behind his breastbone – a hot indigestion of baffled desire. He wanted to roar with frustration as he leaned against the wall of a giant merchant bank and watched the duo of icy beauties disappear into a subway. Designed like a French cathedral, the bank he rested against had gargoyle faces fashioned into its stone front. They leered down at him. Death masks from communist tyrants of old Europe – the enemies of freedom and capital he'd learned about in school. Their sharp chins, gougy eyes and thin beaks protruded as if in sympathy with the thwarted demon inside him. Not long now, they seemed to say with glee. Not long, comrade.

And indeed, he was close to release. In one of these temples his doctor waited for her blinds to be closed and her legs to be bound. The very thought made his heart pound. But would his cravings for these powerful muse ever be completely gratified, or must he march the Zones eternally panting for a fix until he burned up? He'd not been absolved of his lusts for these women. It was as if there was something else he wanted – something they seemed to promise, but ultimately held back. He walked on, wishing he'd never been given a questioning mind or such relentless cravings.

All about him giant edifices had been raised from the ruins of the old and dead city below. Corporations in the shapes of pyramids, cathedrals, cubes of glass that stretched away from his eyes and were lost in the clouds, mausoleums of marble, skyscrapers, the teeth of giants, and alien domes. Every building a captive from history, or a bold new structure suggesting the future of a new aesthetic order, all of them shimmering up and into the bluey-green vapours of the sky. Strange gusts of wind were created by these monuments to market forces. They blew through the ravines of streets like hot and belching exhausts, forcing people to stop, lean forwards, or drop to their knees, while around them the palm trees were stripped of haggard leaves, and umbrellas were blown from loose fingers. And then the gusts, fresh from so many new deserts, died as quickly as they found howling life and the professionals in black ran back to their business.

Angel left Thatcher Boulevard and took a right turn. Before him hummed the vast reactor of The Surgeon's Tower: a reconstruction of a Holy Roman church, full of the new popes and clerics like Dr Madelaine Sutton. Angel shuffled inside the vast edifice, insignificant beneath the height of the domed Venetian ceiling. White doves flapped through the arches and yellow beams of sunlight shone through the windows in straight shafts before dispersing in a hue of mid-air gold. Angel stared into the space, stunned by grace; a tiny black figure still among the clatter of tipped heels and the swishing robes of the medical soothsayers. About him, everyone ran in straight lines, their equally straight faces committed to self-importance, unless their heads were wrapped in bright dressings – those who had come to this church to be made into the likeness of their youthful gods.

Angel fell into step. He matched his communicator to the identity pad at the first barrier, and then passed through the grid of red lasers when his access was accepted. Choosing the stairs in a moment of hesitation before the appointment, he tried to rediscover the excitement that had captured him out on the street when he walked behind the hard backsides of the career girls, before the winds and buildings had dwarfed his spirits. It was gone. An overwhelming sense of insignificance had replaced it.

He entered the fifth floor. Mahogany and glass. Museum world. Venetian magnificence resurrected.

Dr Madelaine Sutton's terrain. On the wall behind the giant reception counter, and above the two beautiful girls in caps and chic white uniforms, was mounted a large wood and metal fixture on which the names of the staff members were listed. It was a manually operated antique, donated from one of the old universities. Where once the names of the lecturing staff had been, the titles of the surgeons were slotted between brass runners. Next to the name Dr Madelaine Sutton, Genetic Enhancement Specialist, Studio 38, a wooden slide had been moved to the IN position.

A tall man in a bowler hat passed Angel while he stood before the reception desk. They exchanged glances but the man looked away quickly before Angel could stare at his arresting eyes. Like shiny marbles polished into his face, they were completely black, bereft of iris or white. A woman wearing a hat and veil passed him on the other side – her body looked especially frail, as if aged, while her screened face seemed to have recently emerged from out of her teenage years. She walked with a stick and peered at him intently, as if to gauge the reaction of a younger man.

One of the girls, behind the counter, stood up from her chair and moved the slide to read OUT beside the name of a specialist. As she turned around to resume her seat, she caught Angel smitten by the display of her legs. She smiled. He coloured and felt his cock twitch. Immediately, he dropped a hand to conceal the growing tumerance. 'Can I help you, sir?' she asked.

Angel cleared his throat. 'The gents', please.'

'Down there.' She pointed at the central concourse. 'Turn right.'

Angel thanked her and walked away. Both girls watched him. He could see the pretty faces under the little hats from the corner of his eye. Afloat with the joy of a man noticed and desired, his doubts fled and he suddenly experienced an overpowering love for this world. It had seduced him long ago, but now, with smiles on lips such as these, it seemed ready to accept him. For the first time in his life, he thought he knew what it was to have prospects.

Alone inside the gents' bathroom, Angel threw water on his face. Straightening up, he adjusted his tie – he could almost complete a Windsor knot now. He smoothed his hair back and took a mint from a small dish beside the white face-cloths. Inside the third cubicle, he locked the door behind him, lowered the toilet seat and then climbed up to feel the top of the cistern. His reaching hands touched paper. Carefully, he withdrew the padded envelope from the plumbing. As he brought the weight of it against his chest and stepped down from the toilet seat, he heard the jingle of chains inside the envelope. His stomach turned over. What was the fascination with these strange bindings?

He checked the time: three minutes remained until his appointment was due to commence. Leaving the gents', he walked down a plushly carpeted hall of red. Still was the air, sombre the atmosphere. It was as if he walked on hallowed ground. The walls on either side of him were wood-panelled. It had been designed to look unlike a medical facility and made him wonder where the operations were carried out. On this floor the powerful surgeons, the transformers and lengtheners of life, gave consultations. Somewhere behind one of the oak doors he passed, a man cleared his throat. And then a drawer was closed on the other side of the corridor. The sounds were incongruously sharp.

On the door of number thirty-eight, a small brass plaque at eye-level was inscribed with the title of *Dr*

M. Sutton. Outside the door, he smelled a trace of perfume. Had she prepared herself for him? The thought made him shiver with excitement. There could be no error this time. One woman, one room, a locked door and closed blinds; there was little risk. And a doctor; an educated woman. Already, he fantasised about other illicit trysts with this woman and her powerful mind. A lover and mentor who could tell him where he fitted into the scheme of things. His ignorance and clumsiness would vanish and he too could stake a claim in her society.

He held the door handle. It was cold in the palm of his hand. For a moment he paused and inhaled the distilled air of power – sharp with brass, tangy with wood – and told himself he could not have found a better occupation in more spectacular surroundings. For the first time as a companion he truly recognised his own love and devotion for the corporate world. He willingly offered himself as a sacrifice.

Sensing a desire for surprise, he never announced himself with a knock. The office was vast. It was big enough and sufficiently grand to be part of a palace with its porcelain, bronzes, aspidistras, oils, chandeliers and fireplace. Besides the heavy desk there was little to suggest that any work took place in here. But he only allowed himself a fraction of a second to take in the opulence, because a greater prize than the furnishings waited for him. Behind the desk, facing the window, was the figure of a woman. Tall with long red hair, she stood with her back to him and smoked a cigarette – a habit that had returned to fashion since synthetic tobaccos had been made beneficial to respiratory health. She never turned around. Besides what he thought to be a tensing of her shoulders at the sound of the door, she never moved. Angel walked to the front of her desk. The envelope in his hands felt heavy, and he with it suddenly ridiculous.

At last, she turned to face him. Though pale and thin-faced, there was something eminently handsome about her, like the woman who watched a polo match from beneath the wide brim of a hat on the label of a vodka brand he had seen on the subway sidings. The crimson of her painted lips was startling, but the way her mouth thinned in response to his welcoming smile made her seem troubled.

She looked away from him and drew on her cigarette. It was fitted into a black holder. 'So you came,' she said, after exhaling the smoke she held inside her chest for what seemed a long time. 'I never doubted you would, but . . .' She paused and smiled sadly. 'But then, don't you think there is too great a distance between what you dream of and the moment when, supposedly, it arrives?'

He wanted to say something, but the buzzing in his head and the hot wash of self-consciousness kept him mute. The moment was lost. The trace of a melancholy smile remained though, in the creases that deepened at the side of her mouth. It was as if, through his hesitation and silence, he had actually said something naive.

'This is it, then,' she said to herself.

Angel hadn't expected this. His ideas of what to expect were never clear. How foolish he was to think of some connection. She was older, supremely intelligent, a separate species from those left in the townships.

'You know . . .' she began to say, but then stopped again and filled her lungs with smoke instead. To break the silence and the thickness of the air that seemed to be forever dropping slowly to the floor around them, Angel tore open the envelope. She flinched at the ripping sound. He swallowed. Refusing to look at what he poured, silvery and twisting, on to the desk top, she looked into his eyes. The sound of the chains and the wide cuffs, rattling against the wood, seemed unnecessarily loud, as if this inanimate thing were against them.

'I really don't think this can be done,' she then said, her smile nervous. 'Maybe if this is done to me. Then something will start that should never be seen. If . . .' Her sentences were breaking apart like the thoughts that created them, but abandoned them and then made other thoughts jostle forward in a kind of confused crowd.

He understood her doubts and walked back to the door. She never made a sound. It was as if he had felt her freeze behind his back. He imagined the smoke from the cigarette still moving across that intensity in her eyes. Yes, despite her sudden display of reticence, there was something uncompromising about her face. And it was as if she was afraid of just that – afraid of herself. He reached for the handle and then locked the door. Behind him, he heard a quick inhalation from the doctor. He turned around and walked to the window where she stood, still watching him. He kept his face angled down. If their eyes met, he thought, it would be terrible.

Slowly, he drew the blinds and the room darkened. Only a smoky vanilla light from the desk lamp, with a green scallop shade and a brass stem, gave any shape or definition to the furniture or the occupants. It was beginning to be too much for him: this having to assume the power, to dim the lights and turn a room to a prison cell. Inside himself, he seemed to bend like a sapling stripped of bark and made white. Even when he turned to her, his shoulders seemed to dip of their own accord, as if he were prepared to bow. But she never seemed affected by him being crushed by her pressure. In fact, it was as if the opposite dynamic had occurred. She stubbed out her cigarette, her face still stiff with anxiety, and then moved away from him to stand on the rug before her desk. She gave the impression that she was suddenly following orders. She bowed her head and crossed her hands over her stomach, as if commanded into submission.

Between them, their positions reversed, the cuffs developed a special hue in the umbra; greenish – like treasure glimpsed in the depths, suddenly within reach after a long excavation, but only now to be surrounded by unseen hazards and curses.

Angel followed her to the rug, wondering if her strange reaction to him was part of the scenario she desired – this assumption of his control and her reticent compliance. Their eyes locked once he stood before her, and even in the dark, each of them suffered from the glare of the other's stare. A frown creased her forehead. A shiver ran up one side of her face and he felt its ripple inside him too. It made her blink the eye on that side of her face.

'Oh, God,' she said. The colour of her eye make-up was charcoal and matched the faint soot of rouge on her sharp cheekbones. There were some fine lines on her skin that he could see more clearly now, but the beauty and vulnerability of her expression was stronger for them. He liked this face, so close to him, and wanted to see it stirred.

He reached for her hand. Her fingers were limp and cool but had closed in on the palm. So his touch made but the briefest impression on her softness, he held her wrist between the finger and thumb of his right hand. She closed her eyes. Her breath came in quick gusts from her thin nose and broke against his mouth. He could smell mint.

71

'You mustn't . . . Mustn't get into this,' she whispered, and he never knew whether she said it for herself or for him. 'Can I have him? Can I do it? Can I have another one?' she said excitedly, and he felt the question was intended for someone else in the room.

Confused but curious, Angel continued with his assignment, operating on an instinctive level now, unable to think quickly enough. He moved her hand out before her, so her fingertips touched the front of his shirt, by his navel. The hand retained a rigidity inside its delicate bones. He coaxed her left hand out also and placed it against her right hand. Then he grasped them both, suddenly and tightly, by the wrists.

'Oh, God,' she said again. Her eyes opened. 'You must –' she tried to say, but Angel stopped her by resting his lips against her mouth.

Just to touch the slippery, red cosmetic, more than to kiss her. Closing his eyes, he then drew away from her mouth, but only slightly so she could watch him tentatively touch his lips with the tip of his tongue – to savour her taste, and take it inside.

Then, determined to soften her, he kissed her fully. But still, her mouth did not relent. The lips remained parted and soft, but unresponsive. From her chin, he kissed her cheek, her jaw, and then nuzzled the hair off her ear with the end of his nose.

'Oh, God,' she whispered again.

Down her neck, he left the impression of his mouth and then kissed her collarbone. Feeling dizzy and strangely weightless as his arousal was released to flow and then thicken through him, he pushed his face into the angle of her shoulder and throat where it was warm. She could hear his air and feel the rise and fall of his chest against her as he breathed.

72

It was when he clenched his fist even tighter that he heard her breathing quicken. Immediately, his kisses became harder. Through the angle of her head, falling backwards, and in the tremble of the fine membrane of her eyelids, he could see she had begun to fall into the urgency and insistence of his attentions. With one hand in the small of her back, he squashed her against the pronounced edges of his body. Against her long thighs his longer thighs were firm. Into her breasts went the hard ridge of his chest. Along her flat belly, so soft with a promise of wet depths and a tight, nervous clinch, stretched his thick sex. Feeling the significance of his greater breadth, height and strength, she became utterly precious to him. Fragile, guarded, elegant, civilised – he sensed these qualities slowly surrendering their hold on her.

Down to the floor they went; she under him, protected from the hard boards by his hand and then his elbow. She clung to him, her need for a firm touch plainly revealed the moment his hand ventured inside her flimsy blouse. 'Oh, yes. Yes. Be hard there,' she said, her lips lavishing passionate kisses against the side of his face as she spoke.

And after seven days of abstinence he felt imbued with a curious power; his strength seemed to have no limits and she felt weightless in his hands; the hard floor offered no discomfort, and his co-ordination was slick despite the incongruous angles of this new body at his disposal. As his stubbly cheeks writhed in her hair, he pressed his hand against her breasts. Such a pressure against so intimate a place eased the remaining rigidity from out of her porcelain, designer body. When he sought her lips again and kissed her, his hand firmly kneading below, she responded and he felt a stranger's tongue inside his mouth.

Releasing her wrists, he placed a hand under her buttocks and one behind her coiffured head and then

73

pulled her in tight against him. Blind to everything but his lust, he suddenly wanted to consume her, to devour and digest every scrap of her – the long bones and smooth flesh, the lavender and musk, the shiny hair, the long doctor fingers and the wedding ring. All of her. She let him spread her thighs with his knee, like he'd once done to a girlfriend on a staircase in Binton, and then, with a frown, she eyed the thick lump inside his trousers that he tugged her towards, her bottom slipping along the floor.

Her skirt and slip ruffled under her buttocks and displayed her panties. He felt he might explode at the sight of the little gauzy black triangle over a clipped mound. And when his face hovered over her dark brown stocking-tops he saw a peppering of freckles on her inner thighs. Lowering his face, he kissed the freckles on the warm skin and all about his head he could hear the rustle of disturbed silk as she relaxed, offering herself. Pushing his face further under her skirt, he inhaled the doctor's musk. It smelled of soap and hormones. And so rich was her perfume, it made him squint. The salted damp patch at the front of her dark briefs was studied and then placed under the lap of his tongue. Through the thin fabric, he could feel the shape of her lips. Moving her panties to one side, by hooking a finger through the leg, he then plunged his mouth into the heavy sap on her sex. And while he sucked and lapped, he thought of the dark red hole, so close to his face, that he would soon fill and stretch and push through until she wrapped all around him like a pretty anemone in a coral pool. And he stayed between her thighs and ate until his jaw ached, and until she bit her knuckles to stifle her own cries. When finally he sat back to breathe, she moaned and wriggled her buttocks for more.

Driven by this sudden display of her appreciation and this need she possessed to be pleasured during the

74

working day, he was overcome by a need to be free of his tangling, hot clothes. He wanted to writhe naked down there. So off came his jacket, stripped from his arms with the haste of a medic in a roadside emergency. Off came his tie and shirt and trousers and underwear, all of which were thrown aside while she watched, her eyes wide, her fingers busy between her legs until his mouth or cock were ready to continue. Nostrils broad, he dipped his head back between the length of her smooth thighs. Her nylons made slippery sounds against the side of his head, and a full blare of her seasoned sex, peppered and gamey, clouded about his face once more.

His hunger for this rare food made him groan. Under her shiny gusset he lapped, his tongue wide and outstretched again. Screwing up her features, she shielded her eyes with both hands and then uttered a series of quick, feminine sounds, more like whimpers than moans. Pulling her panties across her sex and then stretching them completely out of his way, he uncovered more of her soft down, and all of her wrinkled, dew-plastered lips. Pressing his tongue harder against her teeny red clit-tendon, upon which mere draughts of his breath made her body seize up, he caressed her with a more circular action using the tip of his tongue. Her groans deepened. Pursing his lips, he then pulled this part of her into his mouth and she began to roll her head about on the rug. And, as he sucked so fastidiously, he reached up her body, with his shoulders packed behind her thighs, and seized her breasts.

Her feet rose from the floor and she slid her legs over his back. With the indent of her nipples in the palms of his hands, he gently and slowly massaged her breasts. When his hands and tongue found the rhythm that other lovers had liked, her breathing stuttered. And it seemed as if she were stuck for something to do with her arms; she raised them from across her face into the air and then dropped them back down so she could smother her moans with her forearms. Skating his tongue over the little bead between her legs, or by flicking it left and right across this nucleus of nerves he associated with the very tip of his penis, all of her body gradually softened as if something had drained out from beneath her suit.

'Bastard. Dirty, common bastard,' she whispered, surprising him.

Tongue replaced by the pads of his fingers, Angel tickled and then pushed her clit. Moving up her body, but leaving that one hand behind and busy in her wet fur, he dropped his sticky lips, odoriferous with the fragrance she knew to be her own, on to the doctor's open, hot and blaspheming mouth. Alive to the kiss, with all reticence gone now, she licked her own brine from around his mouth. She took all of it away and then let her head drop back to the rug. She squeezed her eyes shut and then groaned as if the muscles of her womb were pushing something out. Fingernails, red and long and lacquered stronger, dug into his triceps and shoulders, leaving small half-moons of bruising on his brown skin. Angel clenched his teeth on the discomfort and watched her face as the intense feeling passed over it and through her body too; a momentary paralysis, mixed with a sweet pain. It seemed to rise through her and then last for so long, if her screwed-up features were any indication, until the peak then jolted through her muscles, little volts that made her shudder, until they died away too and left her face dreamy and lost.

Angel kissed her neck, before disentangling himself from her arms, to sit back on his ankles and stroke her legs. Remembering his instructions, he reached for the cuffs on the desktop. He slipped his hands under her knees. Perspiration had dampened the stockings and made them cling to her ligaments. He raised her legs and drew her ankles together. After knocking her sling-back heels off, he then placed the heels of her feet on his chest. The doctor stared up at him, her eyes wide and intense now, the expectation in them almost unnerving. Around each ankle, he closed the curved steel bands of the cuffs. They felt so cold in his hands and the sudden embrace of some-thing so hard and confining on her ankles prompted her to prop herself up on her elbows. The clasps in the bracelets locked and the chain between them shook loose.

She snarled at him. He was surprised again. The shock must have been evident on his face, but she never relaxed the hard grimace from her beautiful features. To Angel, she looked like a savage. It pleased him.

Smoothing his hands down her legs, from ankle to thigh, he felt her stockings ripple and tug around the contours of her legs. 'Open your mouth,' he whis-pered at her wild, staring face. She rocked her tousled head back and opened her jaws. He moved around her legs and took the blue, chiffon scarf from around her neck, hanging loose like a sling. A cloud of perfume dispersed from it. Angel put it under his nose and briefly inhaled. Then he stared hard into her eyes and slipped the scarf between her lips. There was no resistance. She even angled her head forwards so he could tie it behind her head. Cuffed and now gagged too, she closed those watchful eyes at last. Resting back on the rug, she placed both of her hands on her stomach and waited, wanting neither her frank stare nor raking hands to interfere with his work.

77

Angel unbuttoned her blouse and helped himself to her chest. Pinky-tipped but so soft, it was almost impossible to grasp them in the palm of his hand and to feel their shape. He put his face into them. Tweaking her nipples with his fingers he rubbed his face in her scented cleavage. With flicks of his tongue, he then tasted her nipples – hard now, the size of pebbles – with just a twist of soap and salt on the puckered skin. Squashing her breasts down into her body, before gently pulling them back out, with her nipples held lightly between the inside of his fingers, he moulded and adored her pliant breast-flesh. And as the action of his kneading hands became firmer, his desire to enter the doctor increased.

'I'm going to have you,' he said to her, in a voice that was low, but firm with intent. 'I'm really going to take you now.' She moved her bottom on the floor, in small rotary rubbings of anticipation. 'Excuse me if I'm rough, Doctor. But I've had to wait for you for a long time.'

She cried out. He heard the word, 'Yes,' muffled into her gag.

He was more excited than he could ever remember now. The front of his underwear was wet with dew and the back of his head tingled cold. Up inside the ruffle of her skirt and creamy underskirt, his fingers rediscovered her now soiled panties, and drew them up her legs to leave them hanging by her cuffed ankles. Her breath suddenly quickened and sounded noisy in her thin nose. Hastily, Angel stroked his cock. It pulsed upwards in his hand, as if pulling back on invisible reins. He smiled. A flicker of something he thought cruel went cold in his mind, as if a shadow had fallen. 'Watch it, Doctor. Watch it go inside you. Then you can see yourself being taken by a servant. By a common bastard.' She was propped up on her elbows before he even finished speaking.

With one hand, he held her legs before his body, and gripped the stem of his girth with the other. The doctor moved her head to the side of her knees so she could watch. Angel moved forwards into position between her raised thighs. When the tip of his cock touched her sex – a gentle skim – they moaned together in the most exquisite moment of all. And then an impatience showed on each face – a need to commence with the quenching of so many basic needs.

Ready for the intrusion of a hired stranger's cock, her sex produced so much moisture that a trickle of her fluid made the cleft of her buttocks sticky. Slowly, Angel pushed the head in, shivering as her floss tickled his purple and sensitised skin. A moment of resistance. More pressure. A stretching of her sex, that almost felt to each of them as if something had been gently torn, and then the smooth slide of his entire length inside her followed. Red in the face, teeth clamped on the chiffon gag, she rubbed the side of her face into the rug.

Inching forwards on his knees, so his hips pressed into the bottom of her thighs, Angel squeezed another small measure of penetration into her womb. Leaning forwards, he snatched her wrists together and pulled her upper body a few inches off the rug and then pressed his face into her ankles. Squeezing her wrists tight, he stroked her silky legs with his free hand, and kept his cock still inside her until the desperate temptation to ejaculate passed. When his sex felt less sensitive in the wonderful flesh of its surround, he began to thrust into her, delivering long and deep strokes, never breaking his rhythm. The doctor bit into her scarf and her nose became all pinched up and her eyes screwy and wrinkled.

'This is what you want?' he asked her, breathless, his pounding relentless. She never replied; she seemed unable.

'Maybe harder,' he muttered, and then rearranged himself so they lay on the rugs, his body behind her, both curled into an S shape with tangled legs, his cock never relinquishing its deep foundation inside her body. The side of her face was hot and her eyes seemed darker to him. 'Now it can be harder.' He clenched his teeth. 'Put your hands on your . . . On your tits, Doctor.'

'Oh, you bastard.' Her voice was louder, sibilating around the gag. Her hands stayed still.

'Do it.' He slapped her thigh, hard. She squealed. Her eyes went wild and she grabbed her breasts, hanging free inside her blouse, and began to twist them with her fingers. 'That's it, feel them,' he whispered into her ear as he licked around its rim. Issuing a groan every time his groin slapped against her buttocks, she plucked and then rubbed at her nipples. He watched her fingers, delighted, but also keen to learn how she wanted them touched if she ever hired him again. 'Go on, harder, Doctor,' he said, and began to bang his pointy hips into her soft buttocks, increasing the speed of his thrusts.

With her ankles locked together, her legs were closed at the thigh and her sex especially tight around his cock. The friction was wonderful. One week of desperation and fevered dreams, when even the sheets of his bed had felt like a woman's hand, boiled inside him. Like an animal, he licked the side of her face, smearing and then eating the make-up off her skin.

'I'm going to put you on your tummy and come in you,' he said, his hands leaving her hips and joining her own fingers on her breasts.

Her breathing was loud in the heat and madness around and inside his head. 'Yes, yes. Anything you want, take it,' she said quickly, in a thick voice that seeped around the gag, now a thin dark strap that pulled the sides of her mouth wide.

Angel kissed her, his mouth aggressive, lingering. Right inside her ear, he whispered, 'You dressed for me.'

'Yes,' she said, her voice urgent.

'You dressed so this would happen right here in your office.'

'Yes. I did. I did.'

This confession made him thrust into her so hard he felt the first ominous pulse at the root of his cock. 'To make me do this. To make me wild for you. To make me want you so much.'

She closed her eyes and squeezed his fingers with her hands and then pressed them into her bosom. 'Yes. You know I did.'

'To make me fuck you on the floor.'

'Yes!'

He rolled her under his weight and began to ram his hips into her from behind. His hands were trapped inside hers now, under the weight of her jolting body, and he could feel the jelly of her breasts on his knuckles and wrists. Powering himself from his thighs and lower back, his exposed stomach and groin made a slapping sound so loudly against her naked buttocks and back, it began to sound like a hand was administering discipline in the doctor's office.

She was crying out, too; every time his sex packed and stuffed itself through her most intimate place, she yelled, 'Oh!' And then the doctor began to mutter to herself in between the deep groans that followed. He pulled the scarf from her smeared mouth so he could hear her say, 'Handle me. Fuck me. Take me. Handle me.' Her eyes had closed and her monologue remained continuous until she came. As she climaxed, she pushed her backside into the thrusts from his hips, grinding herself in tight to increase the friction of their coupling.

He pulled the doctor's hands out from beneath her, and then clutched them in the small of her back with one hand. 'Hard in here,' he said, his face wet with sweat. 'And then much harder in the other place. To teach you what happens when you do this for me.'

'No, no, you bastard!' she shrieked.

'Yes!' he cried out. And with her squashed flat, cuffed and hand-held beneath him, on the rug in her fine office, Angel ground himself inside another of the beautiful creatures that never ceased to haunt his dreams. 'Ready for me? Ready for my come? There is so much.'

'Oh, oh, oh,' she said into the rug, face-down, muffled again.

Out it pulsed and shot; a stream, a gush, a continuous scalding of his pipes. 'There. Oh, yes. There it is. All of it inside you.' Flooded, spread, splayed, squashed, used by the degenerate needs of a savage, the doctor wept, lost in the ecstasy of being handled.

As they lay together in the gloomy warmth of her office, her wrists still clutched in one of his hands, Angel looked at the small red light at the foot of the doctor's desk. Positioned about two feet from the floor, it must have been fastened in the wooden panel at the front. Like the eye of some wild animal of technology it watched him and occasionally winked. Sleepy and pleasantly fatigued, he never thought about what it actually was. Contented, he just stared at it and let his mind wander, mesmerised as if by the last ember of an open fire, until he was roused by a noise. It sounded close, but was muffled. It was the relieved squeak of something made out of wood from which a weight had been removed. The sound came from the other side of her office, behind the wall where her framed medals and her antique scalpels and forceps were framed on red velvet, behind glass. The chair in his own room in the townships made the same sound when he jumped off it after replacing a light bulb. He moved his head to look at the wall from which the squeak originated, but the doctor moved with him and rolled on top of his body. 'When I see you again,' she whispered. 'Not here, but in some other place where I can have more time, we will do other things.'

The request seemed strange to him. It suggested something other than his current ritual of visiting women at work or at home or at their clubs to pay obeisance to their pangs. There was a direction in her proposal, leading him somewhere where intimacy could flourish. For some reason, that he could not define or articulate, it alarmed him.

'Thank you,' he said. 'I'd like to see you again. You're beautiful. And there are things I would like to ask you about being a doctor.' His voice was timorous but he could see that it made her smile. 'Make another appointment for me.'

This final comment displeased her. Her face changed. The colour seemed to sour. Her smile sagged. She looked older. Much older. 'But then I have to take when I want you to give. Don't you understand? I'm offering what you want. What you always wanted. I've been honest; why can't you?' The bitterness in her voice and the spiteful look in her eyes made him recoil. He'd not wanted to offend the doctor by reminding her of his business. He swallowed but could think of nothing to say to make things straight again. The rug no longer deflected the hard polished floorboards from the bones of his hips and knees. He fidgeted.

The doctor threw her head back and laughed. He smiled and wanted to laugh also, but her mirth sounded forced and aggressive. She put a hand on the side of his face and stroked his cheek gently. But then, suddenly, that same hand was in his hair. His eyes watered and his face was shoved into the rug. Instinctively, he wanted to lash out and knock her hand away, but held back, remembering her position and where he was; that he was hers to be dealt with and used as she saw fit. Angel was confused and didn't understand what she was trying to do, but this bullying appealed to a secret part of him. It must have done because his cock began to swell again. She released his hair and stood up, concentrating on maintaining her poise as she rose from the rug.

Slowly, Angel regained his feet also. As he belted himself away, she messed with her hair, and then slipped her shoes back on. Once again, she looked especially delicate to him. But was it a careful elegance she carried beneath the stylish suit, or something fraught that made her totter and made her fingers slow with an earring?

'I know when it's right. When it begins. They must have told you.' She said this without looking at him as she lit a cigarette. Then she turned and offered him one. Frowning from his deepening confusion at what she had just said, Angel shook his head. 'No, you wouldn't, would you? All you do is fuck and swim. So simple.'

He cocked his head to one side. And how did she know about his life in the water?

She laughed again. 'But maybe things aren't so simple now, darling. You must have been told about how some of us like to invest.' Then she sat down in her chair and watched him, smoke rising from her cigarette holder. When she saw him check his watch, his face pale and stricken with a great discomfort, she said, 'Go, then.'

But Angel walked to where she sat and leaned against the desk. Scared she might slap him or clench a hand in his hair, he managed to kiss her. To his relief, her arms closed around his neck and affectionately stroked and ruffled the back of his hair with her hands.

'You're real, aren't you? A sweet boy. My sweet boy.' She was smiling again and her eyes were wet. 'We'll meet again. Soon.'

'Yes,' he said instinctively, out of fright.

This time, his answer pleased her. She laughed. 'They are so clever. They know. They really do know me.'

Sensing madness in these cryptic suggestions, Angel disentangled himself from her arms and kissed her once more on her forehead, just to make her happy until he was out of range of her claws. How had it turned so ugly? If only she knew how much he admired her and all of her achievements. He wished he had the courage to tell her and not stumble. 'I have to go now,' is all he said.

At the door, he turned to look at her for the last time. 'Goodbye, Doctor,' he said, his face friendly but betraying his nerves. But the doctor never smiled back. The pale oval of her face never moved. With those stern blue eyes, she looked at him the way those bitter with grudges tend to watch others with fewer complaints.

Five

She was extraordinary, and when she looked at Angel, as he stood at the front door waiting to be admitted, he felt light-headed. He found himself blushing for no apparent reason and then unable to speak. Now he worried that she'd interpreted his reaction as arrogance. Dressed formally in one of his six suits – black and identical in cut – Angel followed this delightful maid down a long marble concourse to a living room overlooking a fabulous garden lit by green lights.

Seated in the living room – forwards and near the edge of the couch, unable to relax in the silk cushions when he had left a slum less than an hour before – he looked around himself at an exact reproduction of an affluent home from a previous era. As if he'd been run through a museum, led by the hand and only permitted backward glances at the exhibits, he found himself half-dazed by this overflowing but not disorderly penthouse. There were gilt-edged mirrors, patterned squares of black and white swirly marble on the floors and walls, crystal chandeliers, busts made from dark stone, Egyptian carvings, hieroglyphics behind glass, white and gold lamps on table tops, shiny mahogany furniture, and books; so many books with long spines and gold lettering embossed in their red covers, like this was a private library and museum rolled into one. But the maid, encroaching once more on his line of vision, was the most immediate, fascinating and precious thing of all. Like the apartment, she was something he'd only previously seen in library books. Black dress, white apron, black ringlets tied up under her cap, a fine net that fell halfway across her eyes, making them appear sleepy and sultry, her Cuban-heeled shoes with a high polish, and her black seamed stockings – she was from another age. Uniformed domestic help was not uncommon in the higher residential Zones but, on his journeys to and from the centre, he'd seen no girl dressed in quite this manner. And certain features of the apartment reminded him of the mid-twentieth century also, as if it were the home of an archaeologist, explorer or a gentleman-dilettante who read the languages of people and civilisations long dead. Between the wars of that century, he knew the wealthy people lived like this. If only they had known those conflicts were merely preparations for the next one, when everybody inhaled the enemy. On the mantelpiece an onyx sculpture of a long-eared jackal watched him from across its slender paws – Anubis, God of the dead.

'Madam will be with you shortly. She's with the boy,' the maid said, rolling her eyes at the mention of the boy, as if he promised trouble. Angel went cold. A boy? And the maid had mentioned someone called 'Madam', whom he presumed was the client in what was to be, he now presumed, a non-contact domestic visit. For this assignment, the instructions on his communicator had supplied nothing but an address in the exclusive residential spread of Zone Two – a vast architectural tapestry of low-rise buildings built like Greek temples in the Athenian quarter, or Georgian, Edwardian and Regency mansions in the south, sombre red-brick Victorian's north, and even several castles with fortifications and moats in the eastern parts. All of them examples of the revivalist period that begun at the dawn of the corporate age, when technology leaped forwards and architectural style trawled backwards to rebuild the ruins from the silent war. But a family situation here? This revelation did nothing to placate his growing anxiety towards not only his job, but what he consistently proved himself capable of becoming on an assignment.

'Suppose you want a drink,' the maid said, again catching him in a study of her shapely ankles, with those fine seams that disappeared inside her shiny heels. On her left calf muscle the seam was crooked.

'No. No thank you,' Angel said, reddening.

Self-conscious, she looked down at her legs and then straightened her back. She raised an eyebrow. 'Suit yourself.' Harbouring a dismissive frown, the maid remained in the room. Perhaps she'd been told to keep an eye on visitors, considering the many priceless antiques they kept here. Regardless of her motive for lingering, it gave him the opportunity to not just look at her, and more surreptitiously this time, but to bask in the effect she had on a room. Despite the many beautiful objects behind glass or mounted on pedestals, her striking face would have captured anyone's attention. Her features were unusually angular for a woman, her lips were full, and her unfeasibly large and distinctively yellow eyes suggested resources of natural brightness. But her face was a paradox – he almost had to study it to find out whether she was genuinely attractive or not. In an unusual long-nosed way, she was ugly but also beautiful. And this girl had no enhancements. Even her chest was small on her long and lean body, with that interesting, androgynous muscle definition about her slender arms and legs. A township girl, surely, he thought. She was thinking the same of him. 'Come far?' she asked.

He cleared his throat. 'From Binton.'

She smiled mockingly. 'Long way from home, poor boy?'

'I'm a companion.'

'That what you call it?' she said, and laughed. 'Well, you're not the first to have been here. The others never came back. Don't expect you will either.' She'd meant to be vile, but as she finished speaking, she looked at him with some sympathy. 'Be careful is all I'm trying to say to you. Neighbours should look after each other.'

His hopes suddenly soared. 'Neighbours? You live in Binton too?'

She said, 'Close,' and then checked her watch.

He looked at her long nose again. It was aristocratic; Spanish or Persian or Eastern-looking, complemented by her pale caramel skin. And above the nose, her eyes continued to startle him. He wanted to look at them more closely. Her irises really were an extraordinary yellow in colour.

'Come on,' she muttered to herself. 'I have things to do.'

Still wary of displeasing her, but intrigued, he said, 'They keep you waiting?'

'She does. Always,' she said, not looking at him.

'And you're a dancer.'

She looked at him. Her eyes narrowed with a surprise that quickly became suspicion.

'I'm guessing. Judging by your figure,' he offered in a conciliatory tone, but still blushed.

'Salina!' a woman called from somewhere in the elegant distance, from beyond the living room.

The maid snapped to attention and her face smoothed itself back into the haughty mask he'd first seen. She walked past him, between the table and couch. His head reeled, so suddenly full of the swishing sound of her uniform and the cool tang of her fragrant body that puffed over his face like an invisible force with the power to bewitch. 'See ya,' she said.

Angel touched her arm. 'Wait.' She turned and looked down at him, surprised again. He reached down to her left leg. 'Excuse me,' he said, and gently pinched his fingers on the crooked seam of her stocking. Carefully, so as not to ladder the fine black mesh on her dancer's leg, he pulled it inwards, to the centre of her calf. 'There. Now you're perfect again,' he said, hot in the face, from having touched her without permission, and alarmed at his own opportunism with this girl who made his stomach lurch and go sea-sickly when he caught the full beam of her eyes.

She smiled. Was it pitying? And then she was gone, leaving him alone in the room. 'Salina,' he whispered to himself. 'Salina,' he said again, thinking of her long nose and leopard eyes. In his mind, he pictured her in white robes near a ruin in a desert. But before him, the sight of a child's toys, scattered about the carpets, quickly ruined the fantasy. He loosened his collar and became more alert, even panicky now Salina had gone. He remembered her warning and felt weak in the stomach. His work was hardly suitable for a home with a kid in it. As he suffered this fresh crisis, his client entered the living room. Angel leaped to his feet, astounded. Salina was not the only one whose beauty seemed too large for this life.

'Oh, I say. You're rather a pretty one,' she said, her voice girlie and alive with the promise of a squeaky laugh. He liked it. A bit Binton, but posh also. And this woman he knew from somewhere. Yet he also knew he'd never seen her in the flesh before. No, he'd never seen her glide and move like this – that he would have had no trouble remembering – but her blonde hair curling up at the side of her cherry lips, her soft bosomy front, thick shapely thighs, big black eyes and the tiny beauty spot above her top lip, he was sure he recognised. But from where? 'Salina has gone to get my little man from his room,' she said, 'So you can be properly introduced. But I'll be straight with you, and I always speak my mind, he's a handful. So be firm.'

Angel swallowed. Was she talking about baby-sitting a boy? Had she phoned the wrong agency? Was he not going to touch her long body and find out what kind of treasure rustled and warmed itself under the long black gown, so tight around her generous curves? She could see he was confused, but provided no further information.

Over by the drinks cabinet, she poured a clear spirit into a fat glass with a heavy bottom. It made the ice tinkle and the sound seemed to suit her – to be part of her music – like the rap of her red nails on the sparkly glass. 'I won't be out long. I just need a break from him,' she said, and smiled in a sad way. 'Bet this party is going to be full of phoneys,' she added, under her breath.

Salina re-entered the room, holding a long evening coat out in front of her. It was made from black fur which shone glossy and sleek under the white lights. A beautiful thing that Salina draped around the shoulders of her mistress.

'You better take off, sweetie,' the woman said to Salina. 'I'll get the cab to drop you at the station. That's close to your stop, isn't it?'

'Thank you, ma'am,' Salina said, her attitude gone.

'And here he is,' the blonde woman said, turning away from Salina. 'My little man.' She was all smiles and giggles now that her little man was in the room. But Angel went cold with shock. Out the corner of his eye, he could see Salina smiling, revelling in his mystification and anxiety. The 'little man' was in his fifties. Grey-haired and suited in a boy's pyjama set, with a cowboy print on the creased material, the squat figure skipped playfully into the living room. His fat mouth was sticky with chocolate and half of his pyjama top was untucked from the elasticated waistband on his round stomach. Frowning, and squirming his bulbous body, he twisted away from his beautiful blonde guardian, fighting off her attempts to plant those succulent red lips on his gritty cheek. Once free of her long arms, pale and glittering with jewels, he approached the new object of fascination in his home: Angel.

'Now, baby,' the mistress said. 'This is Angel, who's going to look after you until I come home. And I want you to be really, really sweet to the kind man. And don't think you're sitting up all night watching 3Ds,' she added, in a sterner tone that carried no weight and seemed incongruous against her soft beauty. 'Now, Salina, darling. Are you ready?'

'Yes, ma'am,' she said, putting her own coat on.

'I don't want to keep that young beau of yours waiting any longer. But you must remember it's a woman's prerogative to be late. Indifference is the only thing a man has, so why not use it against them?'

Something twisted in Angel's stomach at the mention of Salina's boyfriend. 'See you later, Angel,' the woman called, from the concourse where the heels of her shoes rang loud and spanky-crisp. 'Take good care of my little man!'

92

Salina never looked back.

Sitting cross-legged with his stomach pushed out, the man in pyjamas stared at Angel with an undisguised malevolence. What could he say to this monstrous figure? Did he speak to him as a child or a fully grown man? His unease must have shown. 'I ... I like your toys,' he lied, for want of something to say.

'They're bloody damn stupid!' the little man cried out, angry at what he'd seen in his new guardian's face. Various gadgets were knocked across the rugs by his podgy hands. Then the figure was on its feet, and those strong, destructive hands were busy in the ornaments on a glass shelf above the fireplace.

'No!' Angel shouted, but before he could reach the little man, a vase slipped from the shelf and exploded on the marble floor tiles. White with fear and standing amongst the shards, he said, 'Shit.'

'Shit!' cried the figure in yellow pyjamas, delighted with his reaction. 'You said shit. Shitty, shit, shit.' And off he ran into the apartment, repeating the word with all the confidence and aplomb that assured Angel the word would be repeated and the source quoted when the guardian returned. His movements jerky and clumsy with panic, Angel gave pursuit. Up ahead, in one of the bedrooms, things were being banged and slammed together. Frantic with worry, Angel realised he could have hours with the hooligan to endure. It would be pure containment. And who was this absurd man? A disturbed relative? A child with some strange ageing disorder? Or something else, something far worse?

The figure was in the master bedroom. This room belonged to ... to the blonde woman. He still didn't know her name, or this foul creature's name he was being paid to guard. The moment he'd arrived, everything had blurred in his usual inner chaos of excitement, anxiety and childlike wonder. He chided himself for being so instantly smitten with Salina and then the blonde woman but, even if he hadn't been so fascinated by them, it was forbidden for him to ask questions. Once again, he was defenceless. And to think of how he looked forward to lying with a beautiful Zone-woman tonight, and how relieved he'd been at not hearing from the doctor.

The bed in the room was vast but unmade. There was a dressing screen in one corner before the window. Items of black underwear were folded over its oriental screens. The sight of them made Angel tighten inside. But he only allowed himself to look at the dangly straps and see-through panels and cups for a second. This man-boy was determined to defile his mistress's room the moment she was gone. The figure was now busy in the wardrobes. From the gleeful and fastidious approach the middle-aged child made in disturbing the drawers and cupboards, Angel presumed this area had been made out of bounds to him, and he'd waited, biding his time until an opportunity presented itself to conduct a messy and ruinous search of the forbidden.

'No, no. Not in here. Leave these things. You mustn't touch them.' But his cries were in vain; the battle had been lost in the first exchange of glances back in the lounge. His aura was soft, imbued with compromise, and the delinquent had sensed it.

Grinning, the fat boy-man held up a rubber mask that he'd found in a bottom drawer. Angel had never seen anything like it before, but the saggy eye-holes and the shiny, shower-cap-headpiece alerted him to the presence of unusual tastes.

'No, put that down. Don't touch these things,' he yelled. Oblivious, the fat boy with silver hair hauled what looked to be a whip of some kind from another drawer. Tangled up with the handle was a pair of silver cuffs, similar to those he secured the doctor's slender ankles with.

'Back! Put it back!' he yelled.

In response, an expensive high-heeled shoe was hurled at his head. It cut sharp above his eyebrow. Pain mixed with fear and all of his emotions combusted. 'Stop! I don't have to put up with this,' he shouted. 'You evil shit! I'm going. You're on your own. You fat, ridiculous baby.' And he turned and left the bedroom and its stunned occupant in the wreckage. He marched back through the lounge, and into the marble concourse that led to the front door. There must have been a mistake at the agency. This was clearly an error on their behalf and they had messed up before; the first assignment should have taken place in an empty building and the doctor had tried to bully him into seeing her out of hours, which she must have known was not permitted. And now this nightmare scenario, with the mistress and maid gone and him alone with the rummaging creature.

The sound of someone sniffing, and the pad of bare feet on the marble behind him, caused Angel to pause before the front door. He turned around and stared at the tear-stained face of the man in yellow pyjamas. Stricken with the fear of abandonment, and also a terror of the man in the black suit who had shouted, the little man wiped at his now doleful eyes.

'Yeah, I thought so,' Angel said. 'No, you don't want to be left alone all night. I didn't think so. Anything could happen in that time. Did you know there's an anarchist killer in this neighbourhood? No? Well there is. He has the security codes to all the houses memorised. It doesn't bear thinking about.' The figure's eyes widened, and then his whole unshaven and baggy face crumpled. Angel fought to deny his instinctive sympathy. If he softened now, the priceless trinkets around him would be reduced to shards and dust. 'Go into the living room and sit quietly,' he said. The figure paused, until Angel gave him an assurance that he would follow.

'What's your name?' he asked the creature, once they were back in the living room.

'Quinny,' it said in a deep but naturally churlish tone of voice.

'And who is that woman?'

'M' he said, his eyes alight.

'M?' Angel queried. The figure nodded enthusiastically, excited by the thought of her. In the circumstances Angel thought it best not to pry any further. 'Well, Quinny, any more crap from you, and you're on your own. That's a promise. There will be no warning; I'll just take off the moment you put a foot wrong.' Although he kept his voice low, the Quinnything could not doubt the sincerity in his tone. The figure obediently sat cross-legged on the rug, the violent energy gone. 'Now, I intend to read one of these books,' Angel said, still shaken. 'I'll read aloud so you can hear also.'

The figure shook its head and pointed at the giant entertainment centre, eager to see one of the holographic programmes or films, so popular with those with the space in their homes in which to allow the action to unfold around them. Angel shook his head. 'No. You sit there and listen to me read or I'm gone.' Quinny cowered.

Angel selected a book called *Gods, Graves and Scholars*. Inside the front cover, there was a family shield, under it the date of purchase, and then a man's name: Professor T. E. Wharton. With the book in hand, Angel sat himself in the largest and most comfortable chair, beside a free-standing lamp and a small glass table mounted with a chess board. It was the only remedy he could think of, to both calm his nerves and keep the miscreant in the same place. Reading aloud would also distract him from thinking about the things he had seen displayed in the blonde woman's bedroom. Angel read the story of Schliemann and Troy.

When he finished a surprisingly vivid and lively tale that read like a novel, he was pleased to see that the little man had fallen asleep on the rug. Ruddy-faced, worn out, grey hairs growing in a copse of spidery legs from each cavernous nostril, he snored far too loudly for a child. Angel shook his head with disbelief, but wanted to laugh also at the sight before him.

Quietly, he left the living room to repair the damage in the bedroom. As he straightened the woman's gowns that hung dishevelled from a long mirrored wardrobe, covering an entire wall, or put them back on their hangers, he paused to look at the hundreds of shoes beneath the dresses. She favoured high heels of every style. There must have been three hundred pairs, mostly shiny and strappy and showing no signs of wear. Angel closed the mirrored doors and moved across to her drawers to tuck the rubbery things back inside, to reseal her secrets back in the dark where best they were employed.

Despite his curiosity about this woman and her collection, he wanted to be quick in here and to get out. Being in this room made him nervous. Since meeting the doctor he felt like a jittery trespasser in the chamber of another mad queen. After a final tuck of a black lace-edged corset inside the top drawer, Angel turned to leave the room. It was then that he noticed a picture, framed in silver on the corner of the dresser, amongst the perfume bottles shaped like Ottoman towers. He raised the photo and studied it. Was it the woman who left him in charge of Quinny? This was where he had seen the woman before, in this photograph, striking this exact pose.

Yes, he'd seen this photograph in an old hard-cover book, shelved in the Charity Library's reference section. But it couldn't be the mistress of this house; the woman in the picture had died over three centuries before. His skin goosed cold. The subject of the photograph was laughing and trying to hold down her white skirts. They had been blown upwards by a draught that had come through the metal grate she stood upon. Her open-toed shoes were planted on the grid beneath long, smooth, barely tanned legs: instant lures for the eyes. Even the curly peroxide hair was the same, as well as the wide eyes with the thick, black lashes. She was a movie star and had died young, but that was all he could remember from the film almanac in the library. She had been in the old motion pictures when everything was two-dimensional and the sound came from in front of you and not all around your head. But how had she come to be living again?

He'd thought it a myth, what people said about the new enhancement crazes that copied the bodies and faces of dead people. He'd dismissed it as anarchist gossip. When he first heard about the fashion for resurrecting historical beauty, he'd presumed the cosmetic industry used preserved genes, in the same way they had brought a scientist with wild white hair back to life, who just looked confused and begged to be made dead again, on the giant news screens that everyone had watched live. The corporations claimed the experiment would never be repeated, after his embarrassing performance, and the crazy-haired man in the bow tie was never seen again. But the woman in this house had been made to look exactly like this movie star by the surgeons. Angel left the bedroom, his head swirling.

Back in the living room, he stirred the sleeping man and then led him to his bedroom. Quinny allowed himself to be guided by the elbow. There were gadgets and toys on the floor of his room, and a big virtual reality unit that rich kids spent all of their time inside, until they were treated for addiction. The fat figure curled up on the bed, on top of the sheets, and went straight back to sleep. Counting this as a blessing, Angel turned off the lights in the room and closed the door before returning to the living room, eager to mooch some more. Before he made more than a cursory inspection of the kitchen, with its steels, bronzes and vines of garlic strung from the ceiling, the blonde ghost came home in a fanfare of giggles and noisy stumbling on her stilettos. She was drunk.

Dared he ask for her story? The heels of her shoes twice caught on the hem of her long gown that swept the marble tiles, and she nearly fell. Angel rushed to her side and offered the support of his elbow. Her big eyes were glassy. Gin clouds mingled with the harsh tobacco smell in her furs and he could smell the freshness of cold air on her soft cheeks. 'Darling, I've had far too much to drink.' She paused to suppress a burp. 'And then I got worried, so I came home. Is everything all right? Is the brat asleep? Sometimes, I just can't stand the sight of him.' She raised a hand, loose and useless above her head and then let it drop, with a smacking sound, against her broad thigh. There was no love in her voice now for the 'little man'. 'Where is the monster?'

'In bed.'

She closed her eyes in a moment of rapture, and then placed her cold hands on his face. 'You're a treasure. He's too much for me, you know.'

Angel nodded. 'He broke something, though. A vase.'

She sucked in her breath. 'I've told him to put them away before he . . . But he never listens.'

'Him?' Angel said, helping her into the lounge.

She slipped her arm around his waist. 'Yes. Another idiot –' But then she stopped herself, as if she had gone too far. She flopped down on the couch. 'Pour me a drink, darling.' Her dress opened up along one thigh, and Angel had to fight with himself not to stare. But as he made a drink for her at the cabinet, pouring from the same bottle he had seen her use before she left earlier in the evening, all he could see in his head was the long leg, and the glassy shimmer of the black nylon clinging to it. He imagined it around his neck in the large bed and felt himself go faint with the hots and the swoons and the stiffness.

'Come and sit by me,' she said, once he'd handed the drink to her. 'I'm all dizzy.' She shook her head around and her whitish curls flopped around her beautiful face. He smiled, but could not resist a peek inside her dress at the top where it had been disturbed. She never rearranged the parting. He wanted to ask about the professor, and the 'little man' and how she came to look exactly like a dead woman, but didn't. He was here to obey, not to meddle.

Sitting beside her, she began to babble at him in her high musical, girlish voice about who had said what to who at the club, and what had happened to so and so, and that she had met one of the polo team, who had a metal arm after getting it crushed in a game. Angel only half-listened; he was too smitten with the sight of her long legs poking from her dress, and with the movements of her thick mouth, sluggish with drink, but all the more arousing for it. When she put her head on his shoulder, his body stiffened – all of his body. Carelessly, one of her loose and floppy hands fell in his lap. Angel cleared his throat. She continued to talk at him and her laugh was wild and all of her words slurred. And as she talked at him, her fingers stroked the thickness in his lap, until it became thicker and raised itself under the cloth of his trousers until the lump rested in the palm of her hand. But then she was murmuring to herself, but held his cock more firmly, and then so tightly he winced even though it felt good. Her head fell on his chest.

Although he was on edge, nervous about this next stage of her performance, he began to stroke her hair. Then he put his nose on the nape of her neck where she smelled so spicy. As her murmurs ceased, the temperature in his groin dropped and his lap felt loose. He could not see over her head, but knew he'd been unzipped. His belt buckle rattled slack as that too was undone. And without another word or tipsy sob from the movie girl, the most wonderful lips he had ever felt against his body went to work in his lap.

With his arms outspread along the back of the settee, he lifted himself upwards. It was impossible to remain still and contain the glorious feeling in a motionless state. Shivers bewitched his muscles and skin. More of his cock slipped inside the thickly painted mouth he could not see, but was able to imagine in vivid detail. Little suckling sounds wafted out from beneath her gently moving, rotating head. Her blonde hair tickled his inner thighs where it fell down over her face. Long nails picked up his balls and rubbed them so gently it was like she was cradling the eggs of the near-extinct sparrow in her hand. Pleasure numbed him in limb and joint and sinew.

Angel closed his eyes. If he saw much more of her shiny legs, and thought too hard about her pretty, podgy mouth sucking him, he would come. Was that allowed without permission? To spill inside her plump red-lipped mouth? Would those long and curly lashes flutter back in surprise at the sudden influx of something soupy on her gums and teeth and tongue? Angel groaned. His sex spasmed and then pulsed. Little showers of sparks appeared under his eyelids like soundless fireworks, and his body deflated as its vigour escaped in hot natural springs from the part of him first bleached by saliva and then smeared red with lipstick. Her head dug further into his lap and he heard her suckle, lap and then gulp.

'Oh, my,' she said, and sat up. Slow-eyed, her lids heavy with dopey-sex sleepiness, she swallowed again and then breathed on his face. The gust was salty and pregnant with his baked yeasty smell. 'Naughty, naughty,' she slurred. 'You should have told me there was going to be so much. I'll get fat.' His softening cock hung unsupported in her loose fingers. 'I want my bed,' she then said, her thoughts elsewhere. Angel wondered if she even now remembered what she'd just done. 'Too tired to walk,' she said in a churlish voice. 'Darling, you'll have to carry me,' she added, more theatrical, her voice rising through the octaves.

Angel swept her up from the couch. She was heavy and filled his arms, but he liked her dense weight against his tight and tensing body. Despite his just being emptied inside her wonderful mouth, he wanted to squash this softness and scent under him.

With one finger she pressed at the straining tendons in his neck. She whispered, 'Another drinky first,' but soon lost interest in the drink and began to nuzzle the side of his face when he paused by the hospitality cabinet. 'Too squiffy for a drinky,' she said. By the time he'd carried her into the bedroom and lowered her on to the bed, his stiffness had recovered itself.

There was something about this room now, especially with her in it, that swamped him with a greater excitement than before. How often did her toys come out of the box?

As he straightened up, she hooked one finger inside his belt and pulled him on top of her. Immediately, her smudged and fumey mouth swallowed his lips and her plump tongue worked inside his mouth. Rolling on the bed with her, and wanting to waste no time in case she fell asleep, Angel managed to twist, loop and unbutton until he'd undressed himself and stripped the woman down to her corset, heels and stockings. They said nothing to each other, communicating with their eyes and guiding hands, allowing the fever of arousal to fuel them. Her body was pale and broad, but shapely – so much for his hands to explore and his mouth to eat. And as he traced his fingers around every part of her, he noticed her tendency to look over his shoulders with her big eyes, until he too turned around and saw their reflections in full profile in the mirror panels of the closets. She liked to watch, and he suddenly liked her even more.

For a while they kissed and he thought himself unable to ever tire of this mouth. Jaws open wide, their heads slotted on a side angle, they seemed able to grip each other's lips in full and provide room for their tongues to play between. The more passionate the kiss, the more eager the touches of their hands. Around his cock, her fingers seemed most comfortable. Beaten through her right hand slowly, with her finger joints lazily rolling over the ridge of his phallus, and her fingers touching the tip of its reddy-delight, he thought himself ready to come again.

Angel disentangled himself. He wanted to last and sustain the exquisite energy and expectation that made him glow inside and tingle on the outside.

Rising to his knees, he placed his face deep in her bosom. Her legs wrapped, slippery, around his waist and one of her shoes fell off her foot. She closed her heavy eyelids and rolled her head amongst the pillows as his mouth and tongue and fingers busied themselves with her large pinky nipples.

'Oh, my. Oh, my. Oh, my,' she repeated, and then followed the outburst with a squeaky laugh.

Unable to resist the delights of penetration any longer, he slipped her panties – a gauzy string of nothingness – from under her buttocks and down her thighs, and off her red toenails and the one remaining, dangling shoe. Anticipating his intention, she giggled and then bit one finger between her teeth. After one long ruffling of his tongue through the bitter lips of her sex, Angel placed a hand on the pillow under her head and pushed his girth inside her with the other hand. Snapping her head back, her arms and legs became firmer on his body, as if she were in the raptures of a slight pain she enjoyed, but felt unable to withstand at the same time. Then she relaxed. As the last resistance around his cock softened and her flesh began to suck at him instead, he was planted right at the back of her.

Kissing again, they ground each other up the bed to the wall, back down to the foot of the mattress, rolled to the sides of the bed frame, twisted in the sheets, made each other's skin damp with perspiration, and only broke from a kiss to catch their breath. Angel could not leave her face alone. Thick lips, dark eyelids, snubby nose, beauty spot, pale chin; his mouth and the tip of his tongue touched and loved every part of her beautiful, famous head. Restraining the need to let go and deliver himself inside her, he would often squeeze his eyes shut and clench the muscles at the base of his sex to prevent a sudden climax and end to their loving, until he began to think he had held on for too long and would be unable to ever come. But when she rose, tired but still purring, to her hands and knees and offered her large heart-shaped bottom to his long and shiny sex, and showed her dazed and slow face to the wide mirrors, so even a reflection could adore her the way camera lenses once had, Angel's concern about having held back for too long vanished.

Hands on her hips, squeezing the pale flesh with his fingers, he slipped into her from behind. Head down, little sobs dropping from her mouth, eyes nearly shut, the movie mistress uttered one continuous moan as he pressed inside her. And then yelped with helium-puppy sounds as his strokes became harder and she was forced to put her hands over the end of the bed and on to the floor.

Looking into the mirror, he saw her breasts swing free in little judders, her stockings tighten on her broad thighs, and her greasy reddish lips mouth the words, 'Fuck me,' at him. Digging his fingers under her pelvis, Angel pulled her back at his groin while banging his body forwards simultaneously. Over and over again, struggling to breathe in the hot air, using hidden resources of stamina, he continued to thrust into her and to make her moan harmoniously. Teetering on an edge inside himself until he reached the point when he had to come, hot and strong inside her, she started to croak, and her face tensed up as if she was about to scream or maybe even cry. And then her head dropped, and she squealed, and he released the pressure inside his sex to finally enjoy the constant sensation of lava surging through his pipes. Looking at the ceiling, he gasped, and his body shook from the emptying.

They lay on the floor to dry off, kiss, and breathe each other in. 'Oh, but you're just a boy,' she said in a sleepy voice, as she lay across his chest. For a while he thought she was asleep, but noticed the thin glint of dark eyes watching him through the spiky fronds of her lashes. 'Cos you're young they used you. They'll use you up. But who wants to live for ever? Better to have it this way with gin and sin, don't you think?'

'Yes ma'am,' he said.

'Oh, ma'am this, ma'am that. Stop it, will you? I'm jussa girl. And you're my new bad daddy.' She folded around him, covered his face and body, trapped his arms beneath her, pushed one lazy leg across his front and then squeezed his sex under her knee, hot and wrinkly with nylon. 'Will you tie me up, bad daddy?' she asked, her lips against his face. 'Put the ropes on me?'

He nodded, too alarmed to speak. Slowly, clumsily, she moved from off his body and crawled to her closet space. He watched her lovely shape, round and long-legged, dishevelled in damp underwear, the blonde locks now tousled beyond repair, crawling to her secret cabinets whose contents he'd already seen, but was not opposed to seeing more of. Things were pulled out. White tangled coils with something purple and rubbery in the middle. Then she came back, giggling, her big eyes still sleepy, but alive with a kind of delirium, as if she were out of control at a society party that had descended into a state of half-dressed people; men in tuxedo jackets and socks, women in bras and high heels; an orgy amongst empty bottles and broken glasses and sugar bowls full of white powder.

It seemed to form all around her like a vision, as she came back to him clutching the ropes and the rubber ball. He thought of cigarette filters stained by red lips, camera flashes, the mean, licentious smiles of

106

drunken women, the raspy laughs of ageing men who fingered them, police cars, and bad language from a defiant drunk before her head was covered with a blanket. How many bad daddies had this woman succumbed to? How could anyone survive this world he had become entangled in? High-Zone world. Doctors, executives, corporations: had he seen too much, too many of their secrets? Bad men and lushes in fur; could he fall in with them completely? It seemed so alien; an opposition to the simplicity of his room, food, and the water he pulled himself through daily. A lump formed in his throat.

But sinking through the soft wombs of these women – could he ever stop the addiction?

'Tie me,' she said, and then fell on to her side, giggling. 'Tie all of me up. I like it.' Her voice had gone hissy. She was a spoiled girl gone mad now; a creature re-created to be adored by men. Angel tied her wrists together. Loose at first, but then she made him do them tighter until her pale skin reddened and wrinkled around the twine. Around her ankles he made four loops and then tied them off with hardware store string. And then the rubber ball was slipped between her big soft lips, so it was held by teeth forced to stay apart. After it was in place, her eyes opened fully; they became alert, surprised even. Another character in this insane house had risen to perform.

At first, he was afraid of this side to her – the reckless and desperate need she possessed to submit to a hired underling – and part-appalled at the sight of this young beauty, wound and bound in exclusive underwear and white rope, suddenly turned call-girl and drug-hooker. But he soon lost control of himself to the hot, writhing urges that twisted his insides, and demanded that he take her, have her, punish her, abuse her. His breath shortened and his chest tightened up the more he looked at her.

This contradictory blend of vulnerability and femininity, mixed with a desire for torture and willing restraint, in an absent millionaire's bedroom, made him blind and mad for her. A grotesque and smoky region of his imagination opened up, where visions came like clips from old movies, or like black and white photographs fading green but suddenly discovered in the bottom drawer of a stranger's desk. And that absurd creature next door, put to bed in cowboy-print pyjamas, was now gone and so easily removed from his mind. Bestial in mind, body and deed, he existed in the immediate, shocking present of a professor's apartment. Gone were his thoughts of a flight back to poverty. He learned to stop thinking; to tie the knots and stroke the see-through nylon on this woman's body, to listen to her raspy sounds and like them, to put his fingertips against her hard pink anus and hear the rhythm of her breathing change from behind the gag.

Suddenly angry, as a random thought of Salina's unavailability entered his mind, but aggressively excited by the sight of M's dozy and irresistible face, he hauled her bound and heavy shape from the rug and dropped her over his knees. Sitting on the corner of the bed, with her soft, white belly pressed against his thighs, and with her legs bent at the knee so her pretty feet – one shoe on, one shoe off – hovered in the cloying air of gin, perfume and salty sex, and with her hands tied together under her breasts, Angel spanked her. So loud was the noise of his cupped palm against her buttock, it seemed to echo off the glass and mirrors and all the little bottles of scent in the room. Lipstick sweet, her fast breaths and little moans gathered around his face. Pinky and then rash-red, her creamy bottom tinted in the light before his eyes. Between his legs and against her ribs, his stiffness rose. Laughing, but spiteful-mad at his collapse into deviance, he slapped and rounded his hand against her cheeks until he was convinced the heat they generated touched the underside of his chin.

Her moans went rhythmic, and her chest rose as if she had hiccuped, every time his hand fell. And as he slowed down, with an ache in his shoulder, and saw the saliva begin to drip off the rubber ball in her mouth, his lap and legs became especially hot. On the marble tiles, between the white furry rug and the bed-frame, he heard the trickle-tinkle of a water leak. Angel stopped smacking her and looked down. Clear and sparkly as diamonds falling from a broken chain, her ammoniac-champagne escaped from between her legs, ran over his thighs and tickled down his calf muscles to his feet. The sheets beneath his buttocks became hot and swampy. Over the gag, he could hear her giggling. Sharp to the nose and fried-kidney hot, Angel could smell the steam from her wine. Immediately, she rubbed her wet sex and damp thighs, where the wetness had taken the gloss off her stockings, against his bare skin.

Angel raised his hands and looked at them. The fingers of his right hand were wet. Oblivious to the warm, overripe sensation of the sodden bedclothes, he sat stunned. Giggling more furiously, his lover moved her heavy body about in his lap, squirming in the moisture. Delighted by the squish of her underwear against naked flesh, he realised her wetting had been no accident. Gradually, the full magnitude of what she had done, of what a society girl enjoyed, dawned on Angel. Not even the rubber mask had been adequate preparation. He was not sure how he felt as he sat there in movie-star piss, or maybe he went into denial, but finally, his new erection seemed to represent a perverse delight that shamed him.

Only the sudden eruption of her cries, muffled around the ball gag, broke Angel from his stupor. Using her elbows, she pushed herself from his knees and stood up on her bound feet. Sensing a presence behind his back, and following the direction of her enraged glare, Angel turned his head to his side. He started and then leaped to his feet. In the doorway stood Quinny. Grinning, his chubby hands worked at the short but fat length of his oily-looking penis.

Her garbled shrieks and the way in which she thrust her hands before Angel's face, intimated that he should untie her. The knots he had tied were not good and her hands were almost free. Hurriedly, Angel picked and plucked and unwound until the ropes were gone. She yanked the gag from her face and threw it down. 'You brat!' she screamed hysterically, and then launched herself at the beaming figure, silhouetted in the doorway. Staggering drunk towards the door, she raised one hand to deliver a slap. The tops of her nylons were dark and droplets of moisture fell from her thighs to twinkle on the marble or darken spots into the rugs.

Laughing with excitement, Quinny only released his stubby offering and fled from the door after her first slaps struck his shoulders and neck. 'I'll kill you!' she threatened. 'Always the face at the door, you bad, bad, bastard boy. I'll kill you!'

Fleeing the madness, Angel headed for the en suite bathroom. With the door closed and the hot shower running, the violent noises of the chase, mixed with Quinny's evil laughter, faded. Quickly, Angel rinsed and scrubbed his skin clean before drying himself with a huge towel – lemon-coloured – the size of the hand-stitched eiderdown that covered his own bed.

As he dried himself, he began to laugh, but didn't recognise the sound of his own voice. These were insane, gleeful hysterics suited to this mad place and at the hideous ritual he had seen performed by the fat, fifty-something boy and the beautiful lush.

But he laughed from a curious relief also. Because something fundamental had been demystified for him. All of his life he had feared and coveted the Higher Zones and craved acceptance by them. Elevated in his mind to another dimension, parallel to his derelict existence, he'd thought these penthouse apartments offered the cure to every ill, the gratification of every desire and the promise of eternal happiness through prosperity and beauty. And yet, here he stood in a professor's bathroom, mopping gin-tinted ammonia from his thighs. Exhilarated by discovery, stronger from disclosure, Angel now believed that behind every ornate door there lived deviance, and behind the perfect, genetically sculpted faces, dark thoughts moved like polluting matter. And, somehow, he'd been instrumental in their expression. Could he fear these tyrants any longer?

He left the bathroom and dressed quickly. It appeared the chase had found its conclusion. Down the hallway someone had begun to groan, and between these cries of anguish and passion he heard the unmistakable sound of a bare hand connecting with an unclothed rump. It was as if they had wanted him to stay and to see this scene played out to its end. And who exactly was the client?

Angel proceeded down the hall to Quinny's room. Through the narrow space between door and doorjamb, he saw flashes of blonde hair, hairy arms loose in their compliance, discarded pyjamas, and a long leg in a laddered nylon. As if his hand moved of its own volition, he pushed the door in.

111

Lying face-down like a beached elephant seal with hirsute shoulders, Quinny received the release he had been seeking all evening. A dishevelled movie star, in soiled black lingerie, pelted his backside crimson with a leather belt. 'And that for peeking. And that for prying. And that for spying,' she said, in time with each wild stroke. Her face seemed paler now and her eyes stared into another place. But Quinny roused his scruffy head from the pillows and looked up at Angel. Despite the tears in his eyes, he was smiling.

As Angel left the apartment, he happened across a final revelation. Behind the coat rack he saw a curious gilt-edged picture frame, turned around to face the wall. Something he'd overlooked on his way into the apartment earlier when he'd been distracted by the seams running down the back of the maid's calf muscles. After he turned the picture frame around, he saw a photograph of Professor Wharton, or rather Quinny, in a three-piece suit, receiving a medal of honour from the French Premier.

Six

Angel sensed the doctor before he saw her. Even the knock gave her up; it was an insistent sound and came when he least wanted to be disturbed. When he opened the door to his room, she was standing in the unlit hall against the wall opposite, face drawn and body stiff. He imagined the silent figure's hand, white and thin, and saw it dip inside his soul where it clenched and broke things until that bright spirit of his was reduced to something wet-eyed and obedient. 'Doctor,' he said, to the long silhouette, partially exposed by the natural light that fell from his doorway into the hall.

Into his room she came without a word in greeting. Angel gaped at her outfit. Gone was the dress of business. Now she had been wrapped and constricted more than clothed. Her body was concealed beneath a black, rubber coat – knee-length and shiny. Her head was scarved and her legs were booted tight and glossy too. And it was as if her sunglasses had been donned to shield Angel from the angry glare of her eyes. An ozone smell wafted inside with her. It clung to this strange rubber skin she wore and then filled his apartment, where the air molecules suddenly began to jostle, as if with nervous impatience, and he felt they would continue to do so, long after she had gone.

113

'Don't,' she said, and held one gloved hand up. 'Don't even pretend you're pleased to see me. I'm no fool, Angel. I know you are not truly ready. Be thankful I know it's only fear that makes you avoid me. But that will go, in time.' She looked dismissively around the Spartan interior of his room and then sat on his bed. 'We must get you out of here. It's no place for you. I have something in mind. No good hiding in the dark and using this dreadful place, and those awful women, as an excuse. Why delay?' And once she'd spoken, Angel realised that how he felt would always be irrelevant with her.

He had been packing a sack with his swimming gear, and was about to leave his room and head for the Commercial Canal when she arrived. Annoyance entered his tone, not just at the postponement of his swim, but at the intrusion into his sanctum. 'Doctor, I have to tell you.' She raised her face. He could see her lips were tight with anger and the end of her nose had gone waxy and white. 'I have to tell you, Doctor, that I am not permitted to see clients outside of prearranged appointments. It is forbidden.'

Without a word, she tapped a button on her communicator. Angel felt his strength drain away through his legs and into the bare floorboards. 'Yes, I want him now,' she said to her wrist. 'Yes, Angel. Right now. Good ... No, that's not necessary. I know where to find him ... Yes, you could say I'm satisfied.' Smiling, she terminated the call. On his wrist, his communicator beeped to announce the standby mode and to alert him to await further instruction. He never bothered to read the message that followed minutes later.

'See how simple it is? So easy to order a commodity in this town. I can do what I like,' she said. Angel straightened up and stared at her, his face hard and

114

unfeeling. She stood up and moved closer to him. 'Don't pout, darling. You wanted to start something, but now don't have the guts to see it through. Much easier to get distracted by the others. The drunks. The imbecile girls. Oh, yes, I know all about that blonde. Was the bitch good? Well, there will be no more of them.'

So she'd had him followed. 'Stop it,' Angel whispered.

'What's this?' she said, and gripped the impression of his cock through his trousers with a hard, leather hand. 'See. It's hard, Angel. It knows what it wants. You shouldn't deny it when I'm near. I deny myself nothing.'

He cleared his throat, but couldn't speak. Anger had mixed with arousal and left him confused. She smiled and moved her lips within an inch of his mouth. 'Want to hurt me? Umm? There'll be time enough for that. And you'll do it when I say. Get used to it.' After squeezing his cock she then moved her hand, with all the affirmation of her manner, up and down its length. His breathing grew heavy and he dipped his head. His eyes closed.

When she released his sex – dew-capped and hot with blood – he could not belay a groan, and hated himself for wanting that hand back. Triumphant, she walked back to the bed and sat down. Her voice softened. 'Others were tried before I found you.' She paused to watch his face keenly for something she hoped to see. When she believed she'd found it, she continued. 'You don't like that, I know. But it was necessary. Trust me. Don't be afraid. We're right for each other. Can't you feel it? Ask yourself how often that happens.'

Angel looked away from her and picked up his bag. There must be something he could do. He smouldered at the thought of her coming, uninvited, to his sanctuary to tell him how he thought and what he would do. In this shabby den, he had a world of ideas, an inner life. Sometimes anxiety delivered the blackest slumps of loneliness, but still, he knew both his struggle, and the place in which he endured it, were necessary and indispensable. She should not be here. This feeling of resistance in him had a bitter taste all through his mouth. 'I'm going to swim,' he said, and swung his bag over his shoulder.

Her laugh was high-pitched, derisory, and also pitying. He hated the sound of it in his room. 'Oh, darling, put the bag down.'

Angel's grip on the bag tightened.

'Put the bag down!' she shouted without warning. His heart nearly went bang. He flinched. Her face was bright red and demanded to be looked at. Both of her leather hands had fisted on the bedclothes. A knuckle cracked. Angel dropped the bag. There was silence between them. She smiled again and exhaled slowly. Pursing her lips, she sent her mint and lipstick smell to cloud about him like a strange pollen. 'That's an end to this silliness. An end, do you hear me? Do you hear me?' she asked sweetly. And then, 'Do you hear me?' in not so light a voice.

He only nodded.

'No, that's not what I want. Is it? Is it?' she asked, the edge sharpening in her voice. 'Is it?'

'Yes,' he blurted out. 'Yes, that's an end to it.' He stared at her, drunk with emotion, and suddenly wanted to break something that could never be put back together.

'Good,' she whispered, and unlooped the belt from her mac. Under the long shiny coat, he saw the rest of her knee-length boots, her stockings, a skin-tight skirt and a long-sleeved top made from a thin rubber

116

with the lustre of fresh oil in sunlight. She threw her coat up the bed and then untied her head-scarf. At the sight of her head, Angel's first reaction was that of horror. Dr Madelaine Sutton's head had been completely shaven. The thick and silky red hair was no more. Pale and smooth, her head looked so small now, but was rounded in a not displeasing shape, and the absence of hair enhanced the fine beauty of her thin, sharp features. 'Surprised?' she said, smiling, and removed her sunglasses. 'Or are you guilty of underestimating me?' Angel swallowed, but could think of nothing to say. 'There is so much you must see.' Her voice was pleasant again. 'You'll never be bored. Don't worry about that.'

A vague recollection of something about investment projects and scarification filled him with a thick and giddy dread. What had he done? Quinny and M were nothing compared to the doctor. In his sinuses and along the roof of his mouth, he could taste something cold and hormonal now: rising panic. She could hire him to infinity and he would play her games, but she should never be allowed to own him. In no matter how small or subtle a manner, he had to maintain his resistance to her.

'Come to me,' she said.

Angel approached the bed, his fear subsiding and his frustration mounting. Perplexingly, he was so aroused too, his thick cock strained against its coverings.

'See what I brought for you. Things you will soon not ever want to be without.' From her rubbery bag, her leather hands pulled out tubes. Dull, purple tubes made from rubber. And then she carefully withdrew something pink, that looked like flesh, but was folded up like a dead jellyfish. From it came the smell of drying wet-suits, the bottom of warm boots, and the

117

tang of lubrication. 'These are good things, Angel. When we're together we will share these things.' Then she unzipped him, her face straight, purposeful, businesslike. 'Step out of them. Don't be a baby,' she said, once his trousers had fallen. 'And get that shirt off.'

When he stood naked, she squeezed a translucent jelly on to his penis. His chest seized up from the frostbite. It was a freezy, sticky cold on his cock. Along his spine a thousand pins, tipped with something wonderful, pricked him. Once she'd smoothed the salve along his length, his sex felt like it had swollen and he experienced something akin to a sweet gum-pain under the skin. A medicinal smell that reminded him of aching muscles filled his nose. 'This will keep you hard for hours,' she said. 'And you'll feel everything. And when we are worn out, I will spend at least two days standing up.'

Angel stared, white with shock. At the sight of him, she laughed and proceeded to untangle the purple pipes. They squeaked in her leather hands like the black dinghies he had seen, rubbing against polystyrene buoys in the estuary docks. Now his cock felt warm all over. The skin demanded to be touched. No, it craved a tight embrace. He moved his hips automatically. 'Steady,' she said. 'Look at you now. You can't wait to start.' She was getting excited too; her voice was breathless and raspy. 'Get these around me.' She gritted her teeth. 'Quick,' she said. 'Pull me apart with them.' Her voice was a whisper now. 'Face down. Tie me off. Quick!'

Overwhelmed by the tingling stiffness between his legs, he watched the doctor make her arrangements. Like a starfish, she suddenly stretched herself up his bed, face down; her leather hands pointing towards the upper bed-frame, her ankles, tight in boots, towards the lower frame. 'Now,' she said through clenched teeth. 'Tie me now. Ankles first. Make it tight. You'll find the slipknots at the ends.'

Angel complied, his fingers clumsy with nerves. The purple hoses passed through loops, fashioned into one end of a length, and then pulled taut. Intestinal rubber squeaked on patent leather. At the two bottom corners of his bed-frame, he created the same knot. When he finished, her legs had been pulled straight and beneath the hem of her skirt he could see her glossy stocking tops and the milky skin above them. Unable to resist the tremors choking his sex, he quickly rubbed both his girth and hands against the back of her legs, sheer in hose and delightfully rough against his cock-skin. Hurriedly, sensing his desire, she unpeeled the pink jellyfish material open with her hands. There was a sound of plastic peeled from fresh meat. It was some sort of mask or head covering. When he saw it, the air in his room seemed to become utterly still. A cloud passed over the sun. Shadows crept over them; his pale muscled body became indistinct; her shiny and sheer darkness seemed to disappear in places and yet shine more prominently in others.

'Quick now.' Her voice was deeper, muffled. She turned her head to look at him. Jellied within a fine membrane of tinted plastic, the substance had spread and tightened over her entire head. Briefly, it clouded with condensation on her face, and then the moisture vanished and the material was sucked inside her mouth and up inside her nostrils. Over her eyes, it spread like a film of water. But still, he could hear her breath as it passed heavily through the clinging though permeable membrane. Soon, he could see her face clearly again – the painted eyes and thin eyebrows sharp – though all her features were filtered pink and made to look doll-like. 'Now,' she said. Deep, demoniac, alluring – her voice like her eyes and face had changed. 'Do my wrists.'

'Yesss,' she repeated, and rubbed her groin into his hard mattress, when her gloved hands were tied off and his fingers were free to forage up inside her skirt. Skull-like, her lovely plastic head whipped from side to side. 'Get inside me. Do it!' He sat astride her and raised her skirt higher over her buttocks. It was tight and cut into her thighs where they had been stretched apart. Knuckle-white, his fingers pushed and peeled the rubber skirt until it gave way and slithered passed her hips. Knickerless in expectation, her backside was a brilliant white between stocking-tops and the shiny rubber ruffled around her waist. Between her legs, what he could see of her sex was shrimp-pink and shaven beyond stubble. He put a finger inside the delicate lips. She hissed. His finger came out wet. 'Not in there,' she said, her voice softer now, almost nervous. 'In the other place, where you promised to go before.'

Closing his eyes, Angel widened her buttocks by pressing his weight down on both hands, each cupping a soft cheek. He swallowed and put the end of his cock against the puckered red bud of her anus.

'Yesss!'

Every nerve-tip in his sex made itself known in a ripple of white cold that passed through his now unnaturally muscular girth. There was little resistance he could feel in the doctor's rear with the salve working as a lubricant. But there was much resistance she could feel. Her wrists and ankles pulled tight against the rubber bindings, and her whole body seemed to electrify under its second skin. Going stiff, then trembling, until deep into the mattress her body finally relaxed.

'Yesss,' she said again.

Between her cheeks, he dug his cock, from tip through to base, at the same pace – relentless though even – and only hastened his strokes when she began to croak and fidget beneath him, as if asking for mercy. But she would receive no relief; he felt a need to punish her intrusion, and so made his intrusion inside her as blunt and demanding as the one she had made into his home. But was that not exactly what she wished to provoke? For, as he ground into the doctor, on her plastic face he saw a look of rapture.

Naked, his skin stuck against her rubber back, until the perspiration from his exertions made him slip and slide against her. Embalmed in her rubber from head to waist, and from knee to foot, the heat of their coupling was contained around her body to a degree that would have been insufferable to most. But from the look on her face, and in the whispered profanities that slipped through her surgical mouth, it seemed this was just what she required. And any discomfort he would have normally experienced, he was now oblivious to. Nothing would make him stop until he came. Never had his sex been so sensitised than it was after being touched by the doctor's salve. To then have it inserted into the tightest part of her body, Angel came close to a blackout.

'I need to come,' he said to the back of her sticky head. But all she could manage in response was a deep groan.

Seizing her arms above the elbow, Angel raised himself from her wet back.

'Yesss,' she cried out, sensing his final, aggressive stand after being so long inside her.

And it came as his fingers dug into her skin, and the sound of his groin striking her buttocks would not be drowned out by even the ferocious squealings of the bed. Knowing some seal or signature had been put on his dealings with her, and dreading the commitment that would be forced from him, while also relishing the tryst in a mad and reckless way that thrilled him, Angel released himself deep inside the doctor's bowels.

'Yesss,' she said, and her small rubber head raised itself from the mattress. 'You'll pay for that.'

Head down, goggles fixed, his arms cutting the water in perfect synchronicity, Angel spent two hours in the waters of the Great Commercial Canal. After every four strokes, he'd neatly turn his head to the side in the grey water and steal a breath. Numb from the first icy immersion, and then gradually warming from the exertion of the swim, his muscles had loosened until they resisted the shock of cold, his heart and lungs passed out of pain, and eventually his mind achieved a clarity. And as he had swum through the afternoon, all the way to the lock near the river docks, he'd swum away from the plastic face and doll body that he'd loved until it was limp and face-down and purring with triumph on his cot.

Three hours in the water, his stamina spent, a deep-pit hunger howling, he'd finally achieved the necessary purge and distance to consider, more reasonably, the shocking introduction this doctor had foisted upon his simple life. There was no use in denial; she meant to own him. And his price would be easily affordable to such a professional. He had to prepare himself for the prospect of slavery. The agency, he was certain, would sell him out quickly. For the first time in his life he had a value levied by the Higher Zones. And yet, despite the sudden lava-hot floods of desire for this strange and dark doctor who seemed ready to invest so much in him, he sensed the opportunity for self-destruction. If he allowed her to own him, it would not be long before he was forever changed. More precious to him now than ever before, his curious dreamy way, with its tides of fantasy and hope, appeared to him as something small and bright and spherical, dwindling though still defiant in his centre. Without that, what would he be? Angel thought back to the sight of his maniacal laughing face in the bathroom mirror after an evening with M and her beloved Quinny. He left the water and began the walk home, too preoccupied with his thoughts to appreciate the pleasing ache in his muscles.

'Hello, daydreamer.'

Angel looked up from his slow feet. His surprise turned to elation. It was Salina. She had emerged from the old school house across the street. An unlit sign, advertising a gymnasium, hung on the sagging chain link face. On her feet, below the hem of her woollen overcoat, he could see her sports shoes and naked ankles. Her coat fell open as she stood with her feet apart – her stance easy and no longer aloof. She was wearing a black cat-suit that stopped below her knees and emitted a faint gloss where it clung to her lean body. Smitten by the effect she had on him, that had not waned since last they met, Angel's head blanked. Again he was awed by her odd beauty. Amongst the derelict buildings and the litter and dross of these forgotten corners, her beauty seemed profoundly odd.

She smiled and her leopard eyes worked on him; inquisitive and quickly assessing. 'You been working out, too?'

He shook his head. 'Swimming.'

She frowned, ready to laugh. 'Where?'

Angel cleared his throat. 'The canal today.' She pulled a face and then seemed to be wondering whether she could smell something rotten on his clothes. He reddened. 'The water's good.'

123

'Now that I find hard to believe,' she said.

'Why? All the industry has gone and the water purification started over a century ago. No waste ever gets in any more.' Salina couldn't decide whether she believed him or not, but he could see she wanted to believe in a small miracle amongst the wretchedness in which they lived. 'Would you believe,' he added, 'that today I saw an otter?' She shook her head in disbelief. 'Well, I did. There are salmon, too, in the river. And seals.'

Still frowning, she cocked her head to one side. 'What a strange man you are. I thought that the other night.' But there was no way for him to deduce whether her thinking that was a good thing or not.

'Well, I thought the same thing about you,' he said, the initial nerves subsiding. Salina looked away, and he was glad she did, because suddenly they reminded each other of their association with Quinny, and exactly what Angel did for money. Things, he suspected, that she was not unfamiliar with either.

'Anyway, I've got to get home and change,' she said.

'Sure.' His voice almost broke with disappointment. Angel cleared his throat. 'So weird I've never seen you before. I walk past this old school three times a week to get to the canals. Though it's usually early,' he added as an afterthought.

'I sleep late,' she said, and then shouldered her bag.

'I'm just over there.' He pointed in the direction of home. 'By the old car plant.'

'I know it,' she said. 'It's all coming down. In five years it'll look like Zone Five.'

'I heard that.'

'And in twice that, the likes of you and me won't be born no more.'

Angel nodded. 'It's inevitable.'

124

Salina began to walk away. Now she was smiling again. 'But don't worry, when they pull your building down, some rich bitch will have you installed in Zone One.' She turned her back on him. Her light and springy step bounced her ponytail on and off her shoulders.

Angel wanted to tell her that was not what he wanted. But would it have been a lie to have said that? It was what he'd wanted his whole life. Wasn't he, like the dwindling numbers of his unskilled kind, desperately on the make in the High Zones? And was it just the full force of the doctor that now made him reticent? 'Wait,' he called out, but then had nothing to say. What was the point, he suddenly realised, in pursuing this girl? She had a lover and he was prohibited from even touching himself in an intimate manner.

Salina turned around, her eyebrow raised.

Just knowing her, though, would make him better off. The shocks would be easier to take. 'I just thought . . .'

'You were thinking that you'd like to practise on me. Don't you get enough?' Although she smiled, her eyes scolded him. 'My mistress never remembers a name in the morning, but she remembered she had a good time with you. And I stay away from anything like that.'

Smarting now, Angel snapped back at her. 'I never meant that. It's just good to see a friendly face down here. After everything else . . .' Part-choked with anger and disappointment, he could not finish.

'Easy, tough guy,' she said, smiling now. 'I just didn't want you to assume anything about me taking part with . . . You know?'

'I believe you. But don't break my balls if I do take part. It's good work. And it's all I can get.' Angel looked at the sky: why was it always so difficult?

'You've not done it long, have you?' Salina said, softer towards him, at last.

'Few weeks. Does it show so much?'

She said, 'It does. But that's why it makes me sad.'

He looked up, mystified. 'Why?'

Salina turned and walked towards her end of town. 'Walk with me,' she said over her shoulder. When he caught up with her, she explained herself. 'Most people around here, I must admit, I don't care a bit for. I don't care about them, because they don't care about themselves. I want to see it all pulled down. But every now and then, you see someone –' she paused and looked away from him '– someone who's fallen through every crack. Who doesn't fit in here, and hasn't made it up there.' She nodded towards the towers of the High Zones, golden and vaporous in the far distance. 'You have to fit into one place or the other. If you don't you're lost. And that makes me sad. Because these are good people I see, and they're alone, and so few now.'

Angel laughed humourlessly. 'Misfits like me.'

'No! I didn't mean it like that,' she said, indignant.

And he felt foolish and guilty. He knew she meant well and that she was right. This quick and worldly girl recognised the quality in him, and its inevitable destruction she mourned. But Angel did not want to be pitied by a girl he considered as desirable as any of the high-heel strutters from the corporations. 'Salina. You're right. I'm not mocking what you say. I loved to hear you say it. And it's a miracle I even made it to this age. All I have now is my health and curiosity. They keep me afloat. And I'm curious about you. Though what I do in their world is clearly a problem for you. And that hurts.'

For a while, she stood stunned by his confession. But then, she smiled and touched a hand to his cheek. 'So soft. Too soft,' she said, sad again. 'Just don't get broken.'

'Like you have,' he wanted to say, but knew it would have been foolish to propose such a thing. 'Can I see you again?' is what he did say, and immediately he read the flattery, mischief and sympathy in her face. 'I mean . . . Friends . . . As neighbours,' he stammered.

She laughed gaily, only teasing a little now. 'I know what you mean, silly thing.'

'Silly thing?'

'You make me laugh, Angel. So maybe you can see me again.'

'When?'

Salina shrugged. 'Oh, sometime, I guess. Maybe you can give me the number of that thing.' She pointed at his wrist. 'I work most days.'

'It's just for work,' he muttered. 'And you have a boyfriend,' he blurted out, and was instantly sorry for being so overt. A pall of things remembered – his service and status, and now some pain in her too – came back between them. At this mention of her lover, her jaw reset at a funny angle.

In silence, they walked the rest of the way together, the bright thing between them smitten by the impossibility of their situation.

After another half-mile, she said, 'This is me,' and walked toward the old Fire Station at the edge of the dead park.

It was a squat where she lived. That he could see. She was more marginalised than he had ever been. 'Goodbye, then,' he said, his voice heavy with the sodden state of his heart.

'I will see you again,' she called back. 'I promise.'

And then she was gone, her long body stretching though the broken red door of the station. And just as she made that promise to him, the sun seemed to break through the sky above him, even though he could feel the beginnings of rain against his face.

Seven

'It's one of the best investment projects ever offered. You're a very lucky companion.' The Acquisitions officer who speaks to Angel is all smile and teeth – a money face. Under the strong electric lights in her office, this pretty blonde shines. She shines physically – crimson nails, ice-blonde hair, sun-glossy skin, black suit, hose, patent heels – as if this were all some further endorsement of her goodwill.

Her blue eyes – clear, crystalline, arresting – narrow as they skim over the information on the screen tilted towards her excited face. 'A residential position. Generous salary. There will be travel, of that I'm sure. The doctor is an international specialist, you know. And Madelaine Sutton is a very beautiful woman. A companion's dream.' Her face radiates a pride in him, as if he were a clever pupil in her class. She leans back in her chair and crosses her legs, and doesn't even seem to mind his quick and instinctive peek between her thighs when she is mid-manoeuvre. He is valuable now and such a transgression is overlooked.

If this meeting had taken place two months before, he would have been overjoyed, positively fortified with self-worth at what she said to him and offered him as a path out of Binton. And even now, in this plush, conditioned acquisition office, Angel feels a tug inside him to acknowledge her admiration and to accept the contract because she approves of it – this bikini-blonde with a head for figures and a body for worship, who raved about his performance and employability. 'You've become a very popular man at the corporation,' she told him earlier. But it is not just his reservations about Dr Madelaine Sutton that keep his face straight and his spirits in an anxious state. There is something in this woman's tone he does not care for. A quality he would have forgiven in his previous life. Although she is his age, she speaks to him as if he is a child. Considering her achievements and his status, it is a mandatory attitude, but something he finds increasingly irritating. More alarming still is her choice of title for him. *Companion*: she never refers to him as anything but this. A companion not a man, then, in the truest sense? Of course not. But he's always known this, so why does it rankle now?

'She frightens you,' the woman says, smiling, more like a young teacher than ever now, amused with a child's touching confusion over a simple matter. 'Considering your background, I suspect it's quite a normal reaction to the idea that someone cares about you.'

He swallows; beneath the instinctive anger, he hurts more than he understands.

'She mentions nothing about bodily modification. I would guess she wants you just the way you were made. Do you realise how fortunate you are? Let me tell you a little secret –' she leans forwards in her chair; the leather squeaks and she adopts a hushed tone of voice, a voice you would pay to hear it say sinful things on a communication channel '– I've known of companions who don't recognise their own faces after an investment contract reaches completion. Do you know what it is I'm saying?'

'I know what you mean,' Angel says, his tone sharp.

Brick-walled, the confidential manner fails. She sits back in her chair in surprise. Why isn't the monkey chattering with glee? She manages a smile and tries again from another angle. 'Let me paint you a picture.' Now she reminds him of the man who tricked him into signing on for four years of public service. Back then, in only ten minutes, that man had taken four whole years of his life and put them in the sewers with the spicy shit of the rich. This woman wants the rest. 'Out of the townships. Nice clothes –'

'No,' he says. 'Forget it.'

Under the chic suit her catwalk-body petrifies. The candid act vanishes. She sits up straight as if suddenly roused from sleep. Some of her cheer remains, but only through effort. 'I detect reticence. And, quite frankly, I do not understand you at all.'

'May I speak candidly?' he asks.

She softens. 'Of course.' She breathes out. 'This meeting is confidential.' Maybe she could still close the deal. 'See it as an opportunity to tell me what you want. All I want is for you to find the right –'

Angel raises his hand and stops her. He shakes his head. No more of that. Not another word of the sales pitch. Under her sincerity he suspects ruthlessness. 'There's no need for that. I know the score. I go with her; you make money on the buyout. You forget me. You have no interest in my well-being.' The woman puts a hand to her chest. Her mouth opens but no words are forthcoming. To this woman he would tell all – a representative of the siren masses that lured him into the city of gold. He'd go the whole way too and she would hear every detail from his last two assignments with Dr Madelaine Sutton. Angel continues. 'Understand why I cannot be her . . . her slave. Let me paint *you* a picture.'

Sitting back in her chair, she adopts the sly smile of those who assume superiority. She is ready to debunk his every objection, but he will have his say. When she tries to interrupt, Angel raises his hand to command silence. If he stops to think, he will surprise himself. 'The third time she hired me, she wanted to make me jealous. Make no mistake. That's why there were three of us with her. You see, she's imagined this bond between us. This tryst between what she calls my "naiveté" and her "sophisticated descent". Sure, I'm inquisitive about these interests of hers. You are too. I can tell by your face.' The corporate girl looks flustered: what could he see in her face? His voice softens. 'But it leads to something dangerous.' A mental flash: he sees the doctor, smiling, immaculate in make-up, a face under rubber – a doll in polythene; around her, naked figures move across her, over her, behind her, inside her. He snaps out of the dreamy digression by an act of will. 'If I saw her enjoying other men, it would be a kind of betrayal that would make me want her more.'

'Did it?' the girl asks, keen-voiced.

'No, because as I said, it's imagined. You're missing my point. There is no deep connection between her and me. No meeting of kindred spirits. Sure, she's fascinating and exciting and beautiful, but you have to understand where it's leading. You see, she goes too far.'

'I don't follow,' she says, a trifle uncomfortable. Was he mad? Would another psyche evaluation be required? 'Group situations, I've been told, are common –'

Angel shoots down the corporate discourse before it can become airborne; there is no connection between the word and the deed. 'But the chair. That chair. They don't use those, do they? The other clients

131

who require several companions at once.' And he tells the enthralled girl about the doctor's surgery, and the giant, black padded thing in there, for cosmetic resculpting operations, and how it had an unconventional use in her operating theatre. And as he narrates the tale, he sees the blood come up to her face. Absentmindedly, she begins to rub her silky shin. Watching her caress her own legs, he wonders where those elegant, manicured fingers would rather be.

For his third assignment, five days before, he was instructed on his communicator to arrive at the doctor's private clinic in Zone One, and to undress without delay in an antechamber adjoining the theatre. No one was there to meet him. Late at night, the staff had left for the evening, but a wrist-swipe admitted him to the building.

'We have been waiting impatiently, darling,' she said, when he entered the theatre, naked. 'But sometimes all the pleasure is in anticipation.' Two other men were in attendance: identical blond twins, golden-skinned, with the tight musculature of gymnasts. All of this he could see because they were naked too. A ball-shriveller, a cock-wilter; he'd not been in the company of naked men since the last lice epidemic, and that experience bore unpleasant associations. They showed none of the reserve, however, that made Angel tighten for flight inside. Their interest committed to the woman in the chair, they never even turned to watch him enter the room.

Lit by a huge, steel fixture, suspended above the chair, the room gave him the chills – hospital shakes. Around the room there was an orderly assortment of gleaming computers and the laser cutters, sawyers, and slicers they served. Manual surgical implements polished by steam were on shelves and in cabinets.

Beside cloudy tanks where prosthetic flesh was cultivated, gowns made from green rubber hung from a silver rack. And if that was not enough to deter him, then the smell was; disinfectant on steel slabs and white tiles. An infirmary where old spirits went to find younger bodies.

Lowered to the floor, the surgical chair in the centre of the surgery resembled a huge glove with four fingers. Along each of the fingers one of the doctor's legs or arms had been stretched and then cuffed fast. Sunken into the black palm of the glove was the rest of Madelaine Sutton's body. Plasticated, rubberised – the patient awaited a specialist operation. Her head had been freshly shaven so even the grey stubble marking her hairline had gone. Over her face and head was a tight mask like the one he had seen that time in his room, only this piece was not tinted. Wrapped in a clinging rubber skin, transparent also, from the halter collar on her neck to the red toenails on her long feet, her entire body appeared a milky-pink through the suit. It moulded around her contours like a flawless coating of extra skin. Mummified in plastic, and glossy under white lights, she had been positioned at an angle in order to see the dealings bestowed upon her body.

At her bidding – 'Come on, come in,' her hand beckoning – he joined the twins who stood on either side of the chair, level with her wet-look breasts. One of them shuffled to one side – reluctantly, he felt – so he could join them. 'Now feed me,' she said, and the silent twins immediately fell to their task. For how long had they been tutored? From the ceiling canopy of steel and lights, a mask was pulled down and affixed to the doctor's face. It added another thin layer of clear rubber to her beautiful head. Through this mask it was as if she sucked at some kind of gas.

As if delirium was instantaneous, she rolled her eyes and released a long satisfied sigh. In addition to the face mask, three other rubber pipes descended from the canopy. At the end of each tube was a thick pink nozzle that reminded Angel of painted lips, open to receive. A slick shiver, bright white in colour, ran up his spine.

Warily, Angel held the one nozzle hanging free, after the twins snatched their attachments from the medicinal air. The thing was wet to the touch.

'Hurry,' the doctor said, her limbs tensing in their shackles.

Stunned, he watched the blond men slip their already hard cocks into the tubes. On each face, once their entire lengths had been capped in the pinky nozzles, was a look of ecstasy. One man ran his fingers through his hair. His eyes were closed. The other made to touch the doctor's leg, paused as if contact would equal pain, and then rubbed the outside of his arms instead.

Curious, Angel looked at the pink nozzle in his hand more closely. It was indeed a mouth. Made from what resembled real flesh, it fired ticklish vibrations through his fingers. A living thing. He dropped it and watched it swing free – a snake slipping from a branch. As if alive, it curled upwards at the end and seemed to look at him. He retrieved it and stretched the soft jelly mouth around his sex – still some considerable way from its stiff maturity. But his flaccidity was short-lived. Once the attachment was in place, he experienced an instant and overwhelming state of arousal. Complete and ruthless desire, and he was at its mercy.

His first thought was of the woman M and how good her slippery mouth and massaging lips had felt when her head was buried in his lap. Only this was better than the best. It was like the moment a soft and feminine hand, possessing the profound tenderness of a new lover's touch, collected his cock from his underthings gently, but with some amorous determination, and freed it to the cooler air. And while so deftly cradled in the warm palm of this hand, the sensuous moment ascended to a pitch of even keener lust as if he were also looking into a beautiful pair of heavily lidded eyes and finding in them a passionate desire to be taken by him. It became the moment a man wanted to eat every part of a woman, when there was a maddening urge to bite shoulder, neck, cheek, or to lick nipple, buttock and toe – to tear apart, to devour, to consume utterly.

Overcome by this strange influx of glorious sensations in his body and the corresponding impression in his mind, Angel's head dropped forwards and he accidentally put both of his hands on to the doctor's leg. On contact, his entire body immediately shivered a cold blue as if from the most pleasing of unexpected jolts, and then his balls seemed to have filled with cream and become afloat amongst clouds of golden bubbles in warm water. Just by feeling the doctor's leg it was as if he imagined he'd experienced the brush of a woman's knee on public transport that wasn't at all accidental because behind the pages of her newspaper she was smiling, and the knee would then begin to rub up and down against his knuckles. A woman he felt compelled to sit next to in the first place because of her scent and her beauty. It was the revelation of suspender clips, pressed through a black dress during a slow dance.

Dizzy with these strange delights, Angel fell forwards and his sex, inside the rubber lips, rubbed against the doctor's leg. The effect was immediate. Desperate to discharge, he cried out and then pulled his sex away from the doctor's flesh so this intense pleasure could be sustained. He stared down in disbelief. When his sex had touched her leg, it was as if he'd felt the tip of a long-coveted neighbour's wife's tongue curl around the edge of his phallus for the first time. A woman too desirable to look at for more than a moment without giving yourself away. And it felt like her tongue had come in the night, and was accompanied by the sensation of her curly hair, smelling of apples, on his navel, under a duvet.

Hunched over, desperate for a greater charge of this deep pleasure, even if it were life-threatening, he sucked at the doctor's shiny leg. His tongue touched the top of a battery connection; he wiggled a loose tooth as a boy; he sucked the lips of a lightly furred sex, blonde and lavender-salty. Delicious. He came. The first of the three men to ejaculate into the succulent sucking red mouths attached like pilot fish to their parts. The other two had learned not to touch her and so pace themselves.

Weakened and made sleepy by a particularly powerful ejaculation, his cock softened and he removed the attachment. Semi-delirious, his head still spinning through the delirium of climactic-dreamtime, he watched the doctor's beautiful face suckle his thick bullets of seed through her clinging mask. It was the face of a glutton smeared with party food. Wrapped from head to toe in this strange, sensitising rubber skin, he wondered how he tasted to her.

Soon the twins followed Angel and were soon bent double, holding their knees. As the last of the acute sensations drained from him, he lay on the tiles of the floor. Refreshing as cool water on a sun-baked body, their touch made him sigh with satisfaction and feel ready for sleep. The other men sat beside him, their faces covered with their hands, their long limbs languid. Up in the chair, he heard the sound of a tongue rustling for treats in a sweet wrapper. It was followed by the excited working of an oesophagus and then silence.

All four of them rested for over twenty minutes, drained by the curious clutches of the latex and its equally curious lubricant.

'Come to me,' the doctor finally whispered from where she lay. 'My beautiful boys. Come to me again.'

And it was time to love her again. One of the twins adjusted the chair to the height of his knees, and then sank to the floor to place his face between her thighs. The doctor hissed. There must have been an aperture in her suit through which he had been able to insert his mouth and fingers. The other twin stood astride her chest and then squashed her breasts together, as if he were pushing balls of dough into the centre of a wet, floury chopping board. Between her sticky-rubber bosom he then inserted his sex and began to rub himself up and down.

'Boys, I can feel you all over my body. In every cell,' she said.

Despite his shock, Angel's cock stiffened.

When the gas mask ascended from her face and disappeared back into the white lights, she called Angel to her. Slowly, and needing to swallow hard in order to regain the power of speech, he walked to the head of the chair and looked down at her wild eyes. Her teeth were set in a snarl between the bright red of her lips. Over her face, he could see that the rubber hood had moulded to her skin. It had disappeared and become an invisible film, detectable only by the latex shine it possessed under the hot lights. The warmth of her flesh seemed to have absorbed the material into her skin. Looking him straight in the

137

eye, she opened her mouth wide. Then, with one big doll's eye, she winked at him.

Bending his knees a fraction was all he was required to do. The moment his cock came within reach of that rubber O-shaped mouth, she raised her head, quick as a predator, and swallowed the first half of his length. At first, the sensation was dull; he could feel an interfering layer between her lips and palate and his sex. When the salve in her rubber mouth set fire to his cock, though, he had to grab the chair to keep his feet. His legs had begun to shake and it was as if something heavy and slow had begun to rotate in his mind. At first, he believed he must have come instantly, until he realised the incredible sensation had not waned and neither had the firmness of his sexual flesh.

Gently, she lowered her head back into the cushioned rest and his body went with her. With his hands placed on either side of her head, and with his legs astride her neck, he began to pump his sex into her mouth. Breathing heavily through her nose, she kept her eyes open the whole time he slipped between her tight red lips. Watching him with an intensity he found alarming, even at the peak of his pleasure, her eyes would only flutter when the attentions of the man's mouth between her legs became particularly poignant.

Eventually, when the chewing twin brought the doctor to her peak, she released Angel's cock and began to roll her sticky head about in the leather cushions – shrink-wrapped in her own climactic world. Angel looked over his shoulder. Between her breasts one man thrust in a quick concentrated rhythm to achieve the maximum heat and contact between her squeaky breasts and his long sex. He made grunting sounds and the tip of his penis had greyed with moisture.

When the twins interchanged between her legs, taking turns to thrust their golden meat inside her, pummelling into her groin – their teeth bared, brows furrowed, nostrils wide – the doctor shrieked and laughed to herself with her eyes closed. Watching the bizarre and deviant group, Angel stood back, cradling his sex with one hand, unable to resist stroking it – the tip poised above her impassioned and creased face. When she began to cry out, and her sounds were joined by the pleasure-grunts of the man thrusting between her thighs, Angel came. Angling his girth down, he wanted to see every drop touch the rubber skin on her face. Snatching at the ropy geysers that pumped from his cock, however, the doctor caught his hot strings of come in her mouth and then snapped her lips shut. She rinsed them inside her mouth and then swallowed them down. Behind him, another lover released himself all over her chest.

After two further hours, dipping and grinding his sex into warm effervescent places, where two other cocks had also plunged, he had returned home to the township with the look on the doctor's face indelibly imbedded in his mind. What notions and thoughts and memories had it supplanted in order to stay there for ever?

After Angel completes his narration, the Acquisitions office is silent for some time and the face of the corporate girl is flushed with emotion. She finds it hard to meet his eye. And against her shin, her hand caresses up and down with longer strokes than it had done previously. Without interruption, she lets Angel tell her a second story.

'And the next time we met, she picked me up from my home. She was in the back of a long car. An old car. But a beautiful car. On the other side of those

139

dark windows she was waiting for me. Smoking her cigarette and waiting for me.'

Inside the car there were seats on both sides, facing each other. Two seats behind the driver and the rear seat where she sat. He couldn't see the driver of the car. Dividing the front from the back compartment was a barrier of opaque glass. But, although it was tinted, he felt he was being watched through it. She never smiled or said hello when he climbed inside. She just dipped her head a fraction. Through the fine black veil, her face was inscrutable. Her beautiful stone features were angled as if to take a disinterested look through the window. And through the glass the world was made grey. Even the bright colours looked watery. The world seemed part of her, as if this was how she saw things in between when she rode that chair or was cuffed on the floor of her office.

Angel had misgivings about her silence; it was worse somehow than the way she talked at him and told him how he felt and what he wanted. Their last meeting had added to his unease. If she allowed him to see and share so much of her other life it was because she considered him a part of it; signed up until the last drop of semen or blood. Her employment of him was becoming exclusive; she had been the sole recipient of his companionship in over a week.

But it was the most beautiful his doctor had ever been, and all the more appealing this aspect of mourning made her. She wore a dark fur over an ankle-length dress of chiffon. It would slide around her body when she moved – he imagined it under his hands. At the side of her gown was a long parting, cut from her high-heeled sandals to her thigh. When she crossed her legs he caught a glimmer of something dark and glassy on the shaven skin of her leg, and was reminded of the original cravings that pulled him from the townships. She felt his eyes on her leg and covered it. Not for him. Don't even look.

Riding through the gloam of the townships at twilight, he accompanied a princess. And yet in his dreams of these women, he had never been accompanied by this cold but exhilarating fear of them as much as of himself – at what he too was capable of. That night, under his elegant black suit, little shivers and gut-rumbles would erupt and pass, erupt and then pass again.

Smoking, she sat in silence, her eyes unmoved by the scenes of dereliction in the townships, unrelieved by the occasional pale light, suffocated in the holed and grime-black fronts of locked factory and reluctant home. Few figures could be seen on the streets. An occasional drunk slouched into a lamp-post, or a bum crouched like a soldier over a fallen comrade, filling his pockets with the trinkets of a man spent in body and spirit. Packs of dogs, wiry and too cunning for the catchers and cooks, ran alert in purposeful patrols from one refuse pile to another.

'It makes me feel close to something terrible,' she said.

'Best seen through glass,' he added, having to clear his throat mid-sentence. She tried to smile, he thought, but then decided her lips had not even moved.

Disused factories became disused warehouses, lining the disused docks. She had brought him to the estuary, brown and sluggish with silt. They drove down a flat expanse of concrete where ships were once unloaded of giant crates after slow voyages across useful seas. He had never been down here, not even to swim; it was too dangerous. Beyond his window, Angel peered into the giant stores; locked or broken open, echoing and wet with damp. Under the vaulted roofs and broken windows it was said vagrants and escaped convicts roamed in dwindling colonies. Forced here from the worst of the townships, where air-strikes were once called against the civilian populace, gin economies and societies of murderers had formed. Dread filled him. Had she brought him here to prove something? There was always some element of exhibition in her. What could he say to deter her? Perhaps he should soften his resistance to truly touching her like a lover. The greater his indifference, the greater her madness.

As they approached the end of the pier and were level with the final warehouse, the doctor leaned forwards on her seat and tapped the glass with a ringed finger. Diamonds twinkled on the black velvet of her gloves. Without a sound the car stopped moving. She depressed a button on her armrest and the window lowered. A breath of cold air, tinged with the fragrance of deep water, dark and lapping through the underside of a pier, seeped into the car. Above them, a gull cried out, hungry. Somewhere in the channel, a bell clanged on a buoy to the rhythm of thick, slow waves. Under the car, these same waters walloped and then sucked at the supports, blooded with rust. He felt the vibrations pass through the floor of the car; a strange beat counting down to an end he could fear but not see. The doctor put another cigarette in her holder and waited for Angel to light it.

'Time for me to go,' she said in the forlorn voice of one resigned to a terrible fate.

'Ma'am, it's dangerous here. We should stay in the car.'

As if moved by his fear – excited, even – she turned to look at him for the first time that evening. 'You

142

will stay here.' And then the door was open and she had swung her long legs out of the car. Her heels made a crunchy sound on the ground.

Most of the light came from the early moon. It made the concrete look silvery and the rusty ladders and railings like bits of bone on the extinct bovine creatures that once lowed and shambled through fields of green grass. Standing on the dock, a breeze disturbed her veil and dimpled the long fur of her coat. She shivered and pulled her collar tight around her slender neck.

When Angel moved across the back seat towards the open door, it closed on him. 'Ma'am,' he cried out, through the rising window.

Indifferent to his warning, she took a final glance out to the channel and then walked around the bonnet of the car and away towards the last ware-house, teetering on her thin heels. Angel banged on the glass separating him from the driver. There was no response. He switched to the other side of the car and watched the statuesque figure of Dr Madelaine Sutton walk without haste to the gaping maw of the last building on the dock. Tiny red sparks from her dropped cigarette bounced around her feet and then she was gone, inside the mouth of a giant.

The car moved. It made a wide and slow arc around the end of the pier and then pulled up close to the hole in which the doctor had vanished. Still peering through the glass of the passenger window, Angel could see a fire. Roaring inside a metal cylinder, flames leaped and coughed up sparks to illumine a portion of the ground around the oil drum. It seemed fresh fuel had just been added to welcome a guest.

Shadows on the ground charged and retreated with the flames, and amongst them, he could see movement. Though indistinct at first, when his eyes became accustomed to the light, he clearly saw three figures circling the tall and motionless silhouette of a woman. But soon, the woman in the middle was no longer still.

'No!' Angel shouted, his hands on the glass, then fumbling with the door.

The shapes of three men, stooped like simians, their heads thick with unkempt hair and beards, had begun to yank at the doctor from various directions. She was pulled about between them and then brought to the ground. Then a fight broke out between the men. Silent blows fell heavy in the murk and dull feet kicked up the dross and dust until a victor emerged. Unsteady on his feet, he stooped over the prize. Dragged to her feet by the wrist, she was then taken to a collection of crates beside a mattress. Rough hands shoved her compliant shape back to the ground.

'No, no, no,' Angel said, before swallowing at the sour dry air that crept up his throat and into his sawdusty mouth. Before him, filtered by dark glass, he watched the doctor's legs rise into the air, slightly bent, the spikes of her heels thin against the orange air. And then these long legs fell to encircle the waist of the brute who rutted between them. Unable to look away, Angel stopped pushing at the door and became motionless.

Two other figures, probably those defeated in the struggle, shuffled back into view and began to pace around the aggressive coupling on the mattress. Drawn by hunger for the softest flesh, the spiciest meat, sweetened by perfume and made to whisper in silk, they risked their unwashed necks to see more of, and maybe to touch, the willing captive.

On the mattress, the man on top of the doctor slowed down his frantic thrusts to quicker, more erratic, doggish groin-jabs. Thin arms, gloved to the elbow, rose from the floor and clawed into his matted hair. The head arched back and Angel seemed to feel the power of the deep groan that escaped the black lips and hoary mouth. The figure then fell forwards upon his prey. Spent and vulnerable, he was seized and dragged away by the others, who then placed themselves in his stead between those white thighs.

Twice more she was taken in this manner. Pounded at, mauled with leathery hands, bitten, devoured. And twice more her legs kicked out, ecstatic, encouraging the foul shapes at their business. For a time then, after all three men had finished with her, they crouched near the prostrate shape and passed a bottle around. Between swigs, they reached out and fondled parts of her that appealed to them. Then, with more care, but hardly what could be interpreted as consideration, they repositioned her on all fours – a groomed dog, shampooed and brushed, but now soiled in their kennel.

Stunned, Angel watched them raise the delicate folds of her dress and arrange them around her waist, freeing the alabaster buttocks. The brief nature of her panties was then cut away by the glint of something that shone like steel, in the hand of one brute, against the backdrop of curling flames. A dark hand cupped the back of her sleek head and then a ragged shape settled to its knees before her face. Long and black, a rigid appendage was slowly fed into her mouth, and then thrust through that narrow and intimate gap between painted lips and tangled crotch. Beating to a different rhythm was the figure behind the doctor's pert and raised buttocks. And for a moment, Angel wondered whether he saw her backside quiver with anticipation before the uncompromising lunging began deep inside her clean, pink womb.

The pretty white doe was seized about the hips, mounted and then worked at vigorously for what seemed like an age until the mate had spent itself deep. The next man then tried the potency of his seed and lasted even longer inside her, using slower and more deliberate strokes in and out of this pampered shape before him. Across her back, he too eventually fell after his vitality was spent and left to trickle down the back of thighs, white but made dark through a skin of nylon.

And over and over again, these three figures conducted this sharing of the booty and passed the bottle around in between passes made on the lone and wandering woman who had high-heeled her way, sacrificial, to their lair, until eventually all of their appetites were satisfied. After it was over, Angel slumped in his seat, worn out from emotion. At that moment the front doors of the car sprung open, and not one, but two men, clad in the livery of chauffeurs, disembarked and strolled into the warehouse hideout. Gripped in their right hands were pistols, their muzzles made long and cylindrical with silencers.

Flashes without noises – blue cordite sparks – erupted in the gloom. Five or six shots, maybe more, followed each other quickly and close together as if the men in dark suits were standing back to back when they worked the triggers.

Impassive, the twins re-emerged from the building, their guns holstered in shoulder harnesses, their leather hands stowed inside trouser pockets. And between them, stepping gingerly, but not without the distinctive and characteristic poise of a woman taking short steps on high heels, was the doctor. Hat and veil back in place, over a less inscrutable face than the one he'd seen over two hours before, she came back to Angel.

The car sank down on its luxury tyres once all three parties had climbed back inside, and the engine whirred into life. Beside him, suppressing a smile, the doctor raised her veil and repaired her make-up. Once the smudges had been wiped away, her lips made red again, the mascara tears brushed off, and her lashes smoothed out, thick and curly, she closed her compact with a snap. Both of her gloves were missing, along with the white encrustations of jewels on her fingers. Captured for a moment, these gloves were to be coveted when stories were told around fires, and the lucky thieves would think they had rediscovered the smell of her perfume in the lifeless velvet for years to come. But now they were just a fee for the silent burial party who would come at dawn. Stained milky in places, torn across a breast, and badly creased, she rearranged her dress across her legs, the stockings now running with ladders. There were black smudges on her pale throat and blue-black fingerprints on both ankles.

As the car made a lazy roll out of the docks, she began to smoke again. Inhaling deep, she held the smoke inside her before it then streamed out, thin and blue, from her slim nose. Angel stared at her, silently beseeching her sly face for an answer. 'Good help is hard to find in these softer times,' she said. Angel swallowed. Would he too meet such a swift end after serving his time? 'I'll be feeling them here for a long time –' she patted her womb '– I like that.' Then she looked at him and smiled. 'What a wonderful end those beautiful, miserable things found in me. Don't you think?'

And at his inability to answer her, she laughed and reached out a hand to touch his cheek. His sense of horror impressed her. 'Take off my shoes,' she said, as if they were merely lovers returning home after a night of boisterous dancing. When he controlled the shakes in his fingers, he unbuckled the ankle straps and removed the sandals from her chilly feet. Her nails were painted claret. 'And these,' she said, unclipping her ruined stockings from their silver fastenings. Angel rolled them down her legs and pinched them from her toes. The fabric felt sticky on his fingertips. She opened the window and dropped the nylons outside with a half-smoked cigarette – the filter pink. 'Take this off,' she told him, pinching the dress away from her body, and he unzipped the loose garment from her back. Parts of her skin were red and she smelled of dark earth, freshly cut by a spade. Her panties had gone and he doubted whether she had worn a bra. The last thing he took from her body was the garter belt, thin, its panels diaphanous. When he touched the small of her back to unfasten it, she moaned and moved her head around on a snaky neck.

Naked, save for the small hat and veil, she leaned forwards and pressed a panel between the two seats opposite the deep bench she reclined upon. The panel, padded with black leather, descended on thin golden chains. Inside the open compartment, lit up yellow, there was a crystal decanter and six glasses. She asked him to pour her a drink. As he fumbled with ice and a glass she stretched her legs behind him and rubbed the base of his spine with her cold toes. 'I want to be held. Hold me,' she said, after draining the slug of Scotch in one gulp.

It was like cradling explosives, when he wrapped his arms around the now sighing and nuzzling doctor-executioner. She'd enjoyed her blood sport and now required another kind of caress from a slave. Unaware of what anything meant, or where anything was leading, he did her bidding. Gently, so gently, he brushed his fingertips across her tender skin. Encouraged by her sighs, but feeling as thin and weightless as a frightened child, he explored her and tried to bring the man inside him out again. Tracing the outline and curves of her feet, ankles, legs and then stomach, where so recently another kind of touch had been administered, he thought he could still hear the sound of that bell, struck by the wind, out in the distance of the lonely channel. And in his nose, he thought he could smell the raw rush of the open fire. Yes, he could still smell the fire; it was on her skin.

When he stroked her breasts, she closed her eyes and moaned softly to herself. Then he tickled the side of her neck while he stared at her face, traces of a girl still there, and prayed for an understanding of her. Evidence of the maniac had now disappeared with her frown and superior smile, but he wanted to tell her that she was destroying him. He touched her jawline with a knuckle. Her red lips parted.

'Take me,' she whispered, and put her arms around his neck.

Against her warm thigh, his cock stiffened. He tried to clear his head of every conscious thought and to give all of his awareness to her beauty; to kill the images of pistols in gloved hands, of gun flashes, silver cuffs and rubber faces with their hungry mouths open. It worked for a time.

So beautifully crafted and lain before him on supple leather, he adored the tyrant's flesh. Murmuring things he couldn't hear, she ran her fingers through his hair and down the nape of his neck. Bitter to the taste, she slipped two of her fingers inside his mouth, removed them, and then dipped the wet nails between her own lips. Not once did her eyes open. He wondered whether they had been open in the docks when she lay on that grubby mattress. He bet they had.

A desperate need took hold of him then as if he sought something in her nature and wanted to see it to believe in it. Unbuckling himself felt easy; sliding his cock inside her sex brought relief. In this place, criminal strangers had been invited and then destroyed. And still, after so much illegal traffic, she was hot and tight in there, even though she said, 'Slow,' to him, once he lay on top of her, fully dressed. 'Be slow.' And he had to fight with his desire to handle her as roughly as she had just been handled, as he thought of blackened hands inside her dress. She sensed this tension in him, heard it in his breath, and murmured lovingly. He hated himself for it, but could not stop this slow and deep ploughing. And as she passed from one side of experience to another, from affluence and light to evil and darkness, and took him with her, he knew he would soon completely lose his way the further he followed her. Each time it would be harder to come back and, when he was like her, what then? A bullet.

Deep he stayed inside her, and ground his pelvis into her fur. And while he moved inside her, he kissed her face, until he found himself pressing his head into hers. Muffling her, squashing her, reckless in his aim to be absorbed by her, he seized her shoulders with firm hands, but kept the rub and grind of his cock slow.

'Yes,' she said, over and over again, her face reaching towards his, her mind sensing his desire for aggression from the impressions she had put inside his head.

But, bound by the restraints imposed by her will, he kept his penetrations slow.

'Now,' she finally said, and a frown cut across her alabaster forehead. Sensing his climax, her own had risen gradually, coaxed toward its peak by his slow hands and deep root. 'Stop thinking,' she said, her breath quick, eyelids flickering. 'Let it play.' And he released himself, a confirmed sinner, an accomplice to her crimes. Her hips reared upwards, and her legs strangled his waist. 'Mine,' she whispered, hushing the word into his head. He surged and spilled inside her, another cream in a rich liquor, his final act of submission delivered. But in the thunder and in the red lights so hot against the inside of his skull, he thought her say, 'You are . . . mine.'

When he had finished telling the story, lunchtime had been and gone in Acquisitions. 'And now this. She wants me to sign a contract.' Angel and the corporate girl were sunken in their chairs, drained respectively by the telling and the hearing. They began to stretch stiff legs and pick at the creases in their clothes that felt damp between their joints. Angel stood up. 'And that's why I cannot be owned by her. She'll be the end of me. I'll lose everything.'

By the door of her office, the girl stopped him. She touched his arm. Angel resisted an urge to look down at her hand. If he did, he knew it would have been removed. Instead, he met her gaze openly and let the hand remain on his arm. Her eyes narrowed enough for him to sense her intention. She leaned forwards and kissed his mouth. Never said a word, just closed the gap with her lovely face and put the fruit of her mouth, with its sweet expensive smell, on to his skin.

Dazed for a moment, Angel tried to figure out how much power he held in this situation. Had she just given herself away to him, a mere companion? Passionately, she sucked his bottom lip into her mouth, and then broke away and looked at him, her face darker, eyes coy. She wanted him, but ultimately had the power to engage and disengage. He saw it in her eyes. Excited by what he'd told her, by the dangerous places this man had been, she found some of the doctor's thrill-seeking inside herself, and some of the same need to use up a pretty boy. That's what she wanted; the use of something. Once, he'd read that this was the way men used to make women feel. He didn't believe it. 'I can't,' he said, holding up his communicator. 'This thing will know.'

'Not a problem for some,' she said, smiling. She teetered behind her desk, an urgency in her movements, not so much control, co-ordination slipping now. She tapped the screen on her desk with her fingernails. *Tik, tik, tik, tak,* and it was fixed; he was set into her schedule. 'We have to be quick,' she said, breathless, one hand up in her hair, pulling it free, her blue eyes on his crotch, on his cock. Get it out, boy, she said with that smile that took everything for granted.

Angel flared up inside; angry but aroused. He kissed her hard, pushed her lips back against her teeth. She pulled away: he dug his fingers into her elbows.

'Oh,' she said, and showed him startled eyes.

Into her face he went again to suck out her tongue, to cover her lips, to wipe that red lipstick up her cheek. She fell against him and he let go of her elbows. Stretching his arms down he grasped her buttocks; soft and tight in the skirt he wanted off. He kneaded her cheeks and packed his hard sex against her crotch. She rose to her toes and let him kiss her neck.

They became less frantic; their heartbeats sped up but began to drum in tune; their arms and hands became less clumsy; their snatching mouths began to accommodate the other and their teeth no longer clashed. Held hard in his hands, she let him press her down upon the desktop. Excited breaths made her chest rise and fall quickly beneath the camisole top: no blouse, hard breasts. He weighed them under their coverings; cupped his hands and felt their heavy curves. Wanting all of her at the same time, he ran his hands up her legs, muscled but soft-skinned, and her stockings whispered at his hands as they journeyed all the way up to the shiny tops. Under her tight skirt, hiked up to the hip bone, he seized the black string of her panties and yanked the ripcord down to her heels in one fast motion. Momentarily, she looked frightened; her breath startled into a gasp.

But this is what it is, he wanted to say, when you start these things they go out of control. Each of us has a need so let's hope these needs go together.

As the panties came free, he knocked her shoes off her feet, and as he held the tangle of knicker-bootlace in his hand he realised they were not just damp, but wet; in season. He pulled her bottom, slippery on the marble, to the edge of the desk and sank to his knees. Between her thighs he pushed his face, right into the crispy, blonde fur and tangy brown lips. She moaned out loud and bit a finger. Salted and hormone-heavy to the taste, Angel furrowed and lapped into her until his chin was smeared shiny. Now her head was against the desk top and her cheeks had reddened – the first wave of fever. Inside the sheer fabric of her clingy top, her hands went to work on nipple and bosom flesh, loaded down against her ribs. Red nails on honey skin.

Pressing down on her spot with his tongue, while smoothing his hands across her brown-sugar tummy, he circled and coaxed at her willingness to come, increasing the pressure, making her give him those little yelps. Muscles in her belly tugged free and went loose. When she began to release the last conscious constraints and make those final 'Uh, uh, uh' sounds, he stood up, his cock hard and out.

He placed the bulbous head against her sex.

'Go on. Oh, God, go on,' she said.

'Sure?' he asked, putting it at the gate, about to cross the threshold and accept the warm welcome.

'Go on. Fuck me. Fuck me.' Getting annoyed now. Maybe ready to slap at him. Yes, there it was: her nails in his forearm. A screech of pain. Bitch. Up went her legs, heels and soles parallel to the ceiling, and down came his hand, across her flanks, smacking, echoing off her buttocks.

'Oh, you bastard. You bastard! Oh, yes.'

Again and again, he spanked her upside-down heart of a bottom, while her fingers worked at her own clit, sustaining the high; doing anything, reserve completely gone, to maintain the headlessness. Wanking his cock, he shoved it inside her, pressed through the brief tautness, and then planted himself all the way in. She choked on a sob and slapped one hand against the table. Her ring made the sound of metal chipping stone. Clenching his fingers on her ankles, he raised her bottom an inch from the table top. She felt ungainly; dishevelled and lifted upside-down, like a kitten hauled up by the scruff of its neck, but she only had time to spread her hands across the desk for balance, before the tulip of his penis was packed against the back wall of her womb.

No longer paying heed to her bio-rhythms, Angel went to the mad red place he saw in a dockyard warehouse. Yelps came from her open mouth: her decorum was gone, her hair fanned out. Body shuffled across polished stone, she moved up and down the desk as his cock reamed through her. They slapped like steaks together. Through the mist, he could hear an occasional squelch, or a hiss of air forced from her sex, and the chesty groans coming out of her wide mouth as if she had indigestion. Her breasts shook about, now her hands were in her hair and unable to support them. All of her flesh moved in tremors as his thighs struck the hard edge of the desk.

'Can I come in you? I want to,' he said.

The thought of that excited her. She called him a bastard again and then bit her bottom lip. Momentarily, Angel thought of doing this for ever. Like he had in the early days. Lapsing into the sensual life. Only staying fit for their pleasures. To be absolved from all responsibilities but a dedication to their random needs and occasional excesses. Wouldn't life be much simpler? So why did he fight it? Nothing felt this good. It was the closest a man could be to heaven.

'You want me to come hard? Hard as I come with her?'

She nodded her head, wordless, but moaning, her buttocks wiggling at his mention of come.

'Then I want you over the desk. I need you backwards.'

The girl made another strange whinnying sound and allowed him to rearrange her. Unsteady, her feet shuffled on the floor and her breasts squashed into marble.

Holding her hip bones tight, he nudged back inside her. Returning to the same rhythm, he yanked her backwards while thrusting at speed in the opposite direction.

She looked over her shoulder. 'Harder.' It was a croak more than a word.

Riding over her back, digging in deeper, he seized her shoulders and went at her with an even greater vigour. Not long now. He couldn't hold back. It met her requirements, though. To be held down on this desk and taken backwards like an animal – her sophistication, intrigues and corporate machinations all gone during an unscheduled recreation period.

She made the whinnying sound again. It quickly broke into a choking sound. She came. Back arching, head falling over the other side of the desk, she came hard. Biting into the butt of her hand, she made the hysterical noises that followed tears in a woman on the edge, a woman about to go for the throat, and then her whole being relaxed, exhaled, settled. She laughed and wiped at her eyes.

In her office – the sanctum of his employer and jailer – Angel experienced a sudden need for something base and previously unthinkable. The doctor was strong in him. 'I'm coming,' he said. 'On your arse and legs. All over them.'

She said, 'Yes, yes, yes,' and turned her red face to try and watch it come out.

Never done it so hard to anyone before, he realised, when the come rose, steam-hot, through his pipes, when the muscles in his cock became a staccato of seizures. 'Coming,' is all he got out.

Her cry warbled from the vibrations his thrusts sent through her body. He pulled out as the first ropy ejaculation clotted and thumped out of his sex. Four long pulses of his milkiness struck her buttocks, soundless, sticky, and then plopped on her thighs at the back where her suspenders were taut on her brown skin. The whitey stuff hung, stretched downwards from buttocks and nylons, a messy accident on a woman's behind. Angel fell across her back.

She twisted around on the table, put her legs around his back, and began to lick his hot face, her laughter mad. Angel struggled to breathe. They nuzzled their heads together. It had been too good for strangers. They shouldn't be strangers; they should be in love, he thought now the madness had been expelled. Salina, he thought. With Salina he wanted this for ever.

Eight

'So where do I stand with the doctor?' Angel asks, as he dresses. His hands move fast and he now finds himself immune to the ritual of a hasty departure after a quickly taken thrill. For a while, and it felt like a small triumph, the formality and falseness has been absent from between him and the Acquisitions girl, but he senses it coming back.

She stands beside him, pleased with herself, her panties snug around her waist again. 'By rejecting the offer?' she says, and lets the dark band of her left stocking go with a snap after tightening her suspender clip. She pulls her skirt down over her straightened stockingtops.

'Yes.'

She continues to straighten her apparel while talking. 'Well, there's the snag. You should be aware of your position. I mean, you did agree to the contract.'

Angel stays quiet. He can remember nothing of what was read so long ago. Back then, he would have agreed to anything.

'Legally, we are entitled to sell a companion. You are what we call a "human resource", and we can sell you like we would sell any other commodity. But you can lodge an appeal under exceptional circumstances.'

'Will it do any good?' he asks, his fingers slowing to a fumble with the tie knot. Some part of him refuses to take the contract seriously. That slavery could never be enforced is a notion he has hung on to, like a daydream rehearsed so diligently it feels like a fact. But the notion is threatened now. Something cold and preposterous seems to have grown all over it.

She pins her hair up, using the reflective surface of the computer screen as a mirror. 'Usually not, I'm afraid. But, considering your popularity as a companion, our revenue loss from the failure of this investment project could be recouped through your continuing service. That's the only way out I can think of for you. You're box office, Angel.'

He thinks of Salina and the strange impatience she has with everything around her. 'How long would that take? You know, to pay back what you would lose from the doctor's investment?'

'I can't give you an exact figure. Just a ball-park sum. At your present rate, I estimate another two years' service and we'd be even.'

Who would he be in two years' time? 'Two years!'

'Is that so hard?' she says, smiling, as she dabs at the back of her thigh with a tissue. Missed a bit, her frown seems to say. 'Personally, I like the thought of you being around for a while yet. I may take a more active interest in your portfolio.'

Angel looks at the floor, stunned. 'That would be nice,' he hears himself mumble distractedly.

'But it's not my call. It goes above me.'

To make matters worse, when the girl reactivates his communicator, it announces an impending assignment. 'Shit,' she says. Angel looks at his wrist. It is the doctor's code. He has escaped her for little over two hours with this woman.

'Just in time,' the girl says. 'The request was made ten minutes ago. What are your instructions?'

'She'll pick me up.' His voice is dead sounding.

'Hope I haven't worn you out. Will the client be able to tell?'

'Probably. It's the doctor. She only misses the things she wants to.'

The girl looks worried. 'Oh, no,' she says. 'Oh, no.'

'Relax. It's not your problem,' he says, still preoccupied with the weight of his chains.

'But it could be.' Cornered, her career possibly threatened, her face no longer seems so tanned.

Angel swats his hand through the air. 'I have an hour to recuperate. You'll be fine.'

She exhales; her eyes close with relief now the danger has passed. 'Look, if you're really against the idea, I'll do what I can for you. The doctor is one of our best clients, though. I see by her record she often upgrades temporary positions.'

Angel holds her arm by the elbow. 'What do you mean by that?'

'She offers some companions permanent positions. But only the very best, Angel.'

He frowns at this revelation of the others. 'Others have gone to her?'

'The exact details, I'm afraid, are confidential, but –' her voice drops to a whisper '– it's quite safe. There have been four before you, and they're very, very happy.'

'Four? Who? The twins?'

'I'm not at liberty to say even if I knew. It happened before I achieved this position. Don't be difficult, Angel. Please.'

'How do you know they're happy?'

'I'm sure we would have looked in on them from time to time. It's all fine, really. Always is.' But this sounds vague and insincere to him and she also knows the odds are against him side-stepping the permanent position.

The girl looks at her watch, distracted. 'I can't go into the conference with a sticky bottom.' She giggles. Angel does not react. It's as if she's in a lifeboat and he's treading water with nothing to hold on to. 'I'm sorry,' she then says, feeling guilty after reading the concern in his young face. He knows her sympathy won't last. Then she gazes past him and into space. 'Sometimes we all go too far. It's so easy to do in this city, don't you think?' He nods, but she's thinking of herself again, not him. She kisses his lips. 'Leave it with me. I'll do what I can. I'm sorry, but you really have to go now,' she adds, the brief moment of vulnerability gone from her face.

He leaves in silence.

When he climbs into the back of her car, the doctor is alone but talking to someone else. Discreetly, a communicator must be fixed somewhere in the rear of the limousine. He looks around the leather upholstery and mahogany trim but can't see it. 'Darling,' she says, in her confident conferencing voice. 'I've told you. I can't go into it now. I'm busy. But be assured the refinements have worked. There won't be any more mishaps.'

From somewhere in the ceiling, Angel hears a man's voice. 'Marvellous, I'm sure. But when do I see?'

'You don't trust me.'

'You blame me? Maddy, I find it preposterous that you could even think of keeping samples again –'

'Soon. Soon. I'll show you soon. When the cultures are ready, you'll be the first to know. I promise.'

'How can I be sure?' It is the deeper voice of an older man that fills the car. Angel can almost smell

161

cigar smoke. 'You assured me the last batch was destroyed. But I suspect you've kept one or two back. I'm sorry, but I can't help myself. I know how reckless you can be, but they won't tolerate it again. And now you present another delay on the voluntary inspection.' His voice descends to a hiss. 'Do you know what a risk you have taken? Times have changed, woman. Can't you understand that? You just can't keep doing –'

'Yes, yes, yes. I've heard this before. They wouldn't dare force an inspection. Think of the revenue I contribute.' She looks at Angel sideways, suspicious. He averts his eyes. The car moves off. 'Everything is secure.' She rolls her eyes, exasperated with the voice that questions her.

'Damn it, woman! If you have anything left, it must go. How could you disregard the stipulations of the licence? Have you, again?' The man is close to panic.

'Yes, yes, yes,' she says, bored. 'Must dash, darling. I have someone with me.'

'Someone with you? Who –?' The man's tone changes before she cuts him off. Her red fingernail has descended into her armrest and closed the communication channel, leaving the note of alarm in the man's voice behind in the car. She turns her attention to Angel. 'Every time I see you, you have such a long face. Do desist with this brooding, darling.'

Today, her mood is upbeat. Progress is being made in her life. Something has brightened her spirits. Angel has no idea what she was talking about, but is glad the sombre persona that drove him to the docks has vanished. Today, she looks conventional again, but Angel knows he would be a fool to expect some parallel between her clothes and her attitude. She wears the generic suit of business, all in black: off-the-knee skirt, a one-button jacket, sheer blouse tight on her breasts, knee-length boots in supple leather with a zipper at the sides. He guesses the twins are in the front of the car. She reaches across to Angel. He accepts her hand and moves closer to her on the back seat. 'So, what do you think of joining my staff?' She looks at her lap. She smiles, amused.

'It's very generous of you.'

'I think you're worthy of investment. You know how special you are to me. How fond of you I have become.' Her voice is girlie at first. Then it sounds tearful.

Suddenly, in his imagination, he can see it under rubber, excited.

'I need you, my little man,' she says to herself. 'Knew it the moment I saw you. You have that thing I like so much. Remember that day in my office?'

He nods, but his smile is an effort. He is aroused too, being so near her rustly, perfumed body, but part of him is alert to danger and stubbornly refuses to soften. He hides secrets and intentions of his own. Things he omitted to tell the agency girl also; the main motivation behind his change of heart about being a companion. He thinks of Salina, the girl he has grown to know and love in private. In his constant thoughts of her and through his meetings with her in the townships, he has fallen in love with the girl who has leopard eyes and ballerina muscles in her legs. In between his last two assignments with the doctor, he has seen the Binton maid and dancer three times. Their curiosity about each other is mutual; this fact is safe inside him.

'When we started to alter everything and tamper with everything, to get rid of all the terrible things, and to make all the little ones so bloody smart-alec

163

and precocious, we threw out other things, like what you have. Mmm? You know? Oh, I have another surprise for you,' the doctor says. She squeezes his hand. 'Something you'll love.'

Outside the window skyscrapers stir the clouds; hot winds sweep through ornamental bushes; great stone steps rise to an amphitheatre; four women with the same facial structure watch the car pass. This is the first time career women have looked at him in the High Zones, but they can't see him: he's behind glass. Their interest is specific to the car. The irony confirms his growing disillusionment. He thinks of his predicament and what he must say to the doctor.

At the thought of rejecting her offer, a great welling of emotion comes up from his stomach. It fills his chest and makes his arms and legs feel weak. Short of breath, he wants the window open. He wants to run fast to dispel the panic – the gut panic that surges through him. Now, the great city seems brighter as if the sun has flashed and bleached the stones and metal and glass. Everything is out of his hands. He can't put his thoughts together. He sweats.

The doctor squeezes his fingers. 'Everything all right?' she asks, searching his face for insincerity.

He swallows, then smiles. 'Sure. I'm just a little overwhelmed.'

'I thought you were through all that,' she says, but seems delighted that he isn't.

He breathes in. When he thinks of Salina, suddenly so clear in his mind, his stomach flops over. He can see her waiting for him on the iron foot-bridge that crosses the canal lock. After the brief exchange outside the gym, two days later he found her waiting on the bridge for him to emerge from the silent water below. Wrapped in her long coat, with her hands tucked under her arms, she had called down to him, as he walked up the stone steps to where his bag was hidden beneath a bench. It was the best place to access that particular stretch of canal and it couldn't have been that hard for her to find. That is, if she were determined. The thought had made him warm all over before he even touched the towel to his body.

And she was delighted that he swam in the city's waters. She had her doubts about the story he'd told her, but the moment she saw him down there in the water, he sensed her relax. Small, innocent things pleased her. She'd even seen a bird that morning, and it wasn't a gull either. As she'd told him about it, he began to wonder why his head was always full of schemes. Increasingly, it made him miss these tiny details of life.

They had walked to his home together from the canal, and stopped to buy bread at the baker's – the last one – where the big pink German couple still worked. They ate the bread with apricot jam and a strange coffee he could now afford to buy from the Higher Zones. Besides that, little had changed in his room. What did he do with the wages? Salina had asked. Nothing, he'd said. But he had a plan for the money after it had grown some more. He kept that to himself.

The second time they met, it was as if Salina was completely unburdened of her initial doubts about him. The confirmation of his life in the water had truly changed things. She talked frankly now, seeing parallels between their struggles. He heard about the dancing school and her life as a maid. Requiring distance from Quinny and M, she'd turned down their repeated offers of a live-in position. She was paid badly as a maid, but the bonuses were generous when she took a firmer approach with Quinny. If she spanked him more often, her position would be easier, but, like Angel, she began to worry where it would lead. The boyfriend story was a lie; a bluff buffer to her employers. She'd been alone a long time.

The fire station where she lived was hardly situated in a safe part of town, but two disabled veterans from the colonial wars squatted there too. They had been mercenaries and she ran errands for them and bought their food. In return they protected her as if she were a saint. It suited her in the short term, but Salina was looking for a way out; not just from Quinny, in truth he was harmless, or the townships, but from the entire city. She hoped to join a touring group just to get away. Up against the academy girls, though, her chances were slim. But what she really wanted was a family.

The next time they met, she was about to start work, and he walked with her to the subway station. They walked through the long grasses and between the struggling trees of the last secure park; safe because the surrounding township had been demolished. They had held hands on the way to the subway. Before she left him at the underground station, she'd kissed him too. Until the evening, when he went to the docks with the doctor, it was as if his body had been filled with a golden helium.

During these two liaisons, there had been a tacit unspoken agreement between them not to mention the details of his work; she seemed happy to believe he worked from necessity and not from some illicit curiosity or calling. It suited Angel. Companionship, he'd decided, was something you do for a while, but need to escape from before you go under and can't breathe.

After their walk in the park, he'd slept poorly until the meeting with Acquisitions, his mind too active and the impression of Salina's lips on his cheek too strong. He had begun to believe there was some other place for them to be, where she could dance and he could swim. Maybe, he began to think, if they continued to grow as friends and companions, he could quit his job and they could be lovers too. In a year or two at his present rate of income, he would be financially secure. But would she wait that long and what would he do if not a companion? And now there was the doctor's contract to trap him. If he couldn't evade it, Salina would become nothing more than a memory. The very idea made him feel sick. And he was due to see her tonight after he finished with the doctor. She promised to check his room, before midnight, after finishing with Quinny. To-night, he would have to tell Salina of his dilemma.

In the car, the doctor recaptures his attention. Deftly, her long fingers work in his lap. Blithely, he moves his buttocks forwards on the seat so it will be easier for her to unbuckle his trousers. After she's slapped the belt to one side and unzipped him, she purses her lips at the sight of his thick, brown sex. 'I've been thinking about this –' she curls a forefinger around his girth '– about your hard cock. All morning. And I wanted to suck it.'

Angel's breath catches in his throat. Then he exhales noisily as her head descends into his lap. Stroking her sleek hair, he watches her take him inside her mouth. The touch of her lips and tongue is gentle. She pulls his foreskin back and sucks his phallus, her cheeks going hollow. Through her nose she moans and he feels the vibrations in his tailbone. His cock pulses.

When she comes up for air her eyes are closed. 'You taste good,' she says. Then her head returns to his lap, but not until after she has pulled her skirt up to the top of her thighs.

As she sucks him, he looks down at her lap and wants to come. He can see a thin strip of white flesh, the shiny fabric of her underskirt, the dark welts of her stockings, and then the thin layer of nylon on her legs through which the occasional freckle is visible. She moves her mouth up from his cock and kisses him. Her breath smells of his sex for a moment, and then her tongue is inside his mouth and he can taste lipstick instead.

'I'm spoiling you,' she whispers.

For a while, he forgets about his dilemma and kisses her mouth hard. When he can't help himself and slips one hand between her thighs, he knows a grave mistake has been made. How can he say no now?

She likes this and closes her thighs when he tries to withdraw the hand. 'Ah, yes. I thought you'd missed me too,' she says. This rankles, but in one respect, it is true. Something about her is addictive.

Angel tickles her pussy with one finger. There is a slit in the front of her panties and, by poking his finger through the gap, he finds moisture and warmth. He is his own enemy, he realises.

She coos into his ear. 'Oh, darling, that's nice,' she says in her sultry, after-dinner voice, rich in chocolatey-whispers and cigarette-huskiness. With one long hand – the skin so cool, the palm so soft – she strokes his cock.

Around his shaft he can see a pinky smudge left behind by her mouth. He feels faint with pleasure, but despite the gentle pressure he applies to her sex and the deep kisses he lavishes on her parted lips, is a desire to be hard with the doctor; to punish her for this confusion he suffers, for this dilemma she's worsened. He wants to reassert his will and can think of no way to do this other than through his cock.

When he slips two of his fingers inside her, her head drops upon his shoulder and she suddenly goes limp against the side of his body. 'We should wait,' she says. 'Don't get me too excited. I have an operation this afternoon.'

'Forget it,' he answers, determined to prove something.

'What?' she asks.

He kisses down her throat and up the side of her neck until the light roughness of her scalp scuffs his nose. 'I mustn't,' she says.

'You will,' he tells her.

'Angel!' she remonstrates, but seems pleased with his ardour. It seems to be the most reckless thing he can do, touching her like this, inciting her, encouraging her. She wants to own him, control him, expose him, train him. But, for a while, he will be in charge; he will be empowered. Sometimes, when he looks at her or loves her, he sees total surrender in her face. He sees it now.

On the floor of the car, he kneels down, his hands upon her knees. He has no difficulty in prising them apart. Before she can react, he's pulled her backside across the seat and put her sex on to his mouth. Through her panties he licks her spot and makes her bite her hand. When he sucks the top of her sex between his lips, she stamps a booted foot on the floor. He carries on, humming through his nose, feeling the stickiness increase on his chin, until her legs are over his shoulders and he can feel the calf of her boot on the back of his skull; she is trying to pull his head further up her skirt, so he can be firmer with her clit.

Suddenly, he stops, and makes to disentangle her legs from around his neck. She looks at him, her face flushed and surprised. Her legs stiffen on his shoulders. Slowly, he begins to put his cock back inside his shorts.

'Don't you fuck with me,' she says.

Angel isn't sure what he's doing; he's been impulsive and taken her sex into his mouth. By stopping now, when she's been so close to climax, he guesses he is trying to impress his will upon her. A mistake he will learn from.

'You fucker!' she says through clenched teeth. By bending her leg, she grips the nape of his neck behind her knee. He cries out and tries to pull the leg from around his neck, but she immediately tightens her stranglehold by adding her other leg to the noose. It is like she's sitting cross-legged now, with his head between her thighs and his face pushed, nose first, into her wet sex. He makes a choking sound and clutches at her knees at the back of his head. Her stockings are too slippery for his fingers to achieve a purchase.

The legs tighten. 'You little shit!' There is real rage in her voice now. 'You pissant little fuck!'

Her language shocks him; it is as bad as any Binton girl after a bottle of gin.

Angel breathes deep the cloying musk of her sex. Her lips press into his mouth and he is made to kiss her there, until his whole face is wet. Then her fingers are in his hair and her fist clenches. His eyes water. He panics. Moving off the seat, with his head still locked between her legs, she lowers herself to the floor so he lies prostrate, his legs kicking uselessly between the seats. The back of his neck is cushioned against her leather calves, and her wet sex hovers just above his chin.

'Today, your life starts over,' she says, her face so suddenly full of pity. 'I wanted to do this slowly. Now I have to be hard. I didn't want to. I really didn't.' And then his face is hot.

170

Streaming across his face, over cheekbone, bridge of nose, across lips shut tight, inside his ears, dripping off his chin, welling inside his eye-sockets, her piss smothers him. At first it drops in a thin trickle that comes out sidewards and splashes on his nose, but now it runs all over his head. He can feel warm trickles running across his scalp by the roots of his hair. On his back, he lurches from side to side, and tries to tip her off, but those booted legs just tighten around his head.

'Mmm,' she moans as it gushes out, kidney-hot, acid-stingy, to form a lake under his skull. 'This is what happens to pissy boys,' she says, and then laughs at him. In a quieter, softer voice, he hears her whisper. 'Next time, I may want you to take a sip, you pissy, prissy, prick.'

She moves off his face and disentangles her wet legs. Propped up on an elbow in the spacious footwell, Angel coughs and spits. The heels of her boots are planted on either side of his face. He looks up, dazed, and wipes his eyes. Between her long thighs, he can see the glassy droplets of clear piss falling from the underside of her legs. At the top of her thighs is a shadowy patch of darkened fur. Angel tries to rise to his hands and knees but the toe of her boot touches the back of his head. Slowly, it pushes down. Only when his lips are pressed into the wet carpet will she remove the foot from his head. He looks at her and, when she reads the antipathy in his face, she smiles.

From out of this degradation, his anger and outrage clash with a sudden and inexplicable desire for her – everything becomes chaotic inside his head and he can hardly see for a time. Before she manages to get her hands in between them, he's grabbed the back of her head with one hand and thrust his other

171

hand inside her skirt. When his damp face presses against hers, she opens her mouth and releases a long tongue to lap his sticky chin. His tongue slaps at hers and his fingers began to work inside her, tickling her slick walls.

'That's it,' she says. 'Yes –' but he snatches her tongue and sucks it between his lips before she can say another word.

Pulling her to the floor, he watches her eyes go wide and white with excitement. Slapping her buttocks and then pulling her hips upwards, he moves the doctor into position on all fours. Then he shoves her thighs apart with his knees and rips her panties down the back of her legs. They are sheer black knickers, cut like a man's shorts. With a hand on her shoulder, and another on his girth, he shoves himself inside her. With her head cocked back he can see one side of her face; her mouth open, her eyes closed.

Without a pause for rest or breath, he thrusts quickly, in and out of her. His thighs slap off her buttocks and she makes a deep grunting sound from the back of her throat. 'I'll break you,' she swears. 'I'll break you for this.' And then she makes more of the deep, chesty sounds and sinks her torso to her elbows with her head hanging down between her shoulders. 'And you'll thank me for it,' she whispers. He comes quickly, butting as far into her as was possible, so the force of his final lunges presses her face against the car door, where she gapes like an orange fish, flapping amongst shards of broken glass on wet carpet.

He's cuffed the doctor on the floor of her city office where she gives consultancies, visited a private clinic where she attached his sex to her mouth umbilically, toured the dockside in her limousine, but Angel has

172

never been to her home. Today she remedies the shortcomings in his dealings with her.

From the outside, with its neo-classical pillars, black iron filigree and smooth white stone walls, he recognises it as one of those buildings popular in the excesses of the nineteen twenties. She is surprised by his observation; perhaps trifled by it too, as if his knowledge does not befit the role she's assigned him. He is not here to think. Dismissed as a freakish anomaly, she never refers to it again for the remainder of the afternoon, and Angel bites his tongue whenever he recognises anything else inside the deep, cool building.

Polished marble walls and floors, minimally furnished by black urn-like vases that hold dark green plants and sombre flowers, make him think it not dissimilar to the great French mausoleums. She keeps the communal areas, between the many locked doors and the stairs-wells, lit by simple lights. And there is no clutter, no mirrors, no furniture, or no paintings hung for relief on the funereal walls.

'From time to time, my clients recuperate here in peace,' she says, as they disembark from an elegant elevator on the first floor of the building. The mention of guests makes him feel a little better. 'And occasionally –' she turns to smile at him '– I entertain a special guest.'

But for how long before you tire of them? he wants to ask.

'I have the next floor. All of it to myself,' she says, looking at the staircase.

It was once a mansion hosting individual penthouse apartments, she tells him, and she has re-developed the building to become a home and research facility. There are eight of the old apartments divided in each wing of the ground and first floors; her penthouse exists on the second floor, while the basement is a laboratory. Only the basement elevator doors are dissimilar to the heavy wooden variety in the rest of the building. The laboratory doors are made of metal and accessed by the swipe panels tucked into the walls. The car and its unseen driver have vanished into a subterranean garage.

Just as he is about to ask why they have stopped on the first floor when she lives on the second, in an attempt to feign ignorance as to why she has brought him to the guest facility, Dr Madelaine Sutton opens the unlocked, unmarked door closest to the elevator. 'This is my favourite. It has the best of the natural light in this wing.' He feels the temperature drop in his body. She places a finger under his chin. 'I suggest you wash and change first in the bathroom. Your bathroom. Then take a look around the rest of your new home. Familiarise yourself.'

She stands back and scrutinises his face.

Unsteady on his feet, the palatial marbled walls seem to move around his head. He looks down the long hallway, and absentmindedly counts three doors along its length, before the corridor opens into what he suspects is a large living room. All of this space is for one person. He considers the eleven tenants cramped around the broken facilities in his township building.

'I'll leave you alone,' she says. 'Lunch will be served upstairs in an hour.' She kisses his cheek and walks out of his apartment. A few seconds later he hears her heels on the floor of the elevator, followed by the sound of the trellis door closing.

It goes silent then. Air molecules seem to fall and go numb against his face. He is afraid to take a single step forwards inside the apartment. Looking back, his breath starts to speed up and he thinks of running

174

through the door, left open. The temptation passes but the dampness of his collar tightens around his throat. Reminded of why it is wet, he steadies himself, by putting one hand against a wall – his wall. Does she love him, then, in the way his stomach seemed to dissolve when he thinks of Salina, his Binton princess? What are his feelings for her?

Sudden rushes of adrenalin, instant erections with hot salves around the phallus, cravings for the sensation of leather and nylon and thin rubber in the palms of his hands, the fullness of expensive perfume in his nose, the taste of lipstick in the back of a limousine, bad language spoken in a cultured accent – sex drugs. Half of him wants this, even needs it, can't seem to live without it.

So is it better to live here and then die young; to be extinguished by twins who wear mirror glasses so you never see what is in their eyes when they squeeze the triggers? He thinks of their leather hands gripped on the steel handles, the shadows around the fire in a warehouse, and a doll's face, its thin neck swallowing. All so incongruous compared to this luxury. But it is part of the same world, the same deal. Nothing is inseparable or simple. In this luxurious tomb, he senses the potential for visceral excitement, occurring instantly, passing in moments, all lit by dim lights and destined to end in a splash of red. Before he lingers too long here, and exchanges his soul with this emissary from the devil, he must refute her and get out.

After he showers, he finds a dark suit, in his size, hanging in the wardrobe of the master bedroom. He dresses before the mirrors on the walls, his movements slow and wary as they had been when he handled the soap, towels, touched one of the leather chairs in the big lounge, or placed his feet in the thick carpets in the halls. His thoughts are quickening, though. Everything here presses down on his shoulders and skull, like water pressure from black depths he's plunged into without thought or caution. Taking refuge inside himself, he seems to understand more of himself and knows his desire for simplicity – water, food, books and a woman with jungle-cat eyes – is still greater than his curiosity for the doctor's sophistication and decadence. He should run to the sea with Salina. He has money. It becomes a glimpse of heaven.

The luncheon is sumptuous as expected. Never before has he eaten food like this: tiny blue eggs, little fishes in hot red sauce, bread that dissolves in your mouth before you can chew it, potatoes that taste of mint and butter, pastry that flakes into steaming dust when prodded with a silver fork. If only his thoughts and emotions would leave him alone, then he would eat more and taste it too. His dumb stomach digests it all. And that is what she wants of him – to absorb all of her tastes and thrills and treats until they are his own. She makes people perfect with her hands, but what will she do to his inner life?

She eats nothing; just smokes and watches him. She's changed into another black suit – the beautiful white neck and head of a rare bird leaning forwards toward a glass of red wine. The twins serve the food, not once looking him in the eye. They hate him. He senses something twisted behind their perfect golden faces. Sinister, beautiful angels without wings who would never know free flight. Tube suckers.

'I can't stay here,' he hears himself say, when the twins have gone from the dining room. He keeps his eyes on the clean white tablecloth between his twitchy hands. 'Believe me, I'm grateful to you. I am. For this offer. For all you have done for me. I've learned so much. It's just ...' He looks up. What is her face doing? The suspense is too much. Nothing. She smokes and watches him. Maybe her eyelids are lower, but it could be the smoke, winding up from the cigarette end, that makes them look that way. 'You are beautiful. You know ...' He gets angry at himself, at this stifling in him, around his throat like a hand and this sudden inarticulation it causes. 'But ...'

She raises a hand for silence. A golden wedding band twinkles in the sunlight. 'Why do you persist with this notion of choice? It makes me angry. You know that.' She tries to smile. It's an effort. 'You are part of a transaction.'

'Not yet,' he blurts out. 'I will *appeal*.' The word sounds stupid and useless. 'It's just ... There are things I cannot be a part of.' His voice grows stronger and he's ready to sprint, to finish, to say it all. 'The docks. It made me afraid.'

Her laughter-lines vanish. A dark shape passes over her face. From the angle of her jaw, he guesses her teeth are now pressed together behind her lips, those on the bottom jaw overbiting the incisors at the top of her mouth. He suddenly feels impotent, insignificant, childish. 'And look what we're doing to each other. I mean, in the car. It alarms me. It's not you. It's what I am capable of. I don't know whether I should be capable of it.' He breathes out, but before he can relax in his chair, relieved the words have been spoken, she disrupts the silence and peace of her graceful, spacious home.

'Go.' He never saw her lips move. There was just one word.

A greater stillness descends in the vast dining room. The movement of a fork on a china plate would be deafening – criminally inappropriate. There is no sound at all now. He never even hears the draught that blows a long and silky curtain up from the French windows, open to the sunlight bathing the balcony. He wants to give the food back and the suit. The clothes develop a new weight around his body. He wants to leave here naked, absolved. He sits still. It is wrong to try and speak, but guilt makes you do stupid things and forgiveness is overrated. 'I just don't feel able to –'

'Go!' A tremor runs through the apartment. Every item of furniture or ornament stiffens and straightens up and then settles, an imperceptible distance, back into its place. The building fears her. Even time stops. No woman should have that voice.

Clumsily, he disentangles his legs from beneath the table, takes a quick glance at her ever-watchful eyes, and then walks from the table and through the dining room. The double doors, already open in expectation of a sudden departure, are in sight but the room keeps stretching away from him. When will he get there? There is a twinge between his shoulder blades. She wants to plunge something between them.

Cold air dries the sweat on his face and under his hair once he is back inside the hallway of the penthouse. Almost tripping, he hurries to the front door. It opens too easily. He is out. Three steps at a time, he vaults down the stairs to the ground floor. Looking back, fooled by his instincts that seem to promise him a bullet, he sees no one at the top of the stairs. Across the foyer, his heels ring out – the noise intolerable.

When his hands touch the long brass handles of the front doors, and he is about to pull them open so he can breathe again, he hears a noise to his right side. He turns his head and his vision takes a moment to catch up. There it is again. A dull thump, soft but threatening more power, against the heavy steel doors beside the elevator – the entrance to the research facility.

There is a brief struggle between him and the front door, because he's pulling at the wrong handle. Then he's outside. The sun is being slowly suffocated by thick clouds, black as soot in the hemisphere, that move in from the north, over the High Zones like an invading army, its armour and steel dull. But now he can breathe. Without a single look back he runs from the building, but the thumping sound against those metal doors repeats itself inside his head. A new heart trying to beat inside him.

Nine

This he had not expected. Angel placed his hand on his desk for support. Since his flight from the doctor, he'd spent the rest of the day rehearsing his improbable story, and trying to think of a way of telling a girl he'd only just met that he cherished hopes for their future together. Fresh from maid service in Zone One, Salina stood in his room, no more than four feet away, with her long winter coat held open. Between the black woollen lapels he stared at pure erotic revelation. Pale skin – milk with a hint of powdered coffee stirred through – on her throat and shoulders. The neck slender and tickled with strands of black hair that had fallen, in exquisite disarray, from the pins in her hair. Thin straps of her black bra trailed over her breast-bone and defined scapula, barely touching the unblemished skin. Breasts, pert like little upturned noses in profile, were screened through a black gauze of sheer bra cup. Their brown nipples appeared hard, their pucker smoothed by gossamer. The wide band of her garter belt, with six straps descending, black-framed the slight rise of her tummy. Widening out from her waist, her hips dropped straight to the tops of her nylon stockings, which made her thighs seem set, or cast solid by the dark welts. Over the teeny triangle of black fur, a wispy sheen of panty cloth seemed to move like a veil over a full-lipped mouth, tempting an insolent kiss. Her pussy was set tight into her body and pulled up by the shadowy angle in which her thighs joined her hips. And there was so much leg, entire in display, one foot before the other – the beginning of a dance. Thighs with a pleasant thickening at the top, tapered to perfect knees that rubbed together when she walked in a tight skirt, before the smooth calves, shaped in a long suspension of a raindrop upside down, became sculpted ankles, elevated on Cuban heels, with her long feet machined or moulded into the tight patent leather of the shoes. A simple girl with a dancer's body, who had plundered the perfumed drawers of her employer to see how much of a woman she could be.

'It used to thrill me, wearing these clothes.' She looked down her body, pondering the effect it must have on a man. 'But you forget how good it can look and feel when you wear it every day.' Then she looked up at him, something intense and fixed in her eyes that frightened him and made him feel unworthy of this beauty offered. 'But when someone looks at me, like you do, it brings it all back. It even feels different on my skin. Like the first time when it pulled and whispered under my clothes and made me cautious about how I moved and where I sat. And I would go all kind of delicate inside. You know?'

Angel blinked because his eyes had dried. He swallowed because his throat had gone the same way. Since he first saw her, he'd fought with his imagination against visualising how she looked under the maid outfit. With masturbation prohibited during his corporate service, such thoughts would have been his undoing. And now, with her strong body made vulnerable and tender and sexual before his very eyes, he pitied all men. In every age they had struggled to come to terms with this power in women.

'You like, huh?' she said and then giggled, a part of her bashful. 'Every man wants to know what's under the uniform. Some might prefer it to be left on but, ultimately, I think whatever's underneath is their final goal.'

'I can believe it,' he said, stung inside by this mention of other men appreciating Salina, yet flattered too by the idea that she, with so many choices, was his now.

'Bet you think I came here to seduce you.'

He felt his face sag. Nothing could straighten his mouth. No games. Please, no games.

Mischievous, she smiled; more light in the gold-yellow eyes. 'Quinny made such a mess of my uniform tonight. There was so much trouble. And I didn't have a spare skirt or anything to change into. So I just put my coat over the top.'

'That's all it was?' he heard himself say, in a dry, dumb, monotone voice; all the hope gone with all the force.

Salina threw her head back and laughed. She closed her coat and sat on the bed. 'Don't think I'm that easy, even though you know I trust you.'

He never moved from the desk. Behind him, through the window, the sky was black with unlit night. They looked like aristocratic fugitives here; a man in an expensive suit and a women in designer lingerie, hiding in a scruffy attic. What was their secret? a face at the window might ask.

'My uniform was ruined,' she said. 'It really was, and I came here because we arranged it the other day.' So it was nothing more? Never. Was she cruel, then? Salina laughed again. When she stopped and fixed him with a stare, her voice was lower. 'And you could use a surprise, I thought. You seem troubled.' She looked down at the front of his suit trousers. He followed her eyes and immediately placed a hand over the protuberance. 'That does look nice too,' she said, and in that moment, he realised she had indeed toyed with him, but in the best way – access rights had been temporarily suspended; a little teasing, nothing more. All along her intention had been seduction.

He moved her to this behaviour; playful, coquettish, provocative. He wanted the happy spin, the sudden rush of elation, to last for ever. She wanted him. Salina wanted him. He walked to the bed and kneeled before her.

There was no resistance when he cradled one of her ankles in his hands. It was light, despite the heeled shoe, and her thin Achilles' tendon was slippery under the heel and seam of her nylons. She had strong feet and calves; he could see the long muscles through her stockings, and felt a ripple of power under the skin when she pointed her toes down. But there was nothing overdeveloped about her physique; the strength had merely pushed to the surface of her skin, which stretched around the contours to softly round them off. Finished with a tint of caramel, as if kissed by the sun but not allowed to bake, he could detect a soft brown hue to her skintone under the black of the nylon. One instep was pink-rimmed from the fit of her shoe. His stomach turned over. He looked up and where the electric light struck her knees he was momentarily blinded by sun on glass.

'You like?' she whispered, enjoying but made suddenly shy by his intense scrutiny.

He nodded. 'It's been hell trying to stop myself dreaming about being right here, with my hands on you.' Angel rubbed his cupped hand up the back of her leg she held forward. He felt the seam like a tickling thread in the palm. On the pad of his thumb and the base of his hand, her leg slipped about as if soaped and wet.

Uncrossing her legs, her coat fell from her thigh. She made no move to close it, or to remove her heel from his cupped palm. Blood gushed to his head. It was a foaming weir in there. One or two sparks of light inside his eyes fell slowly across the image of her tummy, rippled slightly, sweet dough over hard cross-springs of muscle that must stretch in an arc when she bent backwards. He imagined the feel of it against the side of his face. And above it, motionless, but anticipating a touch, her caramel breasts, air-brushed over by a dark gauze and close enough for him to smell the perfumes that were never completely laundered out of bras; the musks of bottled scent, the gentle camomile of soap, and the milk of her own woman-smell.

He sighed, his hands feeling clumsy and damp against her stockinged leg. 'There's too much of you,' he said sincerely, but had started laughing, and started her laughing, before the sentence was finished.

'It's nice to be appreciated,' she said. 'By someone you want to be appreciated by.' She broke from his gaze and her face darkened. 'I've thought about you too. I don't ... I never go out, you know. It's too much trouble all the time.'

He nodded, understanding the plight of a disadvantaged but spirited girl who hovered on the brink of becoming a fresh meat commodity as he had. What else was there for them?

But she had kept a tighter grip on her dream. 'I kind of knew you'd be different. At first, I wasn't sure. But now, I think ...'

Angel kneeled forwards and kissed her cheek. Her eyes retreated. She frowned and then her forehead smoothed out. Last misgivings taken away by need.

She'd held back for so long; he could sense that. No grubby Binton hands had rustled on this underwear, but she wanted his, cleansed by wild waters, to hold her. She felt precious – shivers and trembles passed under the transparent black shield of lingerie that was no shield because it invited contact. He'd been operating in a world without restraint. He'd assumed everyone else did too.

Then he kissed her lips and remembered them on his cheek from the other day. Open, soft, wet; her mouth yielded and then explored more than his cheek this time. Their tongues touched; his cock pulsed. Long fingers surrounded the back of his head, their lacquered tips ruffled his hair and then touched the nape of his neck. Icicle dust fell between his shoulder blades.

'Do you want me?' she hushed into his ear, and kissed him harder. 'You can have me, you know.'

He nearly wept. Under the force field, frosting his nose and fingers when first they met, was something innocent but hot with animal blood. Even this goddess wanted to be under a man. The thought appalled but excited him. He imagined her face the moment his cock entered her. And then he wanted to be inside her, right at the back of her – so much he got heartburn.

Along her glassy thighs he spread his hands. Her head dropped, loose, into the gap between his shoulder and neck. Her breath was hot and then turned wet on his skin. Fingers spread, he swished his hands back to her knees from the inside of her thighs. Only the outside of his little finger had touched the softest skin up there, between stocking-top and furred mound.

Down to her ankles he caressed her legs, feeling every teeny crease, every indent from the occasional mole under nylon, the siding peaks of bone. He thought back to the time in her employer's apartment and how he had watched these legs walk across marble and the thick blades of luxury rugs. And when her mistress wet his lap, he had been thinking of these legs. Never would he be able to withstand the sight of her legs walking away from him with something final in their step, or the thought of them whispering under another's hands. They belonged to him now.

With the underside of one outstretched finger, he touched her sex. Her body seized up as if she'd burned her hand on a stove. It was as if she shrank an inch all over. The panty material was thin and damp. He left the finger in place for a few seconds, but when he moved his hand away, he felt the gravity of her long body move after the touch, chasing it.

'I'm so wet. Feel how wet I am,' she said; an apology and a request for the return of the finger.

He kissed her mouth and, when her tongue was being sucked from her face and between his lips, he inserted his whole hand against her sex. Soft lips and crisp floss pressed into his palm. She shuddered and then pulled her face from the kiss. Her eyes closed again and she sucked in her breath – her most secret and protected part touched at last. He pushed the hand upwards, his middle finger only prevented by a millimetre of invisible mesh from slipping inside. Nails, long and painted strong, curled against the back of his head before they reached down to his shoulders and dug into the hollows between his muscles.

By lifting his face, and that was all he needed to do to reach them, her breasts brushed across his mouth. A nipple, pebble-hard, gently pulled his bottom lip down. She made a crying sound inside her long nose. He had to be careful with her – she was letting him know this. They were coming together in more ways than one. Once he'd loved her they would be inseparable. He knew this instinctively and welcomed a momentous responsibility for the first time in his life. She was all he ever wanted.

Between his lips, his teeth held back, he accepted the nipple. It wobbled when he pulled it out a fraction, the areola tenting, and then let it fall back under its screen, now disturbed. Taking his hands from her legs, he cupped the lower half of each breast. He held them up before his eyes and worshipped them, his lips moving in a brief prayer of silent adoration. And then, ever so gently, he kissed each nipple. The nails on his back tensed, became jungle claws. With the very tip of his tongue, he flicked the nipples, side to side, and then up and down. As if her toes had descended through the still but icy surface of winter water, she made a little cry up in the rafters of her chest. And then he brought the pitch of her sounds down through the register, by swallowing a breast. Wetting the fabric of her bra with his spit, he sucked hard, no teeth, just lips and tongue, on one breast, while massaging its cooler twin with a hand. When he swapped hand and mouth, to pay his eager oral duties on the second nipple, Salina began to fumble behind her back with the catch of her bra. She wanted his mouth on her skin.

The bra fell between them; empty, weightless, nothing but a wisp of black with a single memory of smooth skin inside it. Her nipples were dark brown, almost negress purple; dark chocolate buttons on white pudding, set firm. Into them he pressed his face, and inhaled deep. City-girl perspiration, scented soap, and musty, hot nylon made muscle turn to bone in his shorts. Exploring these breasts with his face hovering close to them, he tweaked the nipples between rough thumb and finger, then rolled them, and delivered a flick, but never caused discomfort, just teased the sensitive parts without touching them too much so they ceased being attuned.

Widening her legs around him, she kicked off her heels and put her supple dancer's feet against the bottom of his spine. Down his face swept to kiss the cleft of her belly. He moved lower to nuzzle the hillock of her womb, with its faint smell of vanilla which then spoiled to a pleasing offal-ripeness between her thighs. Overpowering unless you wanted to bask in it, like he had the moment his balls had filled and gone tight, the shaft of his cock fortified itself with blood, and the tingle of a strange electric current passed through every nerve-ending along its length.

The desire to pass into this odoriferous sex took control. Plucking the dark band of her panties from her hips, he then pulled the crumpled, salted jellyfish – a deadly lure – away from her moist sex-mouth. He drew the panties down her legs, black on black, and pinched them off her toes, red under a matt finish of darker nylon. She lay back on the bed, her pretty breasts distant humps now, pale and only to be reached over the ridge of her ribs. Her arms stretched upwards and her fingers spread on the wall behind her head. The damp-stained paint no longer looked ugly or neglected with the impression of her long fingers upon it.

It was a manoeuvre he never rushed, moving his face between her thighs, his eyes half-closed so no detail of her sexual feature could suffer from the blur of eyes adjusting to close range. He took a draught of her fresh dark smell inside his lungs, and felt his mouth fill with saliva, excited by the prospect of food. Lips apart, he put his mouth into her fur. So wet, the lower half of his face felt a film of moisture spread.

Against his tongue and chin, her outer lips were slippery and her floss was matted thick with a glistening brine. He brushed his thumb-clamps through her pubic hair – a gentle touch – and then lapped over the tiny red centre, hooded and sleek under a membrane of liquid salt.

And there it was; the first taste of her, his Salina, in his mouth. He would never forget it, or the whimpers she made, just after she said the word, 'God.' And her noises seemed to pass no further than a few feet into the air above them, as if the warm air in his room had slowed to a breathless standstill, thickened with suspense around their bodies. He'll suck this beautiful orchid, wet with its natural dew, and then he'll slip that swollen, delightfully aching cock inside her. Right through her. His cock juts out from the thought of her, from the taste of her, and soils his shorts with grey preparatory juice.

A white flash between his eyes. A hot wire glows up his arm and then down his spine. He sits back, one hand against his head, the other hanging limp on her foot.

She sits up, worried. 'What's wrong?' she asks.

The back of his eyes smart from a retinal burn. He traces the memory of the brief but painful seizure. It happened so damn fast. From his wrist – the right wrist – it had fired up his arm and then forked – pain going down his spine and up into his skull. A painful jolt from split lightning; a warning when a curious, reckless finger reaches out and touches an electrified fence.

'What is it?' Salina says, her face flushed, her hair now loose about her cheekbones. She lies inside her open coat, the lining shiny. Scene-of-the-crime snapshot; a photograph of a beautiful woman disturbed at the moment of imminent penetration; her panties and bra shed, her legs spread but left sleek in stockings, slightly creased on the joints. 'What's wrong?' she repeats, looking at him, as he kneels between her thighs, his face in his hands.

He says, 'No,' and shakes his head from side to side; the receiver of terrible news. 'It's this,' he says, and then holds up the wrist manacled by the communicator. A continuous whine, like a siren submerged in water, rises into the air from the wrist piece. 'I can't do it. I'm not allowed. My contract.'

Salina withdraws her legs up, away from him, and curls them underneath her body – scared closer to the fire by a wolf howl. She tugs her coat around her breasts as if they are suddenly cold. 'They know.' Her voice is thin, on the verge of tears. 'How do they know?'

'The scanner. There must be a scanner for my heart-rate or something. For brain activity. I don't know. It's never happened before. They must deactivate it when I'm with a client.'

But that is the wrong thing to say. She sits up, bundled into her coat, a refugee out in the cold. He can only see one naked shoulder. Sniffing, she turns her head to the side and looks at the wall above his pillows. Her nervous fingertips wipe the tears of disappointment from underneath her eyes, bitter with salt.

Now. He had to tell her now. Would she listen to him? Would she believe his story? His refusal of the doctor's offer, and his desire to run with Salina to some kind of new start, seemed preposterous to him now, like a desperate line fed to a woman who was at the point of deserting him. 'I forgot, Salina. I forgot this would happen. I got carried away. They own that part of me. In fact, they own all of me.'

'Don't.' She shakes her head. Her eyes look wet and bloodshot.

'I have an idea. All day, I've been thinking about how I should tell you. I guess, I should just say it. Tell the truth –'

With a crash that makes each of them flinch and gasp, the door to his room blows in and smashes against the old refrigerator with the loose icebox. From the floor where he crouches, he turns his head and sees a figure step into his room. The head is covered with a scarf, the eyes mercifully shut away behind dark glasses – they must be full of hate. The doctor's coat is belted tight around her waist and falls to her leather ankles – they shine against the wooden planks of his flooring. Her hands are inside her pockets, but one emerges. It too is covered in leather. It moves into the air in a quick, jerky motion. Blue-black, the muzzle of the gun looks cold. The pistol handle makes a little squeaky sound in the palm of her hand. Her lips tighten.

'No,' Angel mutters to her, staring at those slick-oily lenses in her glasses.

'Oh, God,' Salina whispers.

'Bastard,' the doctor says, her voice thinned by grief, anger, betrayal.

There is a tiny flash of orange at the end of the barrel. The zipping blowpipe sound seems to leave the gun in her hand and stretch into him. A big hand has punched him in the chest. It goes right through him and slams his body backwards. He gives Salina a shocked, useless look. She stares at him with horror. The pain then blinds him with white light. A black shadow of sleep is pushed down and through his mind. It just happens; he has no choice. The bed in his room telescopes away. There are two more flashes and two more blowpipe sounds he hears whiz into his body. Never feels them. His last thought: it's over now.

Ten

When you wake and cannot move there is an instinct to panic. Especially in the first stage when you thrash between sleep and consciousness. It's an insubstantial dimension you exist momentarily within. Between two worlds, you are never sure if what you see is real or not. When you look up at a white ceiling and see a bright striplight, and then look down and see the machines monitoring your vital signs with the coloured wires attached to your body, your breath seizes; you freeze. Hospital shock. You are tempted to close your eyes and then reopen them. You do this, but things are the same when you take a second look around. This is for real, then. If you move, it could hurt. Some part of your body will start to scream. Stay still. Not that you have a choice. Thick white straps, made from rubber, keep your arms and legs firmly pinned to the tubular metal frame of your bed. Is it some kind of traction?

Slowly, you flex a toe, a foot, then the muscles in your leg. No pain. Now try the other. That's it. Same thing. Now a hand. And then the other, as you did with your legs. Good. But what about your chest and stomach? Beneath the tight wrappings, you feel mostly numb, but sense that your parts are delicate inside. You have a vague impression that damage has been inflicted to that part of your body, but no actual recollection of it occuring. And whatever did happen, you are reluctant to remember. Your will to recall anything is weak. All you can think in, and therefore exist in, is the present. You're in hospital and alive and feel like you have been asleep for a long time. It seems a heavy sedation has been applied also. Even lifting your head from the big pillows makes you break out in a sweat and struggle to breathe. Any exertion will wear you out. Stay still. Rest. You are safe now. Sleep.

Was that a dream, or did somebody just bend over your bed? They were talking, but not to you. Another person was nearby also. And what is it you remember about their faces? They were odd; long white ovals with bright red cheeks and lips, and the outlines of their eyes were pitch-black. They were women, yes. One them wore a bright white uniform, and the other was dressed in blue, but their clothes appeared to be extraordinarily shiny under the lights in your room. In fact, their clothes exhibited a gloss similar to that of their faces. And when one of these women touched your forehead, her fingers felt tacky and you smelled rubber. She must have been wearing a glove. You flinched when she touched you.

But the most peculiar thing of all were their expressions. They never changed. Their mouths never moved, and yet they were talking all the time, and their eyes never blinked. Things began to grow more vivid at this point in the dream, but a plastic cup is placed over your mouth and nose. And now, in this endless daze, the whole thing seems like one of those fragments that stays with you in the morning after a deep-sleeping night.

Another woman has been here. A third woman who stood near the bed. You could smell her perfume; it seemed familiar. You're not sure, but you had a sense of her being glossy too, like the others, only this woman was thinner and her head was pallid, as if she had no hair. Dressed in a shiny black suit, she sat at the foot of your bed and watched you. You were frightened. You passed out.

And if this is also a dream, you do not want to wake up. This feels so good. That whole area around your groin is so sensitive. Soft hair brushes the inside of your thighs. Careful hands cup your hot, full testes. Another hand slowly slips up and down your length, holding it loose, as if time is of no consequence and your pleasure is being lengthened deliberately, but subtly, so the chances of you being disturbed from sleep are slim. Yes, whoever is touching you does not want to wake you, and takes every care to make sure that the pressure of their lips on your tingly phallus is slight. And when you are taken fully inside their warm mouth, and you know that is where your cock resides even though you keep your eyes closed as if the continuation of your pleasure is dependent on you doing so, you hear a voice. A woman's voice. It comes from the distance. There is alarm in this voice. Outrage even.

'Nurse! What are you doing here?'

Damn it! The mouth is withdrawn from your cock; the hair goes from your inner thighs and you are left cold down there. Despite your sudden disappointment and frustration, you can hear talking. Same two voices from that first time when you thought you were dreaming. So the long-faced women with the glossy faces are real, then?

'Bed-wash, Sister. Ssh, he's sleeping. You'll wake him. The doctor says he's not to be woken.' Then a cold flannel is applied to your parts and you suspect

194

a thick ring of red lipstick is being removed by the girl whose mouth smeared it there.

'Very well,' the other woman says, the one called Sister, but she doesn't sound convinced. In fact, you suspect there is enmity between these two women. 'You are dismissed, Nurse.'

'But, Sister, I've only just begun –'

'Dismissed, I said.'

'Yes, Sister.' The flannel and the lovely rubber hand are gone. Nurse's heels retreat from your bed and travel across the linoleum to the door. You keep your eyes shut. After the sound of Nurse's heels fades, the woman called Sister hovers beside your bed. You can hear her breathing, smell her strange rubbery scent, and sense her face drawing close. Your eyelids flicker – nearly a giveaway – but you just manage to keep them sealed. Damn it, what is she doing?

Her breath is pleasant; medicinal, more menthol than sweet, and it feels good against your right cheek and ear where the hair is feathery around the lobe. Between your legs, you stay hard for the presence of Sister.

'Are you asleep?' she whispers, and then waits for you to respond.

Your chest rises and falls; you say nothing.

'She had your cock. I know she did. That bitch had your cock. It belongs to the doctor. No one but the doctor can touch this.'

A finger is placed on the end of your sex. The breath disappears from your cheek. The pressure of the finger develops into the embrace of a cold hand. Involuntarily, this gentle contact starts a contraction of the muscles in your shaft. You want that hand to stay right where it is and you want it to relieve you. It's been a long time since you were pleasured this way. There seems to be a lot of pressure inside you; more than there has ever been.

'She had this in her mouth.' The woman keeps her voice low, but there is anger in it. 'I know it. She wants it for herself.' The hand strokes you.

Your breathing quickens and your buttocks clench. Some more. Please, please, some more, you want to call out, but can't give yourself up. Your hands are tied off fast to the bed and only these women can touch you down there.

The hand releases your sex and you feel the first heat of anger spread through you. It pebble-dashes your forehead with more perspiration. Your teeth grind together. The sound of Sister's high-heeled shoes click-clack back across the tiles and you hear the door to your room close. Just as your hope is about to sink and you are about to groan with this immense bafflement and frustration, her footsteps echo again in the room as she returns to your bedside.

'You had a nasty accident, my lad,' she mutters. 'You need rest and care now. Lots of it. You're very special, the doctor says. So every bit of you needs looking after.' Her voice draws closer to you again. 'You hear me? That's right,' she says. 'Special treatment should only be performed by the very best, like our doctor. It's a miracle what she's done for you. How she's healed you. And now it's our turn to make you stronger.'

Suddenly, something is jammed between your lips. It pushes your jaws apart and lodges itself between your teeth. You can taste rubber. 'To help you recuperate,' the voice says, and then the sheet is pulled over your face. 'You just relax. Just lie still and let me help you.' And as she says this, her voice is more distant again and it labours just a little, as if she's moving something heavy, or climbing steps, but you're not sure. When the bed issues a metallic creaking sound and the mattress dips on either side of your hips, you guess she's about to do something to help you recuperate. Something that will hasten your recovery. Something she requires the door to be closed for. You are thrilled.

Oh, yes. There is the cold hand again, moving your vulnerable, naked sex upright. Something tickles the end of your cock. Feels like hair – a crisp flossy hair. And then you slip inside something you know to be red and slick and moist. Under the thin sheet she has placed over your face, you open your eyes the moment you feel her weight squash into your groin. Her sex swallows your cock down to the base. You wish you could watch. The sheet slips up and down your face as her exertions increase. You hear her breath sharpening and then she makes these little 'ahhh' sounds, stretching them out of her mouth as she arches her back and neck.

It won't be long before you come, not with the embrace of her sex so tight around your starved cock. She senses this and moves her sex slower, and then in tiny circular movements that progress into a delightful grind against the bones in your groin. This is good and she keeps it up until she gets really excited. Her nails clutch beneath your buttocks. They find a purchase and dig in. It would be painful were you not so aroused. She's eager to get more of you inside herself – wants her whole womb filled up – so she begins to pump herself on and off you so quickly that before long she's bouncing on and off your body, and the force and weight behind her plunging thrusts your erection right up and inside her. The bed shakes too and you can hear the metal frame making a noisy rattle. Then the headboard begins to strike the wall and her moans have a hard sound to them. Little yaps of delight follow whenever her body slams against your pelvis and a little judder is passed to her clit.

This is good; you feel you've always liked this – a woman just shoving your cock inside her body.

Lancing herself to release your sleepy suffering, she begins to bite her hand. You can tell because her hard sounds become muffled. You think of her red mouth biting into a rubber-gloved hand and you cannot hold back. Up it shoots; hot, thick, a flood that eases the pressure from inside you right away, and deflates your body back down to the bed with her weight right on top of you. Sweat dries. She kisses your belly. If that gag wasn't stuck between your teeth, you would have said, Thank you, Sister. Thank you.

The sheet comes off your face; you close your eyes just in time; the gag is taken from between your teeth; the rubber cup is applied to your nose and mouth . . .

Nurse has woken you up. 'Ssh,' she says, from behind your head, 'or you'll be in trouble.' Sleepy, you look around. You blink for focus and become aware of how dry your mouth is. The lights in your room are dim; the door has been shut. Beside you, the machines softly purr the rhythm of the hospital night – the stabilised heartbeat. Where is she, then? And why has she woken you?

There is a squeak near your left ear, that makes you think of a rubber sole twisting on a rubber floor. You turn your face to the side and peer through the gloom. Someone all wrapped up in shiny clothes – white clothes – stands at your bedside. She is lit up by the tiny monitor display of your headboard and by the dimmed side lights on the walls. You see the taut plastic of her waist, her hard-looking breasts, her shrink-wrapped throat, her . . . her face? Is that make-up on her face? How did she get such perfect skin? So beautiful. She's so beautiful with that long smiling face, the thick lips of shining cherry, the high cheekbones smudged with rouge, and her eyes, so wide and green and clear with the longest and thickest black eyelashes you have ever seen. They don't blink. No, they just watch you and study you when she tilts her perfect head to one side. Not even her blonde hair moves, pinned up under that little nursey cap of white rubber.

Smiling, forever smiling, her shiny face moves closer to your mouth. Her long hands move up your biceps to your shoulders. Then her fingers tickle across your throat and move under your chin until they press against your lips. You shiver; you know yourself to be terribly vulnerable. But this touch feels so good and her perfume clouds around you – it smells sweet and girlie. You sigh. Beneath the sheets, you feel that sleepy cock thicken and then flop to the other side of your thighs. She seems to hear it, because the nurse turns her head to look in the direction of your lap, and you glimpse the side of her milky face with its tiny alabaster ear. She's so pale, but there are no blemishes on her smooth cheek.

When she turns her head to face you again, her lips brush against your lips. They feel slippery and you know they will leave a stain on whatever they touch. When she opens her mouth, without making so much as a crease at the sides of her cheeks, her tongue appears. It goes straight inside your mouth. You suckle it until her lips push down and find a fit against your own. For a long time, until you're almost struggling to breathe steadily, though it is not an unpleasant sensation, the nurse with the perfect face kisses you. Instinctively, you try to move those damn hands of yours, so you can clutch the tight breasts that look so good in her white suit, but it's no good, the straps keep your arms still. Nurse does the work. She knows how to deal with her patients.

When she breaks from the kiss and you gulp at the air, she moves her face down the bed until the red smile is level with your hips. Bending over, her lovely head descends into your lap. You groan. Forming an 'O' shape, her deep mouth slides down your sex, and then ascends, agonisingly, back up and along it. Her long tongue slaps and slips about the gorgeous red fruit at the end. You shudder like a breeze has just brushed your still-wet back after climbing from cold water. As far as you are able, you move your head to peer over the side of the bed to see more of her as she sucks you. She's naturally tall and made taller still by the heels she wears; white spiky heels with little straps to hold her feet on to the thick platform sole. Not what you expected a nurse to be wearing, but you like the way she challenges your expectations.

And then her long legs rise up to her tight buttocks, glistening all the way within a thin, shiny layer of rubber that coats her body as if she's grown a new skin made from latex. Over her hips and up to her breasts and throat it goes, this one-piece second skin. It's almost as if she is naked except for the shoes, and this is her real skin you're seeing. But it can't be, even though you cannot see any seams or a zipper on the smooth, plastered body. It's so good to look at, though, as she sucks you; just to stare at the shining curves of her buttocks pushed out and her chest so pronounced, and the tautness at the back of her thighs as she bends double to get her head inside your lap.

And soon one of her sticky hands begins to work you down there too. It makes a fist, a close embrace, and the tacky palm of her hand ripples over your hard ridges and stiff swellings. The more she sucks and the harder she pulls at you, the louder her snarly feeding noises become in the dim room. As though you suddenly want to get thrusting into her all-overshininess, you begin to push your buttocks upwards before the straps force you back down to the mattress. The muscles in your arms strain against these bindings too. Your mouth opens and issues a long moan, and then you collapse, dizzy but delighted, and the nurse guzzles your milk without spilling a drop. And as your cock pumps you can hear her throaty swallowing sounds. An expert.

She releases your cock from her red 'O' mouth and looks at your flushed, perspiring face. She smiles at you. Her eyes never blink.

'She's been at you again, I know it,' Sister says, rousing you from sleep, from too much sleep. You are exhausted by sleep now, and of the discontinuity of these indoor seasons and days and nights. How long have you been here? Where is this place? You know who you are – that is, you are comfortable with your body and emotions – but cannot remember anything else. This should trouble you, but it doesn't seem to. Sleep and the infrequent moments of waking, when their plastic faces and rubber hands are busy with your cock, seem to be your only concerns. Perhaps you sensed it was temporary, this stage of the recovery when you were enjoying both the rest and their attentions, but it just goes on and on. You want to move freely again. You want to wake up. You fidget.

Sister takes your temperature. 'What did she do to you? Did you like it?' As she sticks something thin and glassy in your mouth, you get a better look at her face. Same perfect skin as the nurse, smooth and shiny, but Sister's eyes are blue, narrow at the sides like an oriental, and her eyebrows are straighter and don't have the graceful curves that soften up Nurse's face. Sister's brows dip towards the inner corner of her eyes like a frown is about to begin on her face. She's always at the point of interrogation, it seems. And this stern beauty of hers is unnatural also; where are the pores, the laughter-lines, the tiny individual creases in her skin? Like Nurse, why does she never blink or close her eyes? But these eyes are not dead – they are crystalline and have astonishing depths. They lure you inwards. They exist to enchant. Your mouth reaches for her lips. She moves away and prepares a syringe.

You look at her body instead, still hungry for her, intoxicated, greedy, looking to engorge. Pale and institutional-blue in colour, her uniform has been rubberised. Cut like a dress and as tight as a skin-suit from the halter neck to her knees, where it stops. How can she walk in such a clingy, inflexible outfit? Below her hemline, she wears shiny white hose. Her legs glimmer as they catch the hospital lights. They are long, too, like Nurse's, but end in shoes that aren't sandals and you guess the heels are spikier also. How did she get that dress up around her waist, then, the time she straddled your invalid lap and relieved you inside her tight, waterproof body?

'Where am I, Sister?'

'Soon we'll have you up and about,' she says, as though she hasn't heard you.

'How long have I been here?'

'Then, we'll start the exercise programme. The doctor has just posted your new regimen.'

'Am I well now, Sister? What happened to me?'

She takes blood from your arm. You wince and look away from the needle in your vein. 'Now, now. Don't make such a fuss,' Sister says. 'If you're good during your bed bath, you might get a little sugar.'

Bed bath? You feel clean, so do the sheets. How do they maintain you and feed you when you sleep all the time? Perhaps they do things while you sleep. More than once you have woken up with the strong scents of their perfumes on your skin. And around your mouth you can taste their lips too. Sometimes, the end of your tired, flaccid sex is moist, like it has been purged without your knowledge. Did you discharge in your sleep, or are you helped?

'Sister?' You ask for her attention. She hasn't heard and just continues to bustle about the bed. 'Sister?'

'You're a long way from recovery. It's going to take a long time before you're fit again, and I shall need you to be very brave. Can you be a brave boy for Sister?'

'Sure, yes. I can, Sister. But what happened to me?' you ask, a pleading tone enters your voice.

'There's lots of vitamins and nutrients you need before we move you on to solids. I'll feed you before your bath.'

You flop your head back. What's the use? But then she recaptures your attention. The bed starts to move in the middle. Your head and torso are elevated. The bed has made you sit up. She tucks a napkin under your chin and then sits, side-saddle, on the edge of the mattress beside you. Her glossy red nails, cut square for work but painted so prettily, pluck at the top of her skin-dress, by her neck. You hear the sound of two sheets of sticky rubber parting, and she opens her breasts to you. You start to breathe heavily. You moan. Between your legs you feel your cock-pole itself upright, as if the single eye is trying to force itself through the sheets so it too can see her large, milky breasts. They are too weighty for her teeny waist, surely? So big, but somehow still perched pertly over her slender ribs. She pushes this bulbous softness at your face. Her nipples are dummy sucker-things, the areola wide and pinky, but going orange at the rim. Business-like, she holds them up to your face. You do not even have to move your head. She squashes them in. They round over your nose and lips. Greedy for something you expect to be sweet and creamy-thick, your teeth lock on to a nipple. 'Gently,' she says, her tone sharp. You settle your lips around the thick pink nugget and then suck.

Hot milk. Sweet in taste, frothy in texture, fortified with goodness, you suck it from her rubber body. Your eyes close in rapture and her frowning face moves about, studying your suckle. You moan when she takes the first breast away. 'Steady,' she says, and then puts the other fat nipple into your mouth. You suck the liquid in long concentrated streams right to the back of your mouth, swallowing most of it before you get to taste it.

'I've just come to do that!' Nurse calls out from the door.

'Well, it was Sister's turn,' you hear Sister coo, and you keep on feeding, right up to the point when your cheeks ache from such a furious suckling.

'You really shouldn't put yourself out like this. It's what I'm here for. It's my job.' Nurse sounds petulant and about to cry at the same time.

'Just this once won't hurt,' Sister says.

The breasts are removed from your face. You breathe out, your tummy full. It was good. Before your eyes, Sister tucks her breasts back inside the blue rubber of her dress. She seals them inside with a squelch. She turns to Nurse. 'Don't you have other duties?'

'They're done.'

'Well, you can take a break, then.'

'No. I'll finish up here.'

'I'm nearly done. You run along.'

'I'd rather –'

'Run along, Nurse!'

They stand face to face; full lips set in eternal smiles, unblinking eyes clear as mountain lakes, necks unruffled – margarine-smooth and latex-slick.

Nurse starts to sniff. She's smiling, but it's a smile that works hard to mask grief. Unable to bear up to that slight frown above Sister's blue eyes, she turns away. Unsteady on her white heels, she walks towards the door. Her head is lowered. Today, she wears a dress that stops up around her tights buttocks. You feel sorry for this beautiful nurse, but cannot resist leaning your head forwards to look down at the back of her long thighs. They shine in white tights. If that hem goes any higher you'll see her pussy-fur through the gauzy crotch.

Sister sees your hard, straining cock, and becomes aware of your interest in Nurse. 'Well, if that's how you behave, like a big baby, you'll be in here for ever. We'll never get you well again.' She untangles a transparent tube from a machine above your head. Her actions are jerky. You blink and flinch as the sharp angles of her elbows move near your face. At the end of the tube is the plastic cup that always brings the deepest, soundest sleep.

Nurse stops walking and turns around to watch. 'Oh, he can be a handful,' she says in a teary voice, and then sniffs. 'I know. I know he can.'

No. This time you will not sleep. You hold your breath when the cup goes over your mouth and nose. You find you can hold your breath for a long time. For you it's easy – you're used to holding your breath. You know this, but can't remember why. You close your eyes to make it look like they have put you out. You count to thirty and the cup is removed. You hear Sister sigh; perhaps disappointed that such drastic action was necessary. 'Nurse, will you assist me with the bed bath?' she says, in a reconciliatory tone of voice.

'Oh, yes, Sister. Of course, Sister.' She is elated. You can imagine the smile. There is a peace between them now; a cease-fire in the war of bed manners and patient control. 'I'll do this side, shall I?'

'Yes,' Sister says. Immediately, the pressure on your limbs and your chest eases. The straps are loosened, then removed. Fighting the temptation to move makes you perspire. But will it hurt if you move? What is actually wrong with you? Cooler air seeps across your body. The sheets are being removed from the bed. Then you are rolled on to your side and lifted up by plastic hands. From beneath you, the sheet is whipped out, and your limp body settles down on to a rubber sheet. It sticks to your skin in places.

'Well, will you look at that, Nurse? All the scars have gone!'

'Oh, she's clever. That doctor.'

'You're not wrong, my love.'

Sponges dripping with hot water and a soapy foam, that smell of lemon and antiseptic, are bathed across your body. They tickle parts of you and in this pretend sleep you are forced to sustain you cannot resist a smile, and must clench your teeth to stop the giggles. The final place they wash is between your legs. That has been saved until last. First they rinse warm water under your balls and then two sponges get busy with your thatch and hard cock. You can hear the two women breathing harder now. Under their squeaky clothes, they seem to rustle more. You can imagine the bright red blushes on their cheeks.

After the sponging, you are dried with fluffy towels. When they work at your legs and feet, you dare to look through a tight squint. Stretched out before you, your body looks so pale and your cock so red. The tight bindings are gone from your chest – you can see the hairless skin now. Both of their unmoving faces are distracted by what stands between your thighs. It looks like Nurse has raised her eyebrows in surprise, and Sister has adopted an anticipatory frown as if calculating how to proceed. You begin to wonder what your face looks like. You thought you knew, but no, you don't. Your face is a blur, a smudge in your memory. But, without that last gassing, your mind is slowly wakening. It's like layers of cotton wool are being unwrapped from your thoughts. The inside of your head feels cooler.

Once they are done with drying you off, they move to your waist. They both lower their smooth faces to study your erect cock. Their tight backsides stick out on either side of the bed. You clench your cock muscles. One of the medical staff makes a little 'ooh' sound. You think it was Nurse. But it is definitely Sister's breath, coming so fast from her mouth and nose now, that makes your groin hot. Slowly at first, but then with more confidence and relish, they lick your shaft. Even at the root where it joins your sac, where the shivers start, and between your balls and legs, two tongues go to work. And now Nurse has plopped both of your testes right inside her mouth and is making an 'mmming' sound through her perfect snub nose. It's like there is a scent or taste to your parts that makes them ravenous. They seem starved of this peculiar meat. Occasionally their heads knock against each other and there is a hiss or snarl. They back away from each other, angling their heads, with their rubber hands going into tight little fists. The stand-off never lasts for long; their greed gets the better of them. Tentatively, they always resume the licking.

First Nurse sucks your cock, then Sister takes a turn. She won't let go, though. You like Sister's mouth for sure, but like to watch Nurse sucking even more. It's the way she bends over with one foot placed behind the other, her weight supported on the toes of the first foot, her shiny thighs all tight and her hard buttocks sticking out from the bed. Nurse really puts her entire body into the sucking, whereas Sister maintains a sort of poise with her ankles locked together and one little finger on her left hand sticking upright, as though she is sipping a fine tea.

Nurse loses her patience with the inadequacies of the clumsy sharing arrangement. She struts up to your head and lowers that part of the bed. Slowly, you feel the top half of your body descending. She has lowered you back to the horizontal. Through the tight squint, you see her clamber up on your bed and then kneel astride your face. A wide valley of shining thigh muscle confronts you. At the apex, the crotch of her tights is see-through, but there is no dark triangle of fur behind the sheer fabric of her hose. Instead, you can see a pinky, hairless slit, squashed flat. She lowers it on to your mouth. You smell her; rubber, nylon, perfume, soapy salts. Unable to resist, your tongue gets busy. She sounds surprised. 'Oh, gosh,' she says to herself, when your tongue laps and flicks at her pinky inverted lips.

Sister continues to fastidiously suck you with even strokes; the pace never alters. Up and down goes her bright, frowning face. At the base of your cock, that she has taken all for herself, she rings a finger and thumb and then massages you with little squeezes. You feel yourself approach climax and suck harder at Nurse's sex, wishing you could break through the thin sheen of her tights. Nurse is rubbing herself on your mouth too, quite vigorously. You stop sucking and let her wet your nose, chin and mouth, her tiny pip looking for just the right ridge to rub against. Opening your eyes, taking a risk, you look right up and into her green-gem eyes, as big and bright as ever. They stare right back at you. She has placed one of her fingers between her pouty lips. Girlish squeaks drift out of her mouth. She knows you are awake but continues to pleasure herself, until she comes, squealing.

You groan. Thick bolts of cream pulse from your sex. Sister's lips are at the bottom of your cock. You can feel them forming a tight circle. All of you is inside her head when you come. She keeps her head still and takes it all. Greedy bully.

When Nurse sits herself at the foot of the bed, fanning her slick face, Sister makes ready to clamber on to your head so that she too can rub herself into a frenzy, but the door opens. Sister snaps her body rigid and stands away from the bed. Discreetly, Nurse pulls the sheet up to cover your naked lower half.

'How is he?' the intruder asks, her tone sharp. You hear her high-heeled shoes tap and rap across the cold tiles towards where you lie.

'Very good, Doctor. We were just bathing him,' Sister answers.

'Such a strong boy,' Nurse adds.

'Good.' This doctor's voice is familiar. For some reason, your spirits sink when you hear it. 'Is he under?'

'All the time, yes,' Sister says.

'Very good. Make sure he never misses a treatment. Any display of defiance, resistance, disobedience?'

'No, he really is an angel,' Sister says.

'No post-traumatic stress? Flashbacks?'

'Not at all, Doctor.'

'Very well. Don't let me stop you or he'll get cold. And get the chair ready. I want him out of this bed tomorrow. We don't want his muscles atrophying. He has to be strong for the operation.'

'Yes, Doctor,' Sister says, and you feel her hands, soon joined by the longer fingers of Nurse, as they begin to remake the bed. The straps are reapplied.

'You can leave me with him now,' the doctor says, when they are finished.

As Nurse tightens the last strap across your breastbone, she whispers, 'I know. I saw you,' in your ear. You freeze and feel all cold under the sheets, but she leaves with Sister and does not appear to have told the doctor that you held your breath back on the gassing.

The doctor pulls a chair up to your bedside. She reaches out and holds your hand. You dare a squint. A mistake. You nearly make a sound at the sight of her face. Unable to remember specifics, you still manage to associate its thin beauty with extreme emotions; terror, intimidation, excitement, desire. She has no hair. This too is familiar, but today, her skin is plainer-looking than that of the other staff. There is no gloss to it, and yet you remember a time when it was shiny like the faces of Nurse and Sister, as if it were wrapped in a layer of something invisible but for the shine. It's all so puzzling.

'Oh, my Angel. It's so good to have you here,' she says. Her voice makes you feel warm. You dismiss your initial caution. She is kind; she even called you an angel. 'We'll never argue again, darling. Once the treatment is finished, you'll be so happy here with me. Like the others are.' She leans across you and kisses your forehead. Her lips feel good. You want them on your mouth. She kisses your mouth. It is so tempting to return the kiss; to respond to your doctor, your healer, your protector, but you don't on account of fooling the gassing. You feel guilty. She strokes your forehead. 'It's always difficult in the beginning. Your nurse and the ward sister were the same too, a long time ago.' She laughs. A high, musical laugh. 'They were so angry when they saw how beautiful I'd made them. They had difficulty comprehending how perfect, how ageless they had become. The world would never have understood such beauty. So I keep them here with me. Like you.' She kisses you again and then lays her shaven head on your chest.

Eleven

Sister is walking in front of your wheelchair. You like the way she walks with her chin up and her dainty arms held straight against her body. She is moving with mincing steps because her blue skin-dress is so tight around her thighs. Through the shiny rubber clinging to her bottom is an impression of the suspenders she wears underneath. As her knees rub together, they hiss. You can't see her face, but you know this fearless woman is frowning her way down the long white corridor.

You are strapped into a wheelchair and Nurse pushes you. Just now, you cheated on the gassing and held your breath. That makes six times and your head is much clearer for it. And if you look down to your right, you can see all of Nurse's long feet. Her toenails are red; her stockings white; her shoes are spiky platforms with toe and ankle straps made from clear rubber. You like this new clarity of mind and vision; you see all the little details on Nurse and Sister's outfits.

After a long bath, and an even longer suck from two slippery mouths, they lifted you from the bed and sat you in the wheelchair, cuffing your ankles to the frame and then your wrists to the padded armrests. The cuffs are made from dark leather. They wheeled you out of your room – home for so long now – and into this corridor. You guess the doctor wants to see you.

At the end of the corridor, on the right side, you are wheeled to a door. Sister holds a wrist up to an ID pad. With a swishy sound the metal door opens and you are wheeled through the door. This new room is huge; you only get a quick look because Sister turns around and you have to close your eyes again. What you glimpsed, though, was a vast room with many lights set into the ceiling. The whole thing was tiled white. There were computers on one side, a big operating table in the middle of the room, and in the far corner you saw bars – steel bars – but had to close your eyes before you were able to determine was this curious thing actually is. It looked like a cage.

Like your room and the corridor, this place is a sterile white. But there is a strange smell in here that doesn't match the bleached colour. Damn it. From where do you know this smell? Like wet straw. Yes. And meat. That's right. There is a meaty smell in here also. Like fresh sweating meatiness. Just a whiff of it. It's coming from the corner with the bars. You are about to steal another peek, when you hear the doctor's voice. 'You've done so well, girls. Our Angel's looking much much better. The colour's back in his cheeks.' You keep your eyes closed because you sense they are all looking at you right now.

'Yes, thank you, Doctor. See how all that nasty grey has gone from his complexion,' Sister says.

'All the scar tissue has vanished,' the doctor says quietly, as if with satisfaction but only to herself. You have an instinct (or is it memory?) that she often speaks out loud to herself.

'Shall I rouse him?' Sister asks.

'No. Not yet. Take him to my office. I'll deal with him there. I have a few things to finish in here.'

'Yes, Doctor.' You are wheeled around and then pushed in another direction. Behind you, in the distance, you hear something big begin to shuffle about on heavy feet. The sound is distant and you reckon it's coming from that corner of the room with the meaty-sweat smell. What is that? And there's a growl; deep and guttural. Like ... like ... a large animal would make. But this growl you hear is almost a word too. Sounds like 'Dagha'.

Behind you, the doctor speaks softly to someone. 'Magnus, my darling. This is a new member of our community.' Then she says. 'Wait a moment, Nurse.' Nurse stops pushing and wheels you around to face the far corner with the cage. You feel that the doctor and Sister are probably looking at your face, so you have to keep those damned eyes closed. 'This is Angel,' the doctor says. 'He's coming to live with us too.'

Big hands bang against metal bars. Behind you, Nurse gasps. After the sudden explosion of violence, the growling starts up again. It threatens to become a roar. As it vibrates along the tiled floor and comes up through the wheels of your chair, you sense a great strength in this room. You are about to risk a peek at what they keep – this Magnus thing – in the cage when the doctor says, 'Better take him out, Sister. I don't want Magnus upset. It seems he's not quite ready for our Angel.'

'Yes, Doctor.' Sister sounds relieved she has been dismissed.

You are wheeled around again and then pushed quickly through the room. Both Sister and Nurse, who is still pushing, are behind your back. You get a fix on their positions because you can hear them muttering to each other.

'Did you feed Magnus this morning?' Sister asks. 'He seems so restless. More than ever.'

214

Now you open your eyes and see yourself being pushed out of the doctor's laboratory.

'Yes,' Nurse says. 'But you mustn't be angry with me, Sister, when I just throw it through the bars. I don't like him. Not one bit. I'm not going in there ever again with the food. He gets so excited. And it's not the meat he gets frisky about. It's me.'

'I know, dear. I know.' Sister's voice is kindly. 'But don't let the doctor catch you out. You know any tardiness with Magnus makes her furious. We are to treat him like one of us. At least make the pretence. You just keep on smiling that lovely smile when you go in there. Sometimes I know it's hard, but you keep on smiling.'

'Yes, Sister. I will, Sister. But he frightens me. He's dangerous.' Nurse starts to sniff a bit.

'I know, dear. I know. There, there, child. There, there.' Sister is patting Nurse's arm. Behind your head, you can hear the patter of a rubber glove on a rubber forearm. 'He can't get out of that cage. You and me, and this little Angel of ours, are all safe. There's no need to worry.'

Nurse sniffs a bit more, then she says, 'Does . . . Well, it's hardly my place to ask, Sister. But does she go in with him? The doctor, does she?' You stiffen up. You have to swallow to ease the tightness in your throat. Nurse continues, 'Only sometimes I hear things. And in the mornings, when I hose Magnus down, I've seen her things in there. You know, her underclothes.'

'Now hush, girl. You hush up that talk. That talk is nonsense talk. I don't want to hear that talk. Especially with sleepy Angel here. That's none of our business. The doctor knows best. She does right by all of us.'

'Yes, Sister.' And then there is silence behind you.

The wheelchair is stopped by another steel door. Sister swipes her wrist over the plate beside the door. There is a swish and you are pushed into the doctor's office.

You were still pretending to be asleep – gassed into submission – when the doctor waves a metal lozenge, no bigger than a lipstick, under your nose. You know what this object is because Sister once used it to snap you awake from the sleepiness that arises from the gassing. But as you are already awake, and have not taken that dreamy gas inside your body for what would be two days and nights now, whatever shoots up your nostrils stings your sinuses. You cry out and shake your head. The stimulant slips through the delicate membranes at the top of your nose and then disperses right into your brain. Something goes hiss. There is a pop at the back of your skull. A flash of white lightning follows in your head and then your vision swims for a short time. You are left dizzy. The metal lozenge has jolted something loose inside your brain. Your eyes go wide. The doctor is in front of you, but for a second or two you don't see her, you see other things. You look inwards.

You see a dark room with a bed against one wall. There are a few books on a table, nothing more. It looks familiar. But before you can concentrate and force your recall, you visualise a long narrow strip of water and a bridge that crosses over it. It distracts you. Again, this is something you once knew well. Desperately, you want to know where these places are. Too much gas; they gave you too much gas. Will these fragments ever make sense?

The flashes continue. You remember a city where the buildings are tall – magnificent edifices of silver, blue glass and white stone. A hot red sun bakes the beautiful streets and the palm trees between the buildings. Often, black rain falls here too. And when you recall a girl with big yellow eyes and a long nose something twists in your stomach. A tautness, lasting no longer than a hiccup, occurs behind your breastbone, and then the image of her is replaced by other women, many women, who are undressing, or dressing, or writhing under you. But their skin and clothes lack the glossiness of Nurse, Sister and the doctor. Their skin looks more like your skin.

The doctor's face comes back into focus. 'Do you recognise me?' she asks.

You blink the flashing fragments away and say, 'No.' But then you nod your head. 'Yes. I mean . . . I don't know from where, though.'

She smiles. She reaches out and grasps your hand. 'And that's all you need to know. It's all right. You're just starting again.'

'Again?' you ask.

She nods; her expression serious and yet enthusiastic. 'Yes. Once you lived outside of here, in a terrible place, Angel. And you were hurt there. You were damaged, Angel. That's why we brought you here to heal. And Nurse and Sister helped to make you strong again so you can start over. Start again. There is no other place for you. But you're not alone in this. A long time ago, Nurse and Sister had a similar problem and had to come and live with me. They started over, too, and have never been happier. Same with my twin boys. You haven't met them yet. They work upstairs in my house. Like you, they needed a refuge. What I'm trying to say to you is that you are safe now, and that second chances are wonderful. So few are offered new beginnings so they can escape the trauma of their old lives or ways.' For a moment, she continues to look serious, but then laughs to hide the suggestion of immodesty in her tone. This doctor-philanthropist, who seems to have rescued so many people, slows her speech right down as she elaborates. 'And then there is Magnus. A very special guest. Just like you. You'll become friends, too. Do you understand me?'

For some reason that is a question you have always hated. But still, you nod.

'Soon you'll get used to all of us and your new home. You'll like it. I promise you that. You'll never want to leave. We all keep each other company here.' She strokes your hand. She uncrosses her legs. You watch them. Skin-tight rubber, so shiny it catches all the light, covers her from toe to neck. There seems to be no room between this rubber and her real skin underneath, like with Nurse's white suit. You think the doctor's skin must be so warm underneath. Over her lovely face and hairless head there is a pinkish gloss, too. It's as if she wears a very fine hood of rubber, but you're damned if you can see any creases or joins.

The doctor unbuckles your cuffs. First on your wrists, then on your ankles. She helps you stand. Then she leads you over to the bed beside her desk. There is a green plastic curtain on a narrow rail, scrunched up in one corner. When you stand beside the bed, you are unsteady on your feet. It's been so long since you stood upright. As you totter and waver on your bare feet, she peels your tight T-shirt up your body. You raise your arms and she gently tugs it from off your head and then from your hands.

Her long fingernails trace red impressions down your hairless chest and hard stomach. The nails are painted black and look good against your pallid skin. They go inside the waistband of your white shorts. One finger touches your already stiff cock. The contact creates a shiver that travels up your spine to the back of your skull. Her shiny face comes real close. Her glossy lips part. You watch the pink tip of her tongue hover between her lips. Using both hands, she slides your shorts down. As she lowers her face to push your shorts down to your ankles, she keeps her eyes on yours. They look deep.

'Here, no one is ashamed of who they are. You'll see lots of new things, Angel. Here, you can experience so much. See it as an adventure. Keep that fresh, new mind open. Take a leap of imagination. The rest of us have. Sometimes, we may even hurt each other, but in a nice way. You should see Sister go at that lovely smiling nurse. You'd think she hated that poor sweet girl, but they are in love. They have been since the time I helped them to become so beautiful.'

She stops herself. 'Look at me, confusing you with so much information all in one go. After all you've been through, I should know better. But having you here gets me so excited. In time, it'll all be clear. I promise.'

She continues to look into your eyes until her mouth is right beside your cock. She touches her lips with her tongue. Now they look wet. She lowers her long-lashed eyes and stares right at your sex. She almost seems to be suffering, like she's looking at something that hurts her, and yet you feel she would never be without it. You feel good about this part of your body. All the girls in this place have helped you to feel this way. And this bit of you feels so good when it's inside their mouths. Like this one right now. Her lips flatten around the hard muscle behind your phallus; an unseen tongue lashes the underside of your shaft; saliva pools; there is a sudden loss of air and atmosphere down there, and you feel a gentle tug around your sex, like you've just dipped your sex into a river current. You sigh.

The doctor moans, as though she's eating something delicious. Her sharp fingers curl around your naked buttocks. The edge of a nail tickles the puckered outside of your anus. You clench up inside and then slip your hands around the back of her head. It feels warm and slippery in your hands. More of you is taken inside her deep mouth. Her cheeks go hollow and you can hear her breathing through her nose. Then her head slides all the way back down your length until only her pursed lips are touching the tip of your cock.

She stands up, smiling with pride and satisfaction. It was just a taster, then; something she needed. Perhaps a test on your response to her. Yes, you feel she is testing you for resistance. Not asking questions was a good idea. Intuition tells you this woman only wants you to listen to her and to accept whatever she provides. She seems to intuit the curiosity you have for her. 'I knew you before you had the terrible accident, Angel,' she says. 'We were in love.' She slides her face against your cheek and whispers into your ear. 'You used to fuck me, Angel.' Her arms slip around your back; you hold her waist. She closes her eyes and you kiss each other for a long time. Although the defined silhouette of her body looks so rigid in the tight black suit, she actually feels soft against your naked front. Gently, she rubs her stomach against your cock.

When she pulls her mouth away and opens her eyes, she says, 'Fuck me now,' then steps away from you and leans against the bed. 'I want your skin on mine. It's been a while since I've felt it all over me.' She peels the black skin-suit from her throat to her waist. As it opens, your eyes are smitten with the small breasts she has; pert, white, pink-nippled. 'Sometimes Magnus can be rough on a girl. He scratches and bites. So I need protection. It's one of the reasons I wear this suit. But I want to feel your skin again, Angel, as you fuck me.' She slips her thumbs under the shiny skin, when it has collected around her waist, and then pushes the rubber down to her knees where her boots begin. The skin-suit peels into a narrow furrow in her hands. Her legs remain black and glassy, though. She has very fine stockings on her long legs. The sight of them and the thought of how warm they must be, after baking inside that skin-suit, make you a little dizzy.

Carefully, you walk towards the doctor and her eyes go wild when she sees how excited you have become. Sitting on the bed, she unzips her boots and removes them from her feet. Then she strips the rest of the suit off her legs and toes. You look down at her and study her pink doll face. It has a similar sheen to that of the faces of the medical staff, only the doctor's features command more movement – more than one expression.

When she is stripped down to her stockings, you feel a little faint with excitement. With her you sense that loving is always good and, even though Sister and Nurse sucked you into a fatigue this morning, you feel not just ready, but desperate to love her.

As she stands up, she kind of jumps at you. You catch her and she wraps her arms and legs around your body. You hold her off the ground and lose yourself in the pleasure of her mouth. Squeezing her body against yourself, you feel her breasts squash into your chest muscles. When her legs encircle your waist, you spread your feet to support her weight. Slipping a hand down between your legs, she grips your cock and then eases it up at an angle so the head goes inside her sex. As she does this she winces. Her mouth opens wide as you penetrate through her, but she doesn't even breathe.

Then she says, 'Oh, God,' and places her hands in your hands and leans her whole body away from you. Her head rests on the bed. 'Stay still,' she says; her stare is so intense you have to look away every few seconds. But you obey her and remain motionless, even though the temptation to really thrust at her is great.

By tightening her legs on your buttocks and waist, she presses her sex against your crotch. The end of your cock is against the back of her womb, and she begins to rub, then grind the edges of her sex around the hard and floss-covered bones of your groin. 'Be soft,' she says. 'Be soft today, Angel. That's right: just hold me up and I'll do the rest.'

When you relax it feels good. The exquisite sensation of your hard flesh inside her sex is prolonged, tortuously, because there is little friction. Her movements on your cock are slow and circular. Slowly, you begin to grind with her. A rhythm is found. She rolls her shiny head about on the mattress and her fingernails dig into the palms of your hands.

'Make me ready, Angel. Make me ready for Magnus.'

This makes you freeze up, unsure whether you like this idea. She senses your resistance because your little grinds have stopped. Her eyes open. 'Sometimes you will be hard with me, Angel. When you're much stronger. Other times it is Magnus who must be rough with Doctor. Don't be jealous, darling. He needs so much attention now. It's not a good idea to leave him without company for long. You see, he longs to mate. That is what he wants.'

She gets excited just talking about it. Her eyes close. 'He must be serviced today. It's only right before I offer him a real companion of his own to keep. A new mate. Someone who will be there for him always. You'll see. So make me ready, my sweet Angel. Make me tender.' Already she is dreaming or pretending this Magnus is inside her. This makes you angry because you are being used, and yet you become excited by her appetite. A beautiful woman having these thoughts and motivations thrills you. You begin to pump at her. 'Slow, be slow,' she says. You comply, but push her further up the bed. Collecting her legs, you put her ankles on your shoulders, seize her hips and then put the short, hard pumps into her.

She bites the side of her hand for a while and then says, 'Tell me when you're ready, Angel.' She stares at you, her face tensing. 'I want you in my mouth when you're ready.' Her saying this makes you ready.

'Now,' you say, and it's an effort to choke that word out. You pull out of her sex, although the temptation to stay inside and to release your seed nearly overpowers you. Dropping her legs from your shoulders, the doctor slithers off the bed and falls to her knees. Two beats from her hand, fisted about your shaft, and out it surges. You drop your head, dizzy. The world goes reddish and then stays dark for a few seconds. Holding her mouth an inch from the tip of your phallus, she readies herself to collect. You watch your cream spit between her shiny, red lips. She throttles your cock up and down, pumps it in her hand, then shakes it, empties it, until a pearly-pool covers her tongue. Her lips and eyes close at the same time. She swallows.

You cannot stop yourself staring at this creature. But to look is to know terror.

Creases furrow the expanse of his brow. Dark eyes, intense like those of a wild dog alert to a presence, peer out from the rear of the deep brown sockets.

Flat-nosed, thick-lipped, black-bearded, the tremendous face on the slightly elongated head moves behind the bars of the cage as he walks sidewards to keep pace with your steps through the room. No sound is made by the ogre's feet as he stalks the straw and cement floor. Held by the hand, the doctor takes you closer to the cage.

His animal smell gets sharper in your nose and you can see his body in greater detail. Only the pale nipples in the shag of his chest-growth offer any suggestion of vulnerability. The rest is bestial. All six feet of the body is hirsute – brushed by a silky down of goatish black hair. On the legs – columns corded and cut by muscle – the hair is thickest and resembles fur. Between the solid thighs grows a tangle of hair and from this undergrowth hangs a purplish-brown trunk. Although it is at peace now, you recoil at the brutish dimensions and at the suggestion of what damage it could wreak.

The savage angles its head – an artist's image of a shaggy prehistoric prophet. You can see the rudiments of intelligence in its face. It ponders and fathoms. Below the cavernous nostrils, widening to inhale whatever scent betrays you, moisture glistens in the fat brush of his moustache. From one great hand a melon is dropped. You are momentarily relieved that it is only fruit that the creature has been eating until you hear the sound of the melon as it hits the cage-floor, like a wet skull, and does not bounce. Magnus grins when he sees you flinch. Black lips peel over yellow monkey teeth. You suddenly want to shriek to relieve the tension, and you want to run, lock the door after you, and pray this thing will not follow you through your dreams.

'Cro Magnus, you are beautiful,' the doctor says. She stands beside you and has tilted her head back, her eyes narrow, her senses overawed. She squeezes your hand to offer reassurance and then moves to the cage on the toes of her boots – an unarmed scientist about to conduct dangerous fieldwork that you are compelled to watch. And only when she is near the bars of the cage do the terrible brown eyes of Magnus leave you alone. Suddenly, they are keen for her – wide, wild – and the vast mouth issues a groan of longing. It dares to reach through the bars for her, but she has stopped just out of its reach. She murmurs soothing words to it. Its groan dies. There is tenderness in its expression now.

The doctor speaks to you. 'Angel. I want you to stay where you are. Strangers can panic Magnus. Don't move when I go in with him. No matter what you see.' Her last words sound forlorn. They seem familiar in tone and also intent. You close your eyes and dip your head. It was there for only a moment and now it has gone. But for a second you saw a dark place near a great body of water. It was like a cave. There was a fire inside. A dangerous place. You sat helpless while a woman walked away from you, towards this fire. Was that woman the doctor?

You watch the doctor unlock the cage door and then slip inside, her heels and suit so shiny against the dull features of the straw and the hairy giant who stands in it, risen to his full height with chest thrust out. His nostrils – white at the rim – flare. The awful lips draw back. Once you watched other figures – matted, slouched, Simian – surround a passive woman. This woman? Yes, it is the doctor you remember. She gave herself to those creatures around the fire. Back then you were unable to look away. Same thing now.

Quickly, the door swings shut and locks behind her. Slowly now, she walks to the creature, her head

225

bowed, her hands held together before her stomach, fingers entwined. There is a strange calm about her. With long fingers, Magnus reaches out and touches her head. Then he moves her face from side to side; a touch of familiarity. A rough mind perceives great beauty. You cringe inside at the sight of the small, pale and beautiful head cradled in those black, melon-crushing paws. How delicate she looks; bone china rudely held by primitive hands.

The doctor has closed her eyes and not because she cannot bear to watch, but because she is so excited; putting herself in the dark adds to her anticipatory pleasure. Handled more roughly, she is then pulled up and against the shaggy body. Her boot-heels leave the floor. Baton-like, hard, unfeasibly long, the great sex is squashed between her shiny rubber breasts and the creature's stomach.

'He is the last of three, my Angel,' the doctor says, her voice strained.

You are puzzled why at this terrible moment she would think of you, but it is important to her that you watch the ritual, as you know you did before.

'People wanted Magnus destroyed. They wanted to hurt him after so much time was spent bringing him back. Like you, Angel, my darling Angel, I had to rescue him. I –'

But the scent of this slender offering, and the softness of it experienced by these savage claws, ends the moment of tense restraint. In a heartbeat, the doctor is seized about the buttocks and raised up to the creature's flat-topped skull. Her legs part and slide over its shoulders. Suddenly inflamed by the scent of you between her legs, the creature buries its long jaw between her thighs and you hear the mouth begin to slurp. She is playing a dangerous game, you realise. It lifted her like a doll – its fragile mate – and

226

has smelled the spoor of a rival. The doctor cries out and her small head drops back between her shoulders; joyously resigned. Shock spreads a frost all over your body. Even the hair follicles in your scalp crackle.

It swings her down to the straw where the great hands begin to maul at the doctor's now writhing body. The thin shield of rubber is stripped from around her throat. Under the noise of its ragged breath and scuffling knees, you can just hear the sounds she utters. They are stilted cries; caught in the pale throat of the female mate who has been set upon and prepared for the delivery of a barbaric seed. Tugged up to her knees, more of her body comes back into view; her slight figure, nipples hard and red, straw clings to her naked ribs, her buttocks are exposed, the tops of her stockings peek above the ruffle of rubber which now acts as a tight restraint around her knees, and prevents her from crawling away or kicking out at the black thing now mounting her curved spine.

She is stuck – held by the shoulders and then seized about the chest – she has no choice but to receive. Her face flushes a bright crimson; her teeth clench; a long and warbling moan issues through her open mouth. Now she is animal, too – joined via vagina and womb to an ancestor. In its cock sinks, a long purple bridge, steadily descending until it completely disappears from view. The dense primate crotch meets the smooth buttocks of the doctor. She becomes wordless and communicates her mating cry through moans and then deeper groans, that gradually become rhythmic as the Cro Magnon man begins to push and then pull at her, his eyes going wide from brown to white. The shaggy hair and long beard begin to sway. The great fingers encircle her waist and then tighten. She is raised from the ground and yanked back on to the hideous spear in its loins. There is pain in her cries, but something else too. Something you have never before heard. A sound so hard and loud it would be difficult to ever imagine it passing through the elegant and painted mouth of a woman – a professional woman – a High Zone woman.

They fascinate you. Always have. You understand this now, but know you have never fully understood them or what they want. And, regardless of what precisely this cry communicates, you will always remember it in intimate moments, and will acknowledge some urge in yourself to truly serve and coax it out from within a woman. Because that is your purpose – to pursue their ancient and unfathomable mystery – and to touch them at this most secret level, as Magnus has done to the doctor.

You stiffen. Through all the shock and horror at what you have seen – this sudden unleashing of ancestral desire on the floor of a cage – you feel the brute force of Magnus rise inside you. Suddenly, you want to possess the doctor. She has trained you, because she wants to be shared.

The two figures buck and writhe in the straw. He slaps at her white buttocks as he thrusts. The wallop of his leathery palms on her skin drowns out the noise of the choking and sobbing sounds she makes, face-down in the cage. Along her back, this creature then stretches his body and she is engulfed, pressed down, until all you can see beneath the rutting beast is the heel of a patent boot, a thin arm, and a clenched fist. When the great face raises from the small pale head of the doctor, it roars, and then moans more softly. Your eyes are drawn to the hairy buttocks of Magnus. You watch these great slabs of brawn tighten and pump until both of the figures become still. And in the end, after Magnus says, 'Dagha,' there is no motion in the cage save the slowing rise and fall of the exhausted lovers' chests.

A hand is placed on your left elbow. You turn your head to look to the left, but quickly become distracted by the impression of a second hand on your right shoulder. You smell perfume. Nurse and Sister have come to take you back to your room. Nurse smiles at you but crowds her tall body behind your shoulder – she doesn't want to look at the creature in the cage, now stroking the head of its exhausted mate. Sister frowns at the sight of the two figures. Perhaps her frown is too contemplative to be disapproving, and maybe those lovely but cruel eyes have lingered for too long on what has befallen the doctor in the grasp of the creature resurrected from extinction in order to mate with her. You wonder, does she dream of submitting to this beast?

As you leave the laboratory, without a second look back, you cannot feel your legs.

Twelve

'Oh, my Angel, I'm so pleased with you,' Sister says, as he steps out from under the shower head, his body cleansed and still steaming. She embraces him with a fresh bath sheet made from white towelling. He pulls it under his chin and smiles a secret smile she cannot see because she has bent over to begin drying him off. Making him lift one foot from the tiles, followed by the other, she starts down there, then does his shins, thighs, bottom, and between his legs – always a good vigorous scrub there – before her thorough hands travel up his back and chest to his face and hair. He closes his eyes and lets her work, enjoying the impression of every one of her water-resistant fingers – hard-working fingers, and yet these digits show no wear. The nails are manicured to an eye-catching gloss that is never tarnished, and the flesh retains a ladylike pallor that no sun will ever brown.

'Never had such a strong one in my care,' she says, with her hand wrapped around his cock, with only a thin layer of towel between. 'That's the truth of it. It's a wonder to watch you, boy. You've surprised us all. The doctor is so pleased with you. I can always tell when she's smiling on the phone, my dear. You know, she checks in every evening and says, "Sister, how is my darling boy? Is he well?" And I tell her how good you've been. Eating all your food, taking your medicine, doing the exercises. And tomorrow you'll be even better than you were before you came to us as such a poorly boy. The doctor is making a special trip down here to fix you. It's your big day. We'll all be sorry when you're off the ward. Nurse, particularly, has a soft spot for you, my lad. I've had words with that girl on more than one occasion.' She lifts the towel and playfully spanks his bottom. Then she guides him from the shower room to the dressing facility beside the swimming pool, where he must put on the white shirt and shorts and rubber flip-flops. 'All this hair must come off tonight, my precious.' Sister musses the hair on his head. 'It'll break my heart doing it. And that Nurse will be in tears, I wager, but it'll grow back soon enough.'

He smiles again, but she doesn't know the real reason why.

Now his scrotum tightens with anticipatory glee — part fear, part exhilaration. He knows what follows his daily work-out and shower. He is led, as usual, to his room for the bedtime ritual. This is conducted before the gassing begins that he always cheats on. When Sister swipes him into his room, he sees that Nurse is already waiting beside the bed.

A glance is exchanged between Nurse and Sister. At the periphery of his vision, he then sees Sister nod once at Nurse before Sister closes the door. Any time now, it'll happen. He can hardly breathe for excitement. He swallows and feels his stomach flop over. This happens most evenings; especially since the doctor has been away. He hasn't seen her since the night Magnus embraced her, behind bars in the straw. But before they gas him, these pretty benefactors like to pounce. And he welcomes the ambush — if nothing else, his compliance convinces these model-medics that all is going well with his treatment, and that he is becoming a big dummy with fat balls, a hard body, and a good heavy poundage of meat between his legs. Just what the doctor ordered. And as far as this pair know, he cannot remember anything because of the amnesia gas. But they're wrong; he remembers everything now. That's why he can't help smiling at some of the things Sister assumes about his fate, as if he's agreed to this future, or as if the doctor's plans are in his best interests. And because they're so confident he's been successfully gassed to a condition of living servitude, they have become negligent. Been a week since he'd last taken the gas inside his lungs and everything he was meant to forget has come back.

At first the recollections were fragmentary – he saw faces and felt the associations, but struggled with names. But it didn't take long for the fragments to swell and then break into a head-spinning gush of recollection that eventually became a deluge of history – his own history. And each morning when he remembered more of who he was, where he was from, and what precisely the doctor had done to bring him to this place, he has gone from terror and panic to a silent despair. But from the heartache for all that he has lost, a rage has grown, and he has done all he can to keep his head and to maintain the illusion of living servitude. While restraining the need for revenge that burns like indigestion behind his breastbone, his spirit has grown stronger.

Complementing his mental recovery has been the re-emergence of his physical prowess. On the running machine, or when lifting weights in a mini-gymnasium, or propelling himself up and down an underground pool, his muscles have quickly grown hard in a matter of days where they had softened in the bed-ridden state. And his heart and lungs have stretched through the pain barrier to regain their prior capacity and stamina.

Accompanied by the astonished and ever-complimentary Sister and Nurse, he has been clever enough to assume the ignorance and gullibility he'd been suspected of throughout his whole life. As far as they know, he too has become one of the unquestioning devotees of Madelaine Sutton. Whenever those beautiful doll faces gaze at his perspiring face on the treadmill, he knows they are searching for any anomaly in his behaviour, such as confusion, or the bafflement caused by flashbacks. They have been trained to look for all of these and he must be careful what he exhibits. He smiles adoringly at them and says nothing. Silence and love are all he reveals – the miracles of the doctor's healing hands.

And fairly soon, after the medical staff have started coming to him every night since his internment – alone or together, but always so determined to retrain his sexuality and realign his tastes to all the good things the doctor enjoys from her servants – Angel has realised these strange twins in rubber cannot hear a word he says. Just as their unmoving faces and unblinking eyes fail to respond to his tongue between their shiny thighs, or his hard cock between their buttocks, or his greedy hands inside their plastic blouses, getting busy with their lactating, doughy balloon-breasts, their ears are dead to his voice. During these long and sticky hours of additional treatment they provide after the day's work is done, he has realised their small alabaster ears have been tampered with. Along with the transformation of their skin, breasts, and faces to sex-doll-loveliness, their ears are now only attuned to one frequency – that of the doctor's voice.

So who had these curious creatures once been? He often ponders, when left alone in the dark, fatigued

233

and often sore after a visit. Were they companions manipulated and experimented upon through an investment project? He'd never know because they didn't know. They had awoken from a long sleep into new lives. Reincarnated in rubber, they answered only to the names of Nurse or Sister from one voice. Blithe and unconcerned pleasure kittens, coated in a sheen of latex; this is what the great doctor has transformed them into – new female companions, one dominant, one submissive, both durable, highly sexed and as deviant as their creator. This is their new beginning. Between their assigned tasks, which they carry out fastidiously, only the incidents of amorous mischief suggest any vestige of free will within their lovely heads. Without the oblivion gas – the pacifier, the repressor, the opiate of her control – Angel suddenly understands their tragedy. The true horror of their lives seems greater than his own grievances with the doctor.

Same thing has happened with those twin boys – she has altered them to the point when she possesses absolute control. They never come downstairs, but Angel remembers their automatic responses and their unquestioning obedience to the doctor before his *accident*. And he too is to join these obedient ranks. That is the plan. The treatment of gas was designed to pacify him and to take away his memory temporarily until the operation tomorrow fixes him on a permanent basis. Almost every day now, Sister makes some comment about him 'needing to be strong for the big day'. And tonight she has spoken of plans to shave his head. He too is to become a living doll in this toy house where Cro Magnon savages have been summoned out of graves gone cold for millennia. It will be a huge disappointment to the doctor, he thinks, when she discovers he has other ideas.

From healers to masseurs to trainers, these curious glossy companions now become his jailers. They are making the most of him while he's here – he knows this. And it always happens so quickly. Nurse gets her hands with the tacky touch inside his shirt and pulls it over his head. For a moment he cannot see, but hears Sister wheel the steel trolley that he used to be fed from across the door to delay an intruder. Then she runs the green plastic curtain all the way around his bed as an additional precaution against a disturbance. Meanwhile, Nurse secures him inside this green, rubber-smelling corral of curtain. The shirt is pulled from his head and then she clutches his wrists. Behind his back, she ties them off with a length of rubber tubing. Between his jaws, she jams her salty knickers – white rubber he can taste for days afterwards. When he was tied to the bed, or strapped into that wheelchair, things were easier for these girls, but now he's up and mobile and so strong after the exercise programme and power diet, they don't take any risks, just in case he doesn't like the treatment.

Their breathing gets hard now and he can smell a sharp edge to the air in his room – like expensive rubber, as if long boots have been peeled down longer legs. Sister dims the lights. Nurse leaps at him.

Sister shouts, 'Wait!' as Nurse whips his shorts down and is about to start the action without consulting her.

Here it comes; third night running. Quickly, Sister covers the ground to Nurse on her heels and slaps Nurse hard across the cheek. Nurse returns two slaps; the first is parried, the second hits Sister's shoulder. Calmly, Angel steps out of his shorts, kicks them off his feet and leans back against a wall to watch the fight. Sister slaps Nurse's face again. Nurse gets her hands up under Sister's hat and screws her fingers into her superior's hair. Sister's eyes water but she does not blink. And though she wears the tight blue dress and black high-heeled shoes, Sister still manages to get her knee into Nurse's tight white-rubberised stomach. At the same time she shoves the palm of her hand under the junior's chin, to push her lovely head back. Sister will win. When they fight, the outcome has become predictable: Sister wins; Nurse suffers the consequences.

Angel watches them squeak and grunt and thump and slap their way around his bed. Their skirts ride up; their hats are knocked to the floor, and their hair is pulled free from the tight arrangements to hang, silky and tousled, about their lovely faces. It amuses him and while he thinks on what he'll do to them – these foolish girls in rubber uniforms – he grows hard.

When the fight squelches to a sudden end, Nurse is bent over the bed, her hair mussed, hands splayed, red cheeks all teary, legs apart, stocking tops on display, lack of underwear revealed. Sister holds the back of Nurse's neck and stands to one side of her buttocks. 'When I tell you to wait, my girl, you better believe I mean it! Every night, you're the same. And now I've got to do this to you. In front of the boy as well. Oh, the shame of it. The shame of it, girl.'

'I'm sorry. I said I'm sorry –'

Sister's hand meets Nurse's backside with a tremendous slapping sound. 'Sorry's no good any more, girl.'

'Well, I just can't help myself. The boy is so nice and all, Sister,' she says, cantering from one foot to the other.

'Aye. But he's not yours to take. He belongs to the doctor, and you'll get us both in a right mess, the way you carry on!' Slaps follow. Many strokes. Sister

236

pulls her arm right back behind her own tousled head and then slams the hand home. Every blow is merciless – no swing is checked, no punch pulled. Furiously, she continues to belt Nurse until her arm tires of dispensing the correctional treatment. When the blows have been delivered and the sobbing Nurse subdued, the frowning Sister rearranges her hair and catches her breath.

Angel smiles. Tonight is perfect for what he has in mind. In mind! His own mind; mercifully recaptured after being gas-diffused for so long. But for how long? He doesn't know. Besides the week in which he's steadily clawed his memory back, he has no real concept of the time he's spent below ground. And if he remains here another day he is lost for ever, and will never know what happened to the pretty girl whose yellow eyes he started to see in dreams, long before he remembered her name: Salina.

Slowly, with her chin angled upwards and her thick lips pouting, Sister moves across to Angel. She seeks his lips and tongue. Both are freely given once Nurse's panties are removed from his mouth. But as he kisses Sister he keeps one eye on Nurse, who has straightened up beside the bed and now gently massages her buttocks. She was in such a haste to leap upon him that she has failed to secure his wrists tight enough behind his back. This has happened before. Angel flexes his wrists and knows he should be able to wriggle his hands free without too much fuss.

Sister's hands encircle his cock. Then they begin to pull at it. He breaks from the kiss and looks down to see her glossy red nails gripping his silky skin.

'You like?' Sister whispers.

He nods. She removes one hand from his sex and unleashes her breasts. The dress parts from an invisible seam that runs between her cleavage to her belly. Soft, white, and thick-nippled, her breasts bobble before his eyes as Sister slowly rotates her chest, hypnotising her prey. Angel lowers his face and takes a hard nipple into his mouth. For a moment it is salty, but then it just feels warm and has no taste. This is such a sensitive part of the ward sister's body. She drops her head back and moans. Angel swaps his mouth to the other breast.

Beside them, he notices that Nurse has crept forwards. Back straight, head angled down as if to hide the keen and devious look on her smiling face, she has already removed her tiny white dress. It now looks like a discarded swimming costume on the white tiles beside a pool. She stalks forwards, dressed in a see-through white bra and matching garter belt, stockings and heels. As Angel sucks on the sister's left breast, he can see Nurse through the gap between the sister's arm and ribs. Immediately, his eyes are drawn to the pinky-edged slit between Nurse's legs. Nurse touches herself there and a little shudder, barely perceptible to the naked eye, passes through her body. Angel grows harder.

With a finger underneath his chin, Sister raises his face. Her eyes seem wider and brighter than ever. She leans against him, one hand around his neck, the other stroking his cock, and turns his attention to the hovering figure of Nurse, who has moved even closer.

Sister turns her face and begins to whisper to Angel. 'I do believe, I know what she wants tonight.'

Angel stays quiet. Down here, his words mean nothing.

Sister continues with her quiet confessional tone. Opposite them, Nurse angles her head, trying to overhear. 'You see,' Sister says, 'she wants to offer you something special. A particular place you have never been before with her. I caught her trying it once when you were asleep. She was trying you on for a fit, but you were too thick to pass through. So when I'm holding her hands together, I want you to slip inside her hole from the back. Do you understand? Of course you do. Don't go into her tight pussy. Try the other place this time. I promised her that you would.'

Angel nods his assent, and then is rewarded with the sight of Sister undressing. She slithers her dress over her hips and then down her thighs. She steps out of the dress, her tipped heels clacking on the hard floor tiles as she moves about. She wears black stockings, high heels, and French knickers through which he can see her white buttocks and neatly trimmed sex.

Both of the dolls have prepared themselves exactingly tonight, intent on pleasing him. He guesses they dressed in secret, each hoping to exceed the other. As it stands, they are both forced to stare at each other in begrudging admiration, until Sister beckons Nurse towards her with one curling finger. Timid at first, Nurse looks about the floor by her feet, but soon cannot contain her excitement at the prospect of being naughty, and tiptoes across to her superior. Sister takes Nurse's wrists and leads her to the bed, where she tries to bend Nurse over as if to deliver another spanking. Only this time, when Nurse displays a feeble reticence and struggles to keep her back straight, Sister corrects with that stern frown. After just one look, Nurse knows better; she acquiesces and bends her body over the bed, her pert buttocks upright.

With a tube of salve in her hand, Sister then prepares Angel's penis. She lathers the lubricant over his erection. It feels cold until Sister rubs it deeper into his flesh. Something similar was once applied to his cock by the doctor. Nervous, Nurse begins to look over her shoulder. Sister has deliberately manoeuvred him into position so Nurse can see her executioner having his tool prepared. Absentmindedly, Nurse begins to rotate her backside, sensing an imminent insertion between her buttocks.

Sister whispers, 'Be hard with her,' into Angel's ear, and then moves around to the other side of his bed, so she can secure the Nurse's wrists within her own hands. Nurse uselessly raises one high-heeled foot from the floor. Angel steps forwards. The tip of his cock nudges her backside.

Nurse suddenly inhales and a rash of prickles runs across Angel's scalp. Sister nods at Angel.

'No,' Nurse whimpers, but it's too late.

Standing on his tiptoes and then lowering himself, Angel works without the use of his hands to centre his slippery phallus against the centre of her anus. When he finds the spot he pushes at it by leaning forwards. At first there is a great resistance, but then he's through the seal and almost feels as if he's disappeared into an incredibly spacious cavity. For Nurse, it seems to have been the tightest fit of all time. She tries to pull her arms free from Sister's hands, but fails. She gives up the struggle and then drops her head to the mattress, where she bites the bedclothes. Sister's face beams with delight: a pre-conditioned sadist getting her own way.

Angel moves through Nurse slowly, balancing his weight on the balls of his feet. He doesn't want to come right away and has to fight the desire to ejaculate immediately. Friction from the tight fit, the sight of Sister holding Nurse down, the additional view of Nurse's penetrated buttocks, and her long stocking-sheathed legs before him, nearly conquer his self-restraint. He closes his eyes and stills the pumping. This is good for Nurse, who it appears is losing her virginity. It gives her a moment to accustom herself to the dimensions of the long appendage being applied through her rear. She takes advantage of the pause and gently eases her backside in a small rotation around the thickness inside her.

She begins to say, 'Yes. Oh, yes,' into the bed-clothes, now smeared red with her lipstick.

Angel's urge to explode subsides. Gradually, he increases the force of his passage through Nurse.

'Mmm, yes. Mmmm, yes. Mmmmm, yes,' Nurse says, and then, 'Oh, Sister. It's so good. You wouldn't believe how wet I am.'

Without releasing the Nurse's arms, Sister leans across the bed and begins to passionately kiss the captive's face. She is excited, and he suspects it was her idea all along and not some illicit craving of Nurse to be taken in this manner. Angel smiles; a part of him will miss them.

He can hear their tongues furiously slapping and all of the little nose-grunts they produce. In accordance with this delightful sound, he speeds up his hip action, until he's ramming himself in and out of the Nurse at some considerable speed. This ends the kiss with Sister because Nurse has so much to concentrate upon. Sister grits her teeth too, but begins to hiss encouragement to Angel. 'Harder. Go on, be harder with her. Harder still. That's it, nearly there. Now harder! Really hard! Hard!' Angel complies. Nurse shrieks, her legs seems to collapse, but then she is laughing wildly, up on her toes and banging her buttocks backwards against his abdomen. He comes, resisting the urge to throw off his bonds and seize her hips.

'Have you? Did you? Is it inside her?' Sister asks Angel. He nods and collapses over Nurse's back, without withdrawing from her stretched anus. Nurse likes the embrace and begins to nuzzle her lovely blonde head against Angel's face. She can still feel him pumping inside her and makes a sweet little sound every time he throbs. He kisses her cheek. She purrs. Amazingly, though he senses it is begrudging, Sister allows this post-coital fraternisation. But not for long.

She makes her way to Angel's side of the bed and bends down to inspect his now softening cock, still buried inside the Nurse. Her breathing quickens. Reaching out, she seizes Angel's shoulders and pulls him around to face her. After sinking to her knees, she then holds his cock before her lips in one trembling hand. She stares at it for a moment, and then feeds it into her own mouth. Stunned, he watches. Behind him, Nurse makes dreamy murmuring sounds.

Finally, Sister sits back on to her knees and begins to pant. With her tongue she dabs around her gums and underneath her lips, savouring the taste from the connection she has forced between her two lovers. This is clearly something she has wanted for some time. Before he can allow himself to be overwhelmed by the strange creature on her knees, with these curious impulses that must flash through her immaculate head, he crouches down in front of her and decides to initiate the next stage of his plan.

He begins to kiss her mouth and smooth, smooth face. As he nibbles her ears and kisses her throat, he shakes the rubber tourniquet from off his wrists. Slowly, while Sister's eyes are closed in delight, he then clasps his hands on to her naked breasts and teases her nipples between her fingers and thumbs. Sister moans and begins to rub her hands all over his back until she feels the need to claw at his hair. When she stands up, she pushes her neat mound on to his face.

At once, his tongue is busy; lazily lapping through her salty folds, or pressing soft lips into her slick flesh. Soon, she is smeared all over his chin. This is the last time he will love her, so he begins to stroke her legs, slippery in nylons, making the most of this body that has both delighted and fascinated him during his stay. Up and over her calf muscles, behind her hot knees and across the length of her thighs his hands explore until he reaches her squishy buttocks. Continuing to pleasure her sex with his mouth – gently sucking her lips now – he presses her anal bud with one inquisitive fingertip.

Instantly, Sister's breath seizes up and her body goes stiff. He removes the finger, licks her clit-pip more vigorously, and then pushes the finger against her anus again. This time she is more receptive and begins to groan appreciatively – even once the finger is inside her tight, hot, rubber body.

But Sister is clever; he underestimates her at his peril. He must do more than just double-guess her desires; he must think like her and yet still proceed with caution. When he stands up he initiates a kiss on her mouth again, while continuing to move her towards climax by burrowing a finger inside her sex and then corkscrewing it in and out. Greedily and appreciatively, she laps at her own salty juice now drying on his lips. Nurse is sitting up on the bed. Over the Sister's shoulder, he sees the latex-minx angle her head to the side in order to watch his untied hands.

Making a split-second decision before Nurse queries his freely moving hands, he is forced to leave Sister, so dangerously close to her peak, and begins to kiss Nurse, who responds with renewed delight at his renewed attentiveness. Gently, he pushes her shoulders down so she is lying flat on the bed with her legs draped over the side. Quickly, he then turns and collects Sister in his arms, whom he senses is already on the verge of a jealous episode. He kisses her some more and reinserts his fingers inside her pushing sex. With her long tongue again active in his mouth, he carefully manoeuvres her between Nurse's legs.

Massaging her breasts with one hand and screwing two fingers from his other hand in and out of her sex, he watches Sister close her eyes and feels her go limp against his body. He then bends her over, puts his hand on the back of her head, and pushes it into Nurse's shaven sex. There is a tense moment; Sister opens her eyes and begins to mentally question Angel's sudden initiative. Before she can speak, he winks at Nurse, who giggles and then eases her exposed sex against the sister's mouth. He has guessed right. Whenever there are no patients to seduce, bully, and generally abuse, Nurse and Sister have learned to adapt to pleasuring each other in the underground facility. He knows the doctor would never have created anything as beautiful as this pair of nightmare dollies that were not adaptable to a host of deviant purposes. His intuition has served him correct: between Nurse's legs Sister begins to pleasure her underling with some passion.

Nurse drops her head and begins to writhe her body about on the bed as a very fine tongue casually writhes around that teeny button that so often leads her astray. For a while they are lost to each other, and, as the lights have been dimmed, Angel unhooks the gas nozzle from the fixture by his headboard. He lets it rest on the pillow and then returns his hands to their business of pleasuring the sister's breasts. Squeezing and moulding them through his hands – these delightful cushions that breast-fed him back to health and vigour – he moves his fully erect sex between the cheeks of her buttocks. Spurred on by the suggestion that something truly deviant is about to befall her, Sister's head begins to move more quickly between Nurse's legs. One by one, he takes his hands away from Sister's breasts. Placing one hand on her coccyx, and the other around the top of his cock, he pushes his penis against her anus. Sister raises her head and cries out. And yet, with one leg, she reaches backwards and twists it around his calf muscle in encouragement: *It will hurt me, but I want it.*

With a smile of victory forming on his face, Angel then breaks into Sister's beautiful body. And he does not stop pushing down with his hips and buttocks until his pubic hair is flattened against her cheeks. For a long time something resembling a wheeze is uttered from Sister's suddenly oval lips. It never breaks into a shriek or a scream, but remains as an almost silent howl.

Filled with a passion for revenge, as he suspected she might be, Nurse squeals like a child with the devil inside her, and immediately seizes Sister's shoulders to hold her down. After pulling her legs behind her, Nurse then rises on her knees and uses all of her weight to anchor the now-struggling sister to the bed by pressing down on her shoulders. Dominatrix of the lower wards take it all, Nurse's smile seems to suggest. And the frowning madam, the dispenser of slaps and reprimands, the strutter on spike heels, the midnight sucker of cocks, the manipulator and the dictator, does just that. Sister takes all of Angel in a forbidden place, deeply too, and while her entire body bucks and writhes against the mattress she realises she cannot pull her arms free.

With one hand, Angel digs his fingers under her hips and holds her backside steady so his strokes can be even, unbroken and plunged to a depth. With his

245

other hand, he reaches down between her legs and feels her sex. Never has she been this moist; the inside of her latex thighs are slick and even the tops of her stockings are now damp. He takes his time and allows the climax to build back through him. With two fingers he gently presses Sister's little tendon down and then rubs it with the pads of his fingers, all the time thumping his solid meat through her slippery rectum. She comes, croaking and spluttering, the moment she feels the muscles in his cock throb, shaking out those long strands of white cream inside her newly plundered rear, that she can see with her mind's eye.

Nurse throws her head back and laughs like a maniac, but stops the noise the moment she inhales the first lungful of gas from the plastic mouthpiece that Angel has cupped across her chin and nose. He has leaned right across the sister's oblivious, exhausted body to do this. When Nurse passes out, silent and smiling, into a foetal position beside her mistress's slowly moving face-down head, Angel removes the cup. Deftly, he then raises Sister's chin with one hand and gasses her mouth with the rubber cup. There is a brief struggle in which she tries to wriggle free, and in which he hears one or two muffled but incomprehensible words collect inside the cloudy rubber mouthpiece, but the weight of his body across her back holds her in place until she has inhaled her share.

Gently, he lifts Sister's sleeping body from the cold tiles and places her beside Nurse on the bed. With the strand of rubber tubing, he ties their stocking-clad ankles together. For a moment, and for no longer than a few seconds, he stares down at them and wonders if his life would have been easier down here with these pretty dolls, never lacking in sensual excess or fulfilment. He leans over and kisses each of his captors, once on the lips and then once each on their impossibly unmarked foreheads. The moment of doubt passes.

Thirteen

Through the white-tiled kingdom of the doctor's
underground complex, he runs free. Barefoot, having
discarded his noisy flip-flops, he scurries from the
room they kept him in for so long. In his left fist he
carries Sister's communicator and has stuffed Nurse's
wristband in the back pocket of his shorts, to stall
their escape when they eventually wake. He finds that
Sister's bracelet opens all of the doors this side of the
building.

Finding a way back to the surface is not the only
thing Angel seeks. The girl the doctor took from him,
the night she shot him in his own home, could be
trapped here too. If Salina is not being held captive,
then she would be dead; there is no doubt in his mind.
And what would the disappearance of two companions from the townships make to anyone? The doctor
had legally bought him, and he had signed a disclaimer
allowing her to modify him in any way she chose.

Salina? Now, that was kidnap. But who would
report it – her employers? He couldn't imagine M
getting it together to make a report, and Quinny – the
professor – would probably assume she'd tired of his
games and run off. He figured the doctor's only
concern was leaving a witness to the shooting. An
investigation of a shooting could lead to an exposure
of what she had been working on down here.

Strict guidelines ruled genetic modification – even the military imposed standards – and for good reason: too many abominations had been uncovered in private facilities. Genes were tampered with for enhanced procreation, or disease prevention, and some cosmetic improvements were allowed, but cross-species hybrids and anything that could further imbalance what remained of the harassed natural world was strictly forbidden. Even Angel knew that. And what would the world make of Cro Magnon and the transformation of two young women to the doll-like entities of the Nurse and Sister? The doctor would lose more than her licence to practise; she would be imprisoned. As for Salina's chances of survival, from what he knew of the doctor, she would incorporate a young and healthy female specimen into her work before she would destroy her. That would be the only reason Salina still breathed.

Body tense, propelling himself off the balls of his feet, he flits along the side of the building he has spent most of his time within. The enormous operating theatre is central to the complex. He guesses other captives would be housed near rehabilitation like he was, in the rooms of the doctor's legitimate patients, if there ever were such things. The first room he opens is the staff quarters. They must be close to any other prisoners.

A hidden camera in his room, he realises immediately, has been piping visuals on to a large screen in the staff chambers all along. Off duty, Sister still had the facility to monitor him. On this screen, he can see that Nurse and Sister are both still curled up on his bed, appealing in their dishevelled lingerie – one in black, one in white. They should be under for hours. Another three rooms are also under surveillance. On the full-colour screen, split into quarters, he sees they are all much the same as his own; white, well lit, and containing a bed topped with medical equipment, plus one chair. Only in these rooms the beds are all empty. He curses.

Desperation gives him the shakes. His hands become frantic. Locker doors are yanked open, steel cupboards banged until the drawers glide out. Rubber. Everything smells of rubber in here. All he can find is rubber; black, red, blue, white and pink rubber. Lingerie, uniforms, dresses, high-heeled shoes, boots, tourniquets and restraints fill every space. Then there are syringes, mirrors, strange metal braces, salves in tubes, measuring devices. In one set of steel drawers, he finds red floor-length gowns, hoods and black masks. In another, a large strap-on penis with a frightening life-like texture to the latex skin. He slams the draw shut and fights off an image of Sister using the device on Nurse. No time for such a distraction. He looks at their beds. They sleep in single cots; small, grey and institutional furniture on each side of the room.

Momentarily, he is overwhelmed by pity for the beautiful doll-women: their sentence is life. He ponders their free moments in here, and imagines both of them endlessly jabbering in their curious childish discourses before they re-box themselves into their truckle beds – sometimes together. And as he thinks on what the doctor has made them, and had every intention of making him, he bangs his way through the inside of the last storage cabinet. It is in here, amongst the green surgical gowns, that he finds the sign he seeks. In a black plastic bag, sealed and tagged, he finds the outfit of a maid: black dress, white apron, Cuban heels, cap, distinctive seamed stockings. Salina's clothes. Not destroyed, as he suspected they might have been along with his blood-soaked suit, but kept back and stored instead by a curious nurse, perhaps, or even a frowning, inquisitive ward sister.

A lump forms in his throat. He could choke to death on the emotion. He sits on a bed. With these empty rags in his hands, he is overwhelmed by a sense of Salina. The sight of her clothes seems to have abolished the last of the apathy and drowsiness from the sedatives and gas he's been pumped full of. Now, he wants to cry bitterly with grief and rage and frustration. Damp rises to the height of his throat and nose, like the smell of rain, and he tastes misery.

If anything has happened to Salina it is his fault. He'd planned to tell Salina about the doctor, the night he was shot. He'd been desperate to voice his fears about his new direction in life, his lack of control, and to declare his love for the Binton maid, but in his typical, libidinous manner, he'd allowed himself to become distracted by her playful seduction. Why was he so stupid, so slow with everything? Too dreamy. Never concentrating. The story of his life. He had nearly been murdered. How did he get himself into that situation? Expendable, he was to be rooted out of the evolutionary scale. Useless and unskilled, his life amounted to a medical sacrifice, awaiting a lobotomy-ceremony to cancel his simple soul.

And now all that remains of that innocent girl he'd lured into his sordid existence is a plastic bag stuffed with her clothes. The blackest self-loathing fills him. Throughout his entire adult life, it now seems he'd never thought about anything other than sexual gratification. He slumps on the bed, his mortified face in his hands, and wishes he'd never become a companion, or an actor, or manual worker before that, or a charity child that couldn't understand the

251

'confusers'. In fact, he wishes he'd never been born. Throughout his whole life, he's either been used or become utterly dependent on others. The water. Only in the water was he ever free. If he survives this night, he makes a vow to live by the water, away from others.

He flees the staff quarters, throat dry, eyes wide, heart beating fast. He wants to destroy everything. Briefly, he entertains images of fire, of sparking wires and melting steel. Not just down here, but in the merciless world above. Every room; check every room for her. Only this desperate motive keeps him going, onwards, down there, beneath the surface of the earth.

The next three doors he swipes open reveal the empty rooms he has just observed from the monitoring screens in the staff quarters. Scrubbed and sparkling, they have been cleansed of any trace of recent occupancy. After looking into the last of them, he runs down the long concourse until he reaches the giant operating theatre. They brought him down this route in the wheelchair only a few days before. Inner darkness turns the porthole windows in the theatre doors to black holes. He peers inside, his face pressed against a circular pane of glass. Most of the lights on the inside of the theatre are out. Through the windows he can just make out the odd glowing terminal screen, or rashes of red light on the banks of computers against the walls, nothing else. This pleases him – the last thing he wants to do is go in there again and see Magnus.

He follows the corridor around the bottom end of the theatre. If his memory serves him correctly from his journeys in the wheelchair, he will connect with a passage on the other side of the building through which he can enter the doctor's office. Yes, there it is. He runs toward it. Nausea begins to chill his belly.

With a faint swish, the office door opens. Gingerly, he steps inside. He goes cold for a moment. Her fragrance hangs sharp in the controlled air. No, he tells himself, the doctor cannot be here. It's just a lingering residue of her scent. It must be. Sister said the doctor had been away. Surely he would have seen her, had she come back underground – considering she had never been in the habit of leaving him alone. It's the thrill of escape making him jumpy, nothing more.

He moves further inside the office. He sees her desk and the bed where they last made love. Before he tosses the desk drawers, he decides to check the second portal on the far side of the room by the cabinet full of tiny bottles, presuming it is another entrance. He swipes his wrist across the panel. The door opens. It's not a passageway, but an elevator; an escape route up to the ground floor. Relief turns to an exhilaration that makes him want to piss with joy. He could run now and get help. No, he decides. Not until he can be certain of Salina's whereabouts. And anyway, where could he run to? The corporate-backed authority managing his township, or the Leisure.corp agency? Both would immediately return him to his rightful owner without hesitation.

He goes back to the desk. Thinking of the twins upstairs with their expressionless faces and leather gloves, he looks for a weapon in the desk. In the draws on the right side of the desk, he finds glass slides and samples tubes, some surgical implements, electronic devices he can think of no use for, a pair of glasses, tubes, ointments, a tiny laser scalpel, and four sheets of the strange jellied rubber, sealed in perspex boxes, that reminds him of the doctor's pink face that first time she came to him in his room. In the top drawer on the left-hand side, he finds the wrist communicator given to him by the agency.

Beside the communicator, he finds digital photographs. Surprised the doctor would keep such old things, he thumbs through them with clumsy, impatient fingers. He sees her as a younger woman in uniform – military colours. She wears the black uniform of a high rating. Her beauty seems colder and more striking then ever. The style of the clothing seems so old, too. He thinks of her age and how difficult it has become to work out anyone's true years. Could the doctor be old enough to have worn the uniform of the colonial forces? Even if she were in her twenties when the picture was taken, that would make her over seventy now.

In another picture, she wears battle fatigues and is standing in some sort of hospital made from green canvas, with fine nets for the doors that he can see in the background. The picture was taken in a hot country. The doctor seems displeased. Could this be Africa, the land that can no longer support life? There is another picture of her receiving a medal – one of the medals he saw in her city consultancy. A wedding photograph follows.

Angel shakes his head, bemused. Even on the wedding picture she refuses, or is unable, to smile. He pauses in his search, taking a special interest in this image. Never has he seen the doctor looking so noble or so beautiful under the white veil, in her fine-boned aristocratic way, but it is her partner, her husband, that fascinates him the most. He recognises the man standing beside her in the dark suit and hat, but cannot think from where he has seen this man before. A news broadcast, perhaps?

When he hears the sound of the elevator, he freezes. There it is – the gentle sigh of precision machinery fulfilling its given task. The moment the red light ignites on the swipe panel beside the elevator door, he slams the desk drawer shut. Dropping to the cold tiles, he then rolls sidewards and under the cot. Voices and a continuous cry of pain fill the room. Beneath the metal slats and bed springs, Angel squashes his body tight against the far wall and holds his breath.

It is the doctor's voice he recognises first; it rises above the cacophony of moans, the scraping of feet and the heavy breathing of those making a considerable exertion. 'Put him down here. That's best. I'll give him something for the pain. I'll stop the bleeding. Yes, my darling. I won't let you suffer.' Her voice is breaking; she's on the verge of tears. Angel sees three pairs of legs assemble at the side of his bed. The people are struggling to walk three abreast – he can tell by the position of their feet. There are two men wearing identical pairs of black trousers and black shoes with a high shine. But one of the men is injured; his feet are dragging across the floor, and his knees are bent. He is being carried between the other man and the doctor. Her legs are clad in sleek flesh-toned stockings. Down the front of her shins, Angel can see dark splashes. They have been shaken from the body of the man held between the doctor and her accomplice.

Above him, the bed-frame groans as the wounded man, whom he presumes is one of the twins, is laid out. The doctor's legs retreat to the glass-fronted cabinet he saw on the wall beside the elevator door. She takes something from the cabinet and rushes back to the bedside. Soon, the moaning stops. 'Go,' the doctor says to the other man. 'And do what I showed you. Start destroying it. All of it! Deactivate the thermostat and it will corrupt. That bastard is having none of it. The bastard who shot my boy is having none of it!' She is going hysterical.

Angel swallows at the thought of her face and how it can tremble when roused. The able-bodied man seems to pause by the side of his fallen comrade. Angel senses hesitation and confusion in the way his feet shuffle but commit to no particular direction.

'Go, now,' the doctor says. 'Go, now. You must hurry. You can do nothing for him. I'll care for him. I promise. I promise. Don't let them take my work. I'd rather it was destroyed.' She is pleading with the other man now, realising that her panic was only baffling him. He moves to the door and Angel hears her last command. He stiffens in terror. 'After you've destroyed the cultures, get rid of the girls. You'll have to. There's no other way. Use the incinerator. They mustn't find the girls. Oh, God, no. That will be the end of everything. And I'll take care of Magnus and his mate. I'll do it. I'll take care of her and the boy we took. But go. We don't have much time. They'll get in any minute. Please be quick!'

The man disappears and, before the door shuts, Angel hears his feet break into a sprint in the corridor outside. The doctor stays beside the bed for a moment longer, making her final ministrations to the wounded twin, and then she leaves the room in a hurry too, her heels skidding as she flees. Angel remains under the bed, petrified. Above him, the wounded man makes no further sound.

Something has gone wrong for the doctor. A man is dripping blood down the doctor's legs – one of the twins? She has fled down here in a rout – he could hear it in her voice. She has descended into the earth to start destroying evidence; things she is making, things she has already made. Nurse and Sister? No! Are they the girls she wants taken care of? Was an incinerator mentioned?

He thinks of a plastic bag he once saw blown on to an electrified fence. The smell of it was terrible. Can't be. It's all too inhuman. No, it's unacceptable, like the things he's read all about in books that happened in history. It can't be what she means. Or can it? And Magnus? Did she mention that he had a mate – a girl – and the boy *they took*? Was that him? He's guessing. So little is clear. He has to know. Despite the overwhelming desire to stay hidden, he slowly edges his body out from beneath the bed. Lying on the floor, facing the ceiling, he sees a foot hanging from the side of the bed in a black shoe; shiny and inert. Fighting his terror and panic as they try to take hold, he stands up, forcing himself to find courage.

On the bed, it looks like the twin is sleeping. His shirt is red; his face pale. One of his sleeves has been rolled up to his elbow. From his fingers, clad in assassin's leather, Angel pries the gun free. It is much heavier than he expected. He points out in front of his body, his elbow straight, one hot finger lightly touching the trigger, knowing that is how he must use it. The gun feels warm and it smells of sulphur. It has already been used tonight. He feels sick. For a moment, his face screws up and he feels ready to break down. It passes and he is left physically weak and certain there is nothing he can do to stop the terrible events that have been set in motion. He thinks of Nurse and Sister lying helplessly on his bed, awaiting the flames. How they will scream. He can almost see Nurse smiling through her terror as she hugs a frowning, disbelieving Sister. No! He thinks of Magnus and what the doctor said about a 'girl'. Angel clenches his jaw to hold back a scream, and then runs from the office, towards the theatre.

He takes no more than three steps when the lights go out. He stops running and crouches down in the dark passageway. Red emergency lights sputter on and turn the underground facility into the hell it really is. In the distance he hears a dull boom. An explosion. A tremor shakes behind the walls, under the floor and along the ceiling where the red lights start to flicker. In the distance he thinks he hears gunfire too. He stands up and runs the rest of the way to the theatre.

In here, the red lights shine also, but it remains darker than the corridors outside. Perhaps the computer banks and surgical equipment and the long upright tanks of prosthetic flesh absorb too much of the blood-light. He walks forwards slowly, creeping along the walls by the glowing screens, circumnavigating the great operating table, approaching the place he knows the cage to be.

Inside his skull, his thoughts go red as the lights in the ceiling and he thinks of firing the gun through the bars of the cage. 'Salina,' he calls out, certain he is alone now. 'Salina. Are you there?' Now he can smell the straw and the meaty smell. He squints and sees the steel bars, looking wet in the crimson hue. Something moves inside the cage, straight ahead of him now. He raises the gun in the direction of the shape he saw flit through the straw, knowing Magnus can be quick and silent behind those bars. But it seems too thin, too pale to be Cro Magnon. Is that a woman? 'Who are –?'

The air is thumped from his body. He is lifted through the air and then thrown fast at the floor. Consciousness deserts him.

Disorientated, he lies still, not sure where his arms and legs are. The thought of a broken spine adds a nullifying terror to his confusion. He never heard a thing until the last moment, when it was too late. He recalls a quick patter of leathery feet, a grunt, something that sounded like a breeze and then . . . Something thick and so incredibly hard struck the back of his shoulders. His eyes still seemed to be looking straight ahead from the same place he had been previously standing even when he hit the tiles; he'd gone down so fast, his body never registered the blow, until the pain erupted on one side of his face and then moved, jagged and hot, through his back. His vision is still blurred but he sees a great shadow rear above him – its smell is strong, terrible, animal. He thinks about the gun, but realises his hands are empty. He closes his eyes and waits.

'Magnus! No!' the doctor cries out.

The great wind stops just short of his nose. He opens his eyes. Everything judders up and down inside the room. The great shadow withdraws; he hears its feet skitter away, back to the cage. Now he can smell perfume – a blessed relief from the animal stench, until he associates the fragrance with the doctor.

'Did you come back for her? Did you?' she says. He can see her long legs, moon-pale in the dark, only a few feet from his face. He looks up and sees her silhouette – the small head, narrow shoulders, slim hips. All he can see of her face is the moist glisten of two tear-filled eyes. The barrel of a gun presses like a cold ring between his eyes. 'Have I underestimated you?'

He clears his throat. 'I had no choice, ma'am,' he says, remembering his ways as a companion.

'You, too. You betray me. After all I've done. The risks. You betray me.' It is becoming an effort for her to speak – she is breathless with rage. 'They come to take away my work, my community. And you ... You too are a traitor.'

'How can you talk of betrayal?' he answers, a challenge in his voice after swallowing the lump in his throat. Convinced this is the end, he suddenly desires a swift conclusion from a bullet rather than from the prehistoric hands that clench out there in the dark. 'I've been betrayed by everyone. And Salina was all I ever had for myself.'

'She is nothing.'

'You're out of control.'

Her eyes are vague; she stares into some vast inner distance. She doesn't seem to hear him. 'The men who have broken into my home. My home and shot my boy. You're the same.' The doctor looks away. He hears her sniff. 'Get on your feet,' she whispers. He stands. With the gun pressed painfully into his back, she prods him toward the cage. 'I want you to see your sweetheart. See who she belongs to now. She's a mate, Angel. For someone far greater and more unique than either of you could ever be.' He knows she is smiling now; he can tell by the sudden softness in her tone. 'The end will be a relief for both of us. The betrayed.'

'No,' he says.

She laughs and then kisses the side of his face. He pulls away. 'Look,' she says, and points at the cage. She holds a thin torch, turned off. 'Before it ends, Angel, you must look.' She switches the torch on. He hears it click and a beam of white light shoots out from her hand and passes between the bars of the cage. The gun presses sharp into the back of his head. He winces. 'Look,' she says in a deeper voice. Angel's eyes follow the light and see where it falls. He can do nothing but whimper.

From inside the den, two pairs of eyes squint at the torch light. One pair, brown and wild, shrink back inside their deep sockets and a stomach-floor groan of anger is heard in the theatre. The second set of eyes – yellow as those of a giant cat and nobly situated on either side of a long Persian nose – recoil as the pretty

260

head, crowned with ringlets of tousled hair withdraws into the broad, furred chest of something that should not be. Magnus has fled back to his lair to protect his mate. Between its great muscled legs, and long corded arms, black with fur, he can see the slender white body of a woman.

The doctor leaves him standing there in shock. She takes a few steps backwards and relaxes the arm holding the gun. 'So what do you matter now, sweet Angel? In the scheme of this world that we have learned to change, what does your heart matter?'

He regains his breath, but it remains taut, emotion threatening to disrupt. 'It stopped me from being evil. Like you.'

The doctor laughs. 'Oh, darling, I shall miss you.' She raises her arm. Somewhere, a door swishes open. He closes his eyes.

'And I have missed you!' a voice calls out; baritone, cask-conditioned by brandy and cigars. Angel has heard this voice before. Beams of light hit Angel and the doctor from all around the theatre; white lights originating from the gun barrels of the figures in black, who stream through the door and then hunch down into combat crouches. Red emergency light from the ceiling glints dully on their weapons. Behind the doctor, only one figure stands tall. He smokes a cigarette and wears a white shirt under his dark suit. 'My darling, had I known you had worked such new miracles I would have come sooner, and alone. But you forced my hand. You've been indiscreet again, my dear. You always did get so carried away.' He moves closer, keeping the doctor distracted with his voice.

She trembles, white with rage. Slowly she removes the aim of her pistol from Angel's face and points it at the chest of the outspoken intruder. All of the armed men who accompany him tense. Angel anticipates gunfire.

The man comes to a standstill ten feet from the doctor. Even in the weak reddish light, Angel can see that his eyes are completely black; as startling as they were the day he first made the doctor's acquaintance in the magnificence of Zone One, and the only detail missing from the wedding photo. 'Why must this always be so dramatic?' he says. 'Can we not argue like an ordinary couple? Why must you try my patience in this way? Have I not been an understanding and tolerant husband?' He smiles as he speaks, unafraid. 'I've seen the girls. You are a genius. Their skin, my dear. You finally refined it. And now they are safe. It was foolish what you asked the boy to do to such marvellous creations. We stopped him.'

The doctor is unsteady on her feet. She loses balance and Angel almost thinks of overpowering her. 'You hurt him, too,' the doctor cries out. 'Both my boys.'

'Yours?' the black-eyed man answers. 'They all belong to something bigger than us. Have you forgotten the debt you owe the company? Have you forgotten just who has protected you thus far, my dear? Allowed you to indulge yourself? To play as creatively as you work, my genius? So put the weapon down, darling. It's so vulgar that we should confront each other in this manner, and my men are very protective. If you even twitch I'll be a widower. And where will I find such an extraordinary wife again?'

'Bastard,' she says.

On the floor Angel watches, bemused, until he becomes conscious of movement, near to the ground, against the far wall. Something catches in his throat when he thinks of great feet stalking through the straw. 'It's in here again,' Angel says aloud. But his warning comes too late.

Suddenly, from the far side of the room, there is a crunching sound – sickening – as if a giant bunch of celery has been twisted in half. One of the white torch beams rakes the walls and ceiling before it drops to the floor to shine a random beam under the operating table. The doctor screams, 'Magnus!' and the room erupts into gunfire.

Angel flattens himself against the floor; his hands cover the back of his head. The doctor is taken down, caught around the waist by her husband and pulled to the ground. From every side he hears glass shattering, metal dinting, and hot cartridges bouncing off cold white tiles. On his belly, he begins to squirm towards the cage. Above him, metal whips and zings through the air. Something bellows. The roar becomes a long, anguished moan, before it falls silent. The heavy thump of a great body striking the ground sends a vibration through Angel's crawling body. The gunshots stop abruptly.

In a sudden and unnatural moment of silence, he reaches the cage and climbs in through the open door. He goes looking for the girl. In the distance he hears a woman begin to wail – the noise of one suddenly ruined by grief. It is the doctor in defeat. He finds Salina in a corner; her golden eyes are wide with terror; her skin is bruised and begrimed. She reeks of meat and straw. She shows no sign of recognition when he smiles.

Fourteen

'Mmm. Gently,' Salina whispers, after Angel unfastens the white bikini bra she wears without a shirt. The silk looks particularly bright next to her skin that has tanned so quickly in the sun down here. He looks at her, his face showing concern; has her body been left delicate there? And is this the start of her remembering the weeks of her captivity?

Salina smiles to reassure him that his fears are unfounded. The bottom drops out from his stomach. She can still do that, make his stomach vanish with that smile of hers, involving such bright teeth and the impression of bashfulness that appears around her eyes, or in them – he's never sure.

She bites her bottom lip when he takes her nipple between his lips. One of her teeth sinks into the thick purple flesh of the bottom lip and she closes her eyes. Softly and noiselessly, he lavishes all the affection and desire he feels for this girl into the kisses and suckles he applies to each breast in turn. Deftly, as he adores her nipples with his mouth, she unhooks her long, wrap-around skirt. The skirt parts at the side and suddenly a long, browned leg is warm against his forearm. Raising her buttocks to allow the flowing material an easy separation from her body, she offers an invitation. She has taken to wearing these skirts from morning until night; on the beach, idling in the hammock on their front deck, walking around the cliff tops, on trips to the village shop, lazing around the house as he attends to her. And, even when she exercises, the patterned silk about her hips and fine legs sways and rustles with this new element of freedom he sees in her, growing stronger as each day passes and as time increases the distance between them and the Zones.

'Can I kiss you now?' he asks. She frowns at the welcome nuisance of his teasing. 'Here?' he says, and presses a finger against the front of her bikini briefs. They feel warm to the underside of his finger. She turns her head to the side, opens one eye, and then smiles down at where he lies, propped up on one elbow, his upper body curled across her waist. 'Well, can I?' he asks, head angled to the side.

'Why do you make me say it?' she says, beginning to laugh.

'I have to be sure,' he answers and, gently, he moves her legs further apart. She frowns again and then bites her finger in anticipation of the exquisite pleasure he has learned to give her.

'Yes. I want to feel your mouth there,' she says, her cheeks flushed now. She stares at him intently, studying the way his eyes widen in rapture after he takes a final, characteristic look up her body, during that last moment before she feels his mouth on her sex. And she knows he adores her and she doesn't want to think too hard about the future in case she imagines a time when they can't be this close with the melody of the sea ever-present outside of their bedroom, lounge and garden – the places where they make love the most.

As is his habit, he runs his tongue about between the lips of her sex – playful, barely touching her tenderness, she never knowing on which spot his tongue-tip will rifle next. As his lazy tongue darts and dabs, she lifts her head an inch from the cushions, and moans. Encouraged by her sounds and eager for the taste of her, he then laps through her lips from bottom to top with the full breadth of his broad tongue, humming ever so quietly through his nose. And at this point she always feels that wonderful shudder in her body, triggered by anticipation and excitement. And he never rushes down there; often won't remove his face from between her thighs until he's made her writhe with her weight on the back of her head and on her shoulders in the twisted sheets or flattened grass of their lawn. Their lawn.

With her little moans and coaxing hands and shuffling body, she has shown him the map of her parts and how they all need to be attended to. This has taken time but, nearing the end of their first month together by the sovereign coast, that commodity has not been in short supply. In fact, for the first time in their lives they have been able to put the anxieties of their old lives aside, in order to enjoy each moment as lovers.

Little thought has been given to the past; less to the future. How they live and how they find meaning and purpose in each day has changed somehow. Perhaps now, they live by sensation far more than by conscious thought, as they once did in the city Zones. But not everything has changed so fundamentally for Angel; some things have not altered. He still needs to express his ever-active and imaginative urges for a woman, for belonging, for being accepted, desired, loved, wanted by her. And it was not more than three hours ago, when he surprised her in the kitchen. Then it was rough, even his approach, coming up behind her like that.

She could tell he was trying to hold back, to go slowly, because of his tender concern for what she cannot remember, for what happened before they were given this little home, so far away from everything. But she let him know she wanted to be handled like that, on the table top, on a hard, thick, solid wooden table top with the kitchen door open to welcome the ocean breeze. Losing herself in his near rage of passion, she had climbed up his back and over his buttocks with her legs and hands like she had never done before. Clawing him, goading him on with the salacious requests that now flow so freely from her mouth, she made sure his lunges were quick and savage. Inexplicably, and more often than ever before, she required it this way. It seemed necessary, as if something buried beneath the surface of her mind demanded a firmer touch.

Right now, this afternoon on their long bed so close to the floor, it is slower. At least it will start that way, and in an hour maybe they would head for a crescendo. But first, he pleasures her with his mouth before anything else can occur. As he licks the side of the reddy hood, at the top of her sex, to push little currents of motion through its protective cowl so they judder and nudge the pip of treasure inside, her legs lock straight and long underneath his body. With two of his fingers probing deep, tickling and slipping through her, she begins to make a moaning sound that fills the room, and she shows no concern for uttering them as loudly as she pleases. And when she comes, as he pushes her further into her peak by moving his whole head for that final, lasting, fastidious, aggressive suckle, tears line her red cheeks.

After she has stopped breathing so hard, and looks so sleepy with her head turned into the pillow coverlets, he strokes her stomach, ribs, the under-curve of her breasts, and then moves further up her body and into a position where he can enter her. By pushing deep inside, all in one long motion – slow but firm enough to suggest no compromise – she rouses and begins to tug at his hair. She always pulls his hair or claws his shoulders. It's like she's holding on. Swept away by the force inside her, one little fragment of her instinct for self-preservation still reaches out and clings to a part of him as if for dear life. And then he whispers to her, and covers her body with the hard shape of his chest, and she is picked up by the strength in his hips as he withdraws, and squashed so pleasingly back down to the bed as he thrusts.

When he comes, she always knows. He tells her. 'Baby, I need to come inside you. Can I?'

'Yes.' And when she gives him the answer, her teeth, as usual, are clamped together. But he kisses her and unlocks her jaw and teeth – insists on kissing her mouth hard as every surge and spurt of his seed bolts into her womb.

Lying together in a half-sleep until an empty stomach or a full bladder stirs them, she keeps him inside, stoppering that cream she wants to absorb. And today, in his post-coital dreaminess, he thinks of the doctor and realises, as each day passes and he manages to love Salina freely and without the risk of intrusion, he can finally think of the doctor without a sense of dread or despair. She was a nightmare that left him hard and yearning for an exquisite but self-destructive game. Sometimes he still dreams of her, and not even these dreams can exaggerate her danger or beauty or power. Is this real? he often thinks too, now he is beyond the force of the doctor's will, and is living beside the sea he had dreamed of his whole life but never actually seen. This life he and Salina possess, is it truly safe from her?

According to her husband, Lord Sutton, they are truly free.

Now, he is even able to visualise the doctor without his chest tightening, and without those reckless impulses surfacing inside – that confusion of terror and longing. The last time he saw her, she was sitting in the back of a long car. Wearing a veil and black pillbox hat, she had looked straight ahead, as if something glimpsed a mile away, through the windscreen, had caught her attention. Disinterested, or perhaps forgetful of what exactly she had done, she never turned her head once to look at him or Salina, as they stood on the windy landing strip at first light, two refugees with a collection of bags, beside the man with black eyes – the lord with the marriage to the doctor Angel had struggled to comprehend, and could only understand through his own contradictory feelings for the doctor. It was like all the intelligence these people had put into changing the world had done something to the way they loved each other.

Wearing sunglasses, perhaps to hide his devil eyes, Lord Sutton waited with them for the transport, intended for a destination he promised would fulfil every expectation that Angel cherished about life beside the greatest body of water. But Angel had remained suspicious with this bargain struck with another being from the highest Zones. This could have been a one-way trip to a secluded location where they, and their memories with them, would have been destroyed. But they had no choice. Another risk had to be taken. After their liberation from the complex, Salina required expert medical help to reverse the effects of the pacifying medication she had been pumped full of, and the doctor's ownership of Angel reverted straight back to Leisure.corp if the investment procedure terminated within the three-month warranty, which it had. Their only chance of freedom and of gaining access to his funds were through the man with black eyes.

Even after Angel had opened the front door of the cottage on the cliff top, where they had been flown – the wood panels painted a light blue like the shallows of the shore when the sunlight was strong – and gone inside to be greeted by the smells of salt-bleached wood, and wind-smoothed stone, he had remained wary. Only after the transport had taken off and left them marooned by the coast, and no assailants were found to be waiting in any of the bedrooms with the wooden floors and long white curtains, nor any tiny cameras uncovered in the simple lights, or microphones embedded in the plain walls, did he finally relax and believe that the doctor's husband had kept his word: that in return for their silence and permanent exile from the Zones, they would want for nothing if all they required was the sea, simple food, peace and each other.

And the doctor's husband spurned Angel's thanks because he believed he alone owed the debt. One week after their rescue, when there seemed to be some puzzlement as to what should be done with Angel and Salina, while they were contained and monitored in a second medical installation, the doctor's husband had made his full confession to Angel. During a walk through the hospital grounds, with two dark-suited bodyguards walking close behind their lord, he admitted that it was he who had altered the course of Angel's life, using him as a probe to entertain, distract and finally spy on his own wife. His life as a companion was this one man's method of monitoring an estranged and eccentric spouse; a genius, an international figure, an important genetic innovator who had gone rogue. And the husband had witnessed everything from the moment Angel was first assessed and interviewed by Leisure.corp, right through to his final encounters in the research facility. Every rendezvous had been filmed; every expression of his curiosity, trepidation, horror and desire had been recorded; every idle moment surveyed. There had been cameras in the offices, cars and buildings, even one in his room and one inside his communicator.

'I was thrilled by your performance,' Black Eyes had said, as they strolled across the unnaturally green lawns of the hospital sanctuary. 'And, for such a hopeless actor, you had me captivated. I had my doubts about you in the early days of the investigation. But you surpassed even the most optimistic predictions. I found myself unable to miss a moment. I feel close to you. Attached somehow. Few have gotten so close to Madelaine and lived. You see I could never be a part of that side to her life. Nothing beyond an observational role is, shall I say, practical.

'And she could never be incarcerated because she is a genius, young man. Even now, I forget some of her achievements. They have been so numerous. And in our age, genius has to be protected. If I was not there to guard it, nurture it, and finally keep it in check, then others would have interfered because of this dark side to her genius. And that side to my wife's nature has become quite extraordinary as time has passed. Both in her work and in her recreation. It could even be argued they are one and the same thing for her now. She has become more of an artist than a scientist. For that reason alone, I am forced to observe her. So I ask you, in all sincerity and with genuine concern for your future happiness, never to mention what you have seen to anyone. It must be as if you have forgotten, or even better, as if it had never happened.'

'You have my word,' Angel had said, acknowledging the warning and grasping at the unexpected leniency from one so powerful – a small price and compromise for paradise.

'Good fellow.' Black Eyes was taking a risk by letting them live. But this man liked his sport. 'Apologies for leaving things until the last minute,' he'd added, with a smile. 'But we lost contact when your communicator was removed after that rather unfortunate incident in your room. And then I waited. Hesitated. It was a difficult decision to break into my wife's home. To be discreet and pull out as if she had never been there. To get in before our employers did. That would have been unfortunate for her. So the thanks, you understand, is all mine. I've seen everything that happened to you. Heard it, too. It could be argued, you even took three bullets for me. Through your sacrifice I learned I had to act. We are still close, she and I. Very close. But time, with so much time we have now, who knows how we will behave?'

'Did she know?' he'd asked. 'About being watched?'

'Of course she suspected. Exactly when and how I was present, she never knew. And for that reason it was vital your performance remained supremely natural. Had you known we were using you as a monitoring aid, it would never have worked. Spontaneity would have been lacking from the venture and she would have intuited your insincerity. As it happened, you were perfect. Once you had displayed such an aptitude for your training, we manipulated the introduction.'

'How does she feel now?'

Black Eyes had looked uncomfortable for a moment. 'She likes to punish me. By going to such extremes with others. There is pride in her defeat.' He had smiled then, with his own pride. 'There have been many other of her adventures I have been forced to chronicle. Understand that in my community, the longer we all live, the more common these rather sophisticated arrangements have become between husbands and wives. It may be hard for you to –'

'No. It's not,' Angel had said. 'I know about your community. You showed it to me. Remember?'

'Yes, quite.'

They had walked together in silence for some time following the lord's confession, and Angel realised the man was considering his one wish, struggling to believe in Angel and the simplicity of his request. It was too good to be true; too perfect for the inevitable cover-up that must have followed the doctor's disgrace. 'And all you want in return for banishment is this place by the sea? With the books and so forth? There are a few freehold towns left but, I warn you, it's an undeveloped region. The Wessex coast has paid dearly for its independence. Entertainments are rare. They still use prehistoric communications. Some say it still resembles the old world in every way.'

'It's perfect. We don't want to come back. Ever.'

'As you wish.' And as he said this, he'd seemed satisfied with Angel's motives, as if he'd read the truth in the young man's face.

Before they departed for the coast and left the Zones for ever, he'd asked Black Eyes a final question, about what had become of the twins, and of Nurse and Sister, but the man had met his inquiry with a sly half-smile. 'They are well and safe,' was all he would offer by way of explanation. The last time he had seen the doctor's creations was on the actual night of his rescue. Two strange figures, dozy and poorly co-ordinated on their high heels, their bodies still clad in tight rubber dresses, their heads concealed under red blankets, were led from the doctor's home by the commandos before being packed into the emergency transport, waiting outside for the hasty evacuation of another private facility. The twins were taken out on stretchers; neither were moving.

'She'll never know where we are?' he'd asked, as he placed one foot inside the transport, ready to take them away.

Black Eyes smiled and said, 'No,' amused by the query.

But we will think about each other, Angel had thought then, taking one final look towards the car and the silent figure who just then, in that final parting moment, had turned her shadowy, veiled face towards him. She and I will remember. And that was a notion he would share with nobody.

NEXUS BACKLIST

This information is correct at time of printing. For up-to-date information, please visit our website at www.nexus-books.co.uk

All books are priced at £6.99 unless another price is given.